Live.
Live,
and
come
save me
once again.

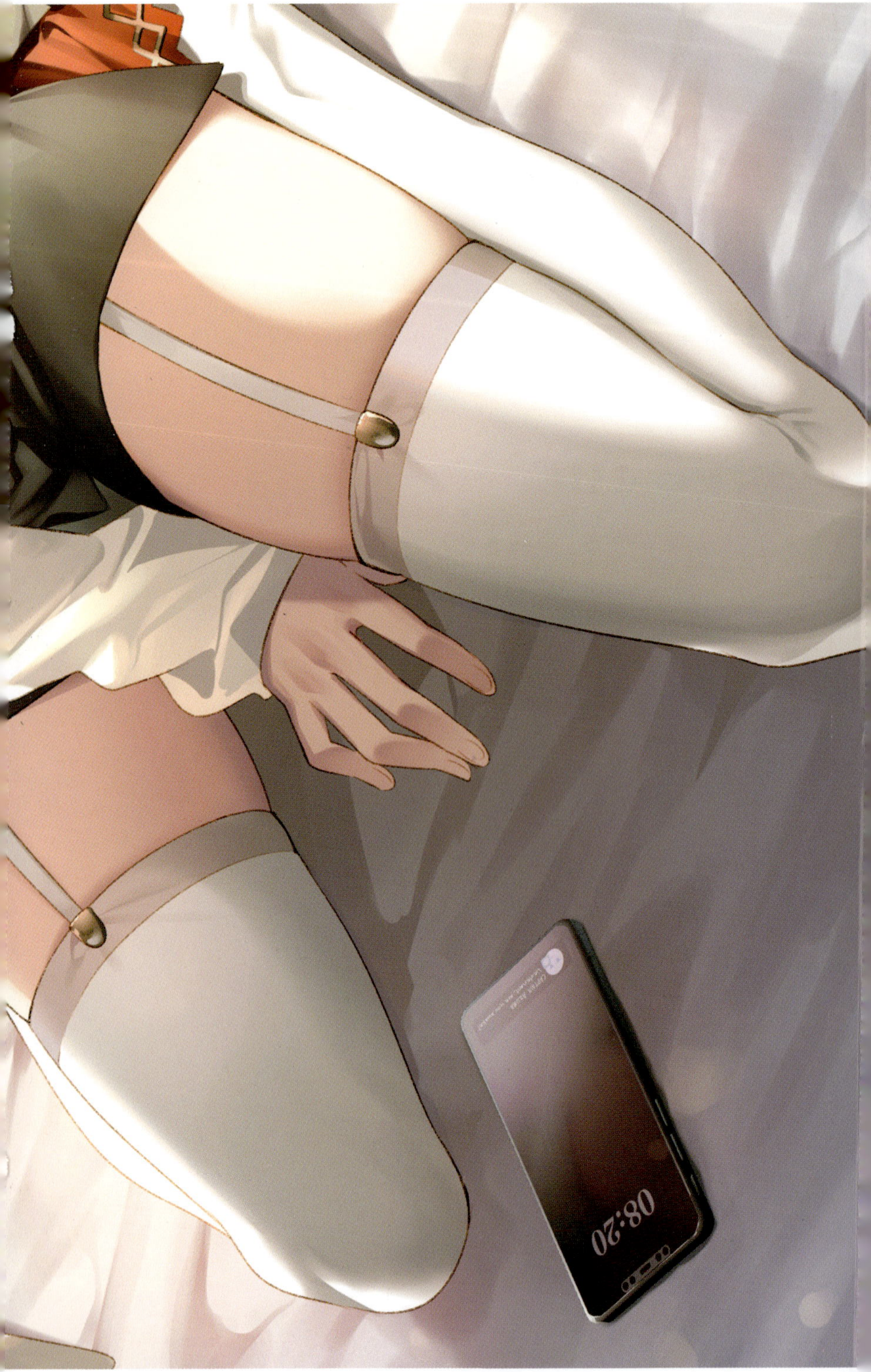
08:20

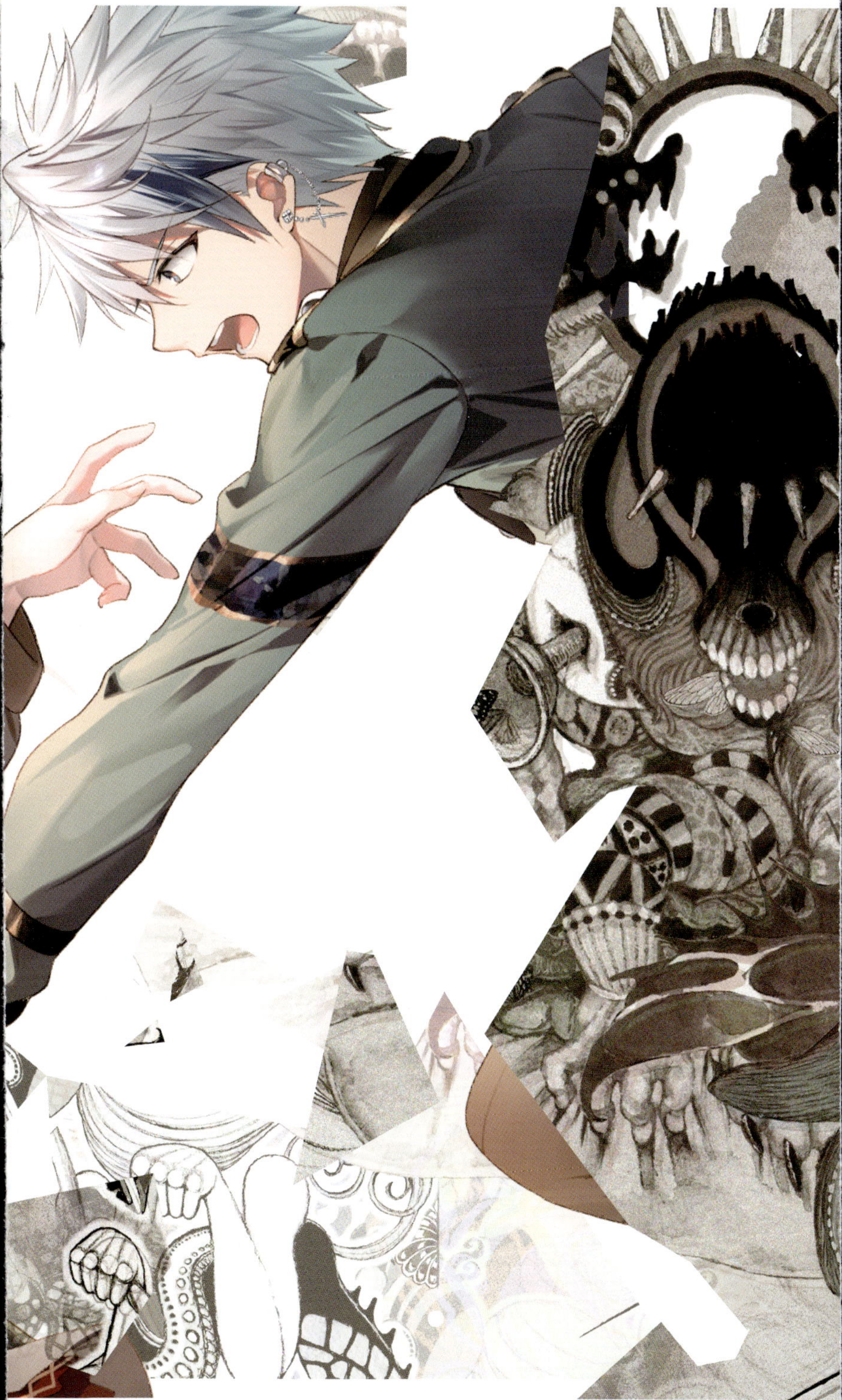

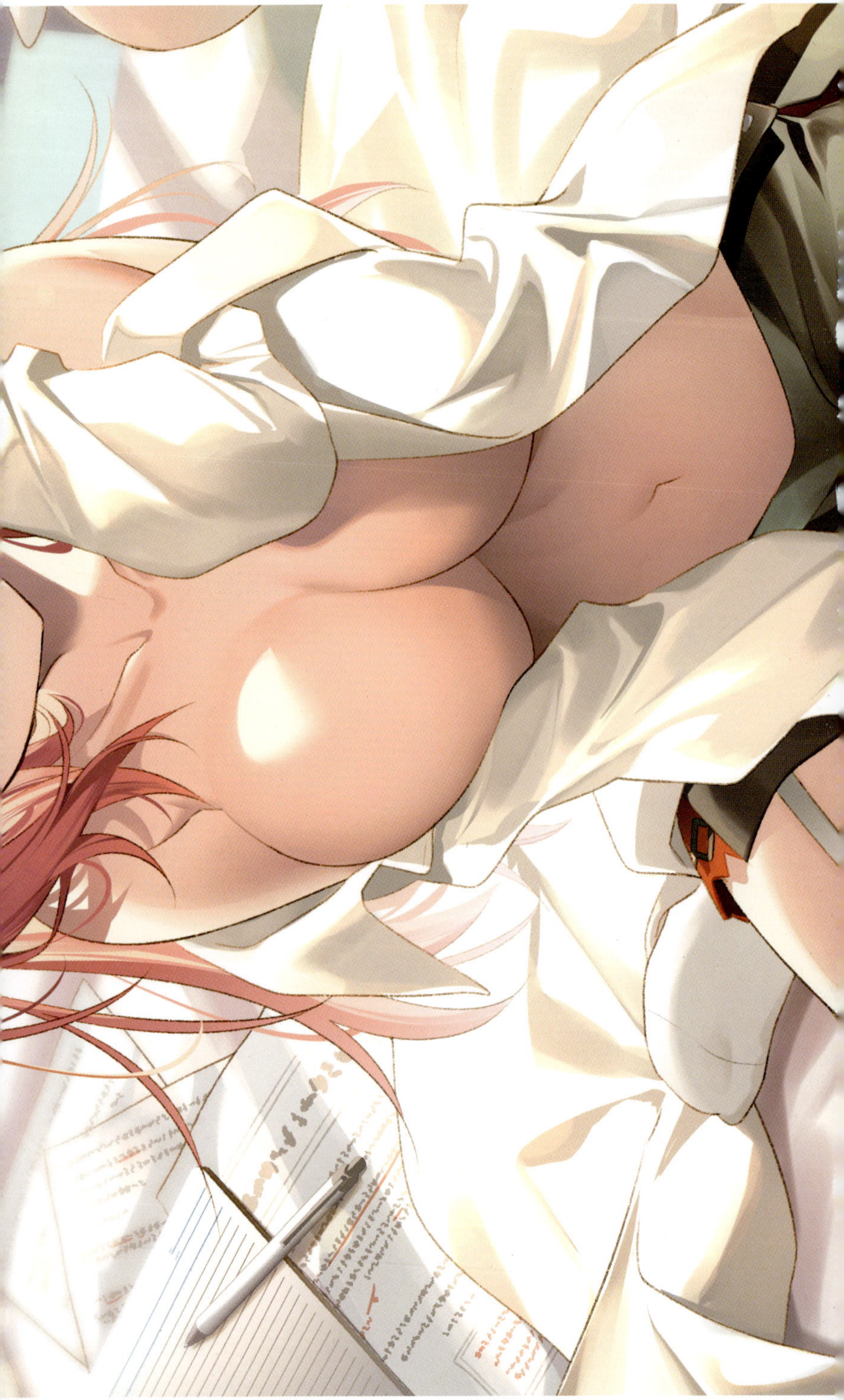

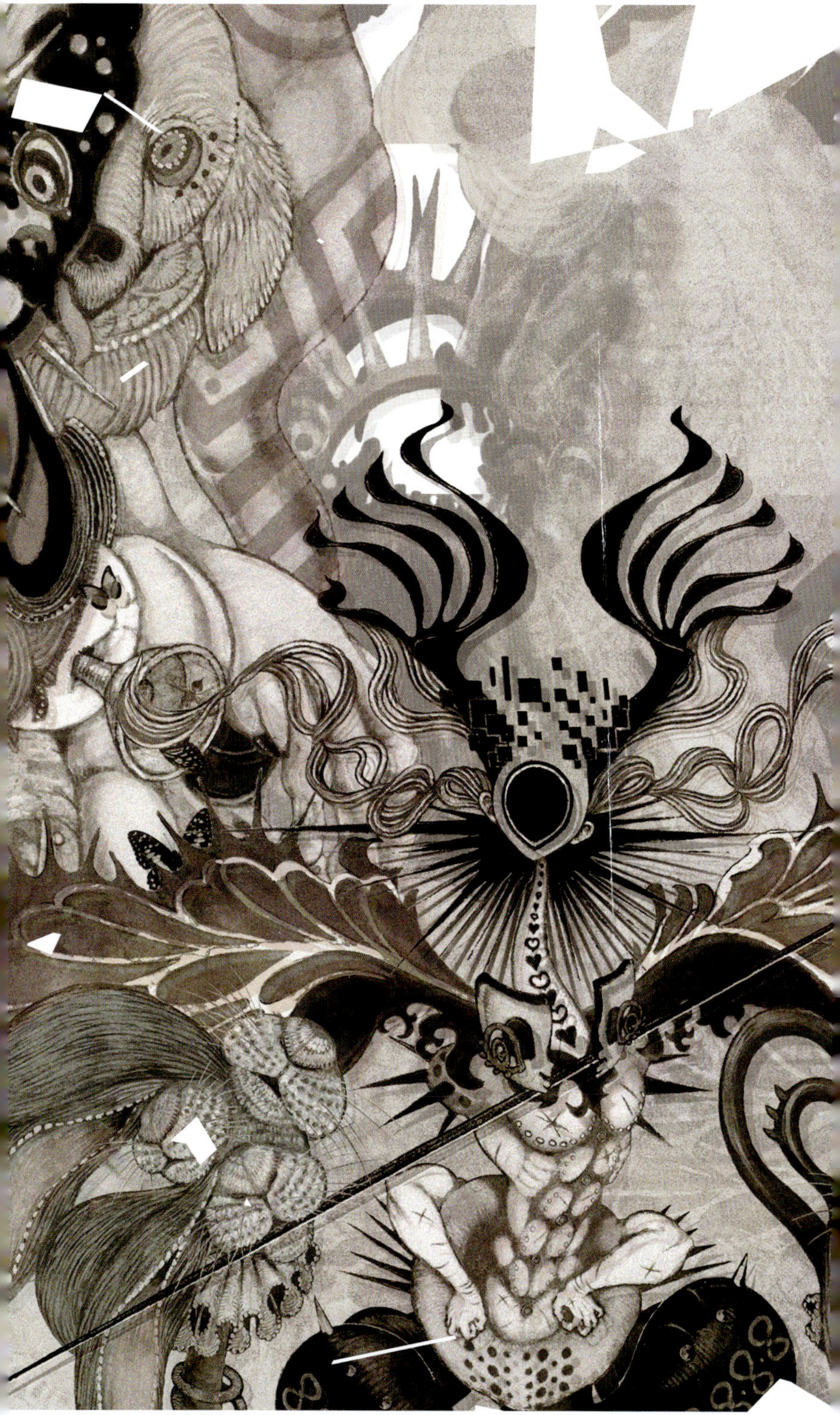

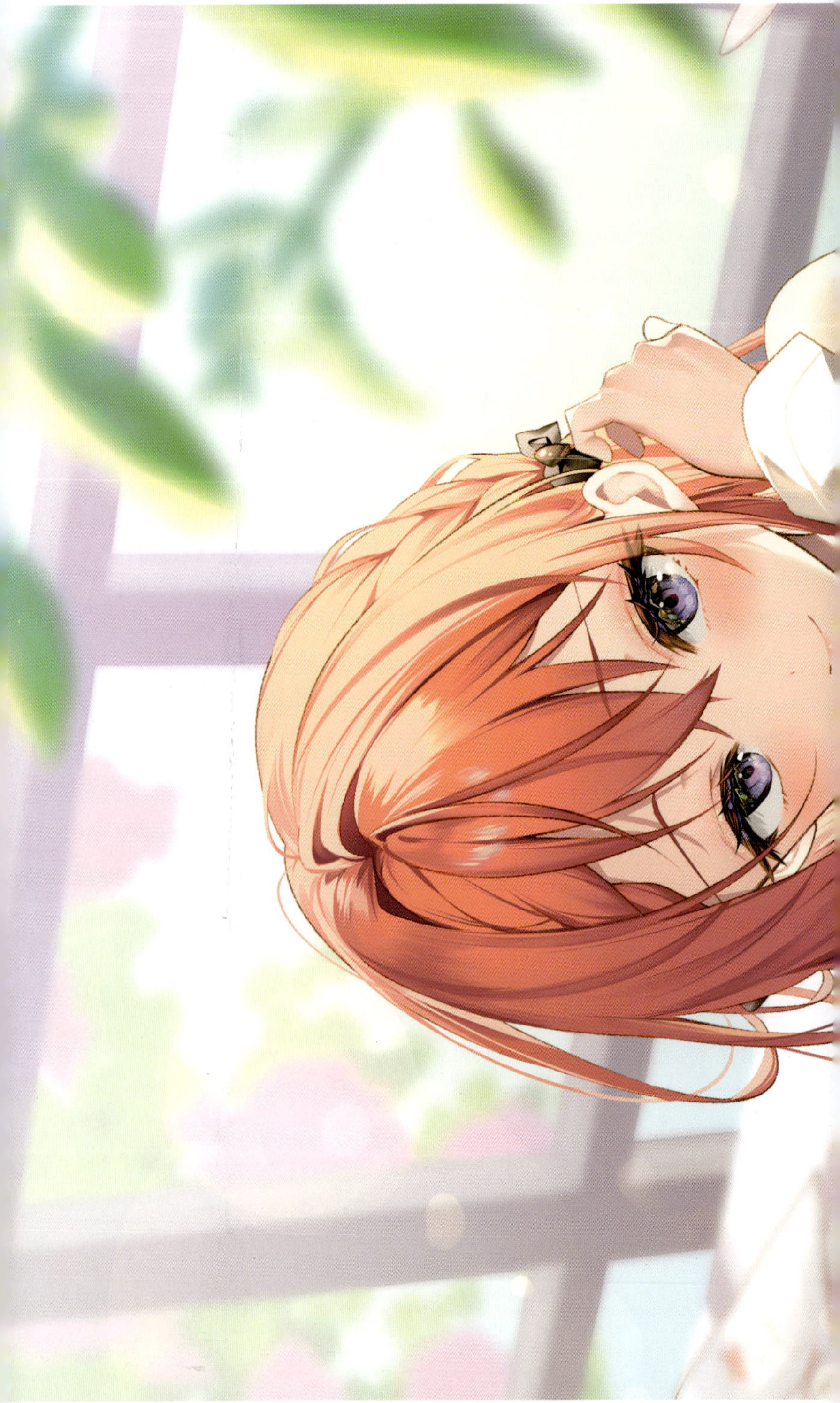

HERO SYNDROME

3

REI AYATSUKI
ILLUSTRATION BY riichu

CREATURE DESIGN BY
GEKIDAN INU CURRY Doroinu

YEN ON
NEW YORK

HERO SYNDROME

3

REI AYATSUKI

TRANSLATION BY **James Balzer**
COVER ART BY **riichu**
CREATURE DESIGN BY
GEKIDAN INU CURRY Doroinu

This book is a work of fiction. Names, characters, places, and incidents are the product of the author's imagination or are used fictitiously. Any resemblance to actual events, locales, or persons, living or dead, is coincidental.

YUSHASHOKOGUN Vol.3
©Rei Ayatsuki 2024
Edited by Dengeki Bunko
First published in Japan in 2024 by KADOKAWA CORPORATION, Tokyo.
English translation rights arranged with KADOKAWA CORPORATION, Tokyo
through TUTTLE-MORI AGENCY, INC., Tokyo.

English translation © 2025 by Yen Press, LLC

Yen Press, LLC supports the right to free expression and the value of copyright.
The purpose of copyright is to encourage writers and artists to produce the creative works that enrich our culture.

The scanning, uploading, and distribution of this book without permission is a theft of the author's intellectual property. If you would like permission to use material from the book (other than for review purposes), please contact the publisher. Thank you for your support of the author's rights.

Yen On
150 West 30th Street, 6th Floor
New York, NY 10001

Visit us at yenpress.com • facebook.com/yenpress • twitter.com/yenpress • yenpress.tumblr.com • instagram.com/yenpress

First Yen On Edition: July 2025
Edited by Yen On Editorial: Rachel Mimms
Designed by Yen Press Design: Eddy Mingki

Yen On is an imprint of Yen Press, LLC.
The Yen On name and logo are trademarks of Yen Press, LLC.

The publisher is not responsible for websites (or their content)
that are not owned by the publisher.

Library of Congress Cataloging-in-Publication Data
Names: Ayatsuki, Rei, author. | riichu, illustrator. | Doroinu, illustrator. |
Balzer, James (Translator), translator.
Title: Hero syndrome / Rei Ayatsuki ; illustration by riichu ;
creature design by Gekidan Inu Curry Doroinu ; translation by James Balzer.
Other titles: Yūsha shōkōgun. English
Description: First Yen On edition. | New York : Yen On, 2024–
Identifiers: LCCN 2024023264 | ISBN 9781975390846 (v. 1 ; trade paperback) |
ISBN 9781975390853 (v. 1 ; ebook) | ISBN 9798855407631 (v. 2 ; trade paperback) |
ISBN 9798855407655 (v. 3 ; trade paperback)
Subjects: LCGFT: Action and adventure fiction. | Fantasy fiction. | Light novels.
Classification: LCC PL878.5.Y38 Y8713 2024 | DDC 895.63/6—dc23/eng/20240627
LC record available at https://lccn.loc.gov/2024023264

ISBNs: 979-8-8554-0765-5 (paperback)
979-8-8554-0766-2 (ebook)

1 3 5 7 9 10 8 6 4 2

HJM

Printed in South Korea

HERO SYNDROME

3

PROLOGUE
Reminiscence

Everything was foggy. She could hear people arguing, somewhere far away, at the edge of consciousness.

She gently opened her eyes. She didn't really mind, but the voices seemed so insistent. Now that her eyes were open, however, she realized she was lying on the ground.

A crimson rain was falling. It smelled like rust.

She listened as the rain beat down on her. The voices—whoever they belonged to—were bickering.

"Wait......this is...again......"

"...Be kidding...did she......?"

"...She's......stop......"

And there, in the middle of it all, *he* stood. She saw his back, large and dark, protecting her where she lay.

When he turned around, she glimpsed a young man with chestnut brown hair and violet eyes. Several other humans were standing around him.

Her hazy consciousness began to sink back into the darkness.

What a strange scene. It was almost as if...she was reliving a memory.

CHAPTER ONE
Hollow

"...Anyway, like I said, it was a very strange dream," said Kaguya Shinohara, frowning in the meeting hall of the Charon barracks. She ran her fingers through her scarlet hair, which was meticulously pulled back, as she described her dream from the previous night.

"A strange dream?" said the other young woman with a smirk. It was Kaguya's roommate, Koyuki Asaharu. "Are you sure it wasn't just something you read before going to bed last night? You have been reading a lot of strange stuff lately, you know."

"Hmm... I'm pretty sure the only thing I read last night was a YA novel..."

Kaguya always had to read something before she went to bed. After first joining Charon, it had been mostly scientific papers and research materials, but lately, she was mostly reading novels. Given her routine, it would make sense for something from a book to seep into her dreams, but last night she had been reading a standard coming-of-age YA novel.

It had been a love story set in a school—a place that Kaguya didn't have much familiarity with at all.

"It seemed like you were having a *bad* dream, though, Kaguya. You scared the stuffing out of me, jumping out of bed in the middle of the night like that!"

"Koyuki, shhh! You don't need to go around mentioning that," said Kaguya, smacking at Koyuki repeatedly, her face slightly red with embarrassment. Koyuki dodged and laughed teasingly.

"It was no laughing matter, Lieutenant Shinohara."

This time, it was the teal-haired Second Lieutenant Haru Takanashi who spoke as she appeared from behind them. She sat down across from Kaguya with an unopened bottle of soda in her hand.

"Try to put yourself in our shoes, as your roommates. I barely got any sleep after being woken up like that," she said, futilely twisting the cap on her beverage, which she couldn't quite seem to wrestle open.

She began to shake it up and down vigorously, growing desperate. The girl next to Haru took the bottle and set it down softly on the table, casting a sidelong glance at the now sullen Haru. The girl was sitting directly across from Koyuki.

"I bet you agree with us, too...," insisted Koyuki. "Don't you... Sakura?"

"Hrm?" At that point, the girl, who had pink hair and was sipping on a juice box, turned her eyes toward Koyuki and Kaguya for the first time.

Her name was Sakura Arakawa, and she was the captain of their special ops squad.

"Sorry, I wasn't listening. What were we talking about?" she asked.

"We were talking about Kaguya waking us up with her nightmares," replied Koyuki.

"Oh," said Sakura, a smile blossoming across her face. "It's not that bad. I think it's cute. It's very Kaguya of her."

"Cute? More like creepy. She really scared us last night," said Haru.

Kaguya blatantly began to sulk.

Sakura flashed her a sisterly smile. "What was the dream about?"

"Um... Someone was arguing with somebody, I think. And then I heard my name."

Kaguya tried recalling her dream, which was already growing hazy as she spoke. With each passing moment, the resolution of the dream continued to fade, and only a vague impression was left behind.

"It was from when I was a kid, I think? Maybe it was my brother...?"

"Your brother? You mean Captain Shinohara? He's with Major Mirai," said Koyuki.

Kaguya's brother was currently one of Major Mirai's colleagues over at the Combat Support Branch.

Kaguya and her brother had not always been close, but after he brought Kaguya back when she had almost turned into a hero, the two reconciled. The dream must have been a memory from that time.

"What was Captain Shinohara's first name again?" Sakura asked.

"Pretty sure it was Ren, wasn't it?" Koyuki offered.

"Oh yeah! That's right. A bit rough around the edges but a pretty nice guy."

Although she interacted with him daily, Sakura had a strange habit of forgetting the man's name.

Ren Shinohara. His role at the Combat Support Branch, together with Major Mirai, was overseeing Charon. He was already twenty-four years old and had not encountered a hero for four years.

A voice suddenly blared over the wireless comms.

"Okay, ladies. It's time to get a move on."

The voice was low, gruff, and devoid of gentleness or concern. It resembled Rindou's voice somewhat, but instead of Rindou's roughness, a cold ruthlessness lurked below its surface.

"R-Ren."

It was Kaguya's brother, Ren Shinohara. He supervised Charon together with Mirai over at Combat Support. He was as curt as always, only telling them what they needed to know.

"Tokyo Ward Seven. Tough luck, but it's close to a nursery school."

In a place where there were lots of children, panic was sure to ensue. They all stood up, realizing what was at stake. However, their squad captain, Sakura, held Kaguya back.

"Kaguya, are you sure you want to go today?"

"What? Yes, of course, I'll be fine."

"There's no need to push yourself... You went yesterday as well, remember?"

Yesterday—for some reason, that word made Kaguya feel strange inside.

"But if I don't go...how will I save the hero?"

"That's a fair point. Back in the day, I knew this was something only you could do, but now we can all do it. I wish you would rely on us a little bit more."

"What...?"

"You can't dive into the heroes' minds and take on their psyches all by yourself. It's too much for you."

"I...guess I forgot."

Kaguya felt strangely confused. She had this sense that she was the only one who could dive into the heroes' minds—as if she had been handling it all by herself because no one else could. Was that... not the case?

"It's too much stress, Kaguya, trying to shoulder everything alone," Koyuki said, her voice scattering Kaguya's doubts. "It was crazy the last time it was Rindou's turn, though, wasn't it? Remember how he stopped the hero? With a punch?"

"Honestly, I think he could do with being a little less violent."

"He does use that violence to save people, though, Haru. Different strokes, I guess."

Oh, that's right. Now Kaguya remembered.

Everyone at Charon could enter the heroes' minds now: Koyuki, Sakura, Haru, and even Rindou. It had been Haru's turn last time, and Rindou's the time before that.

They didn't have a strict system or anything, but Sakura had suggested cycling the responsibility in shifts to ensure that no one got overwhelmed.

For some reason, Kaguya suddenly felt like bursting into tears. How strange. She had already known that everyone could do this, hadn't she? And yet, for some reason, she felt as if she had been juggling everything by herself.

"In that case...maybe I will take you up on your offer and stay back this one time."

"Good idea. You can hold the fort down for us while we're gone."

With that settled, Sakura reached for the long weapon sitting by her side—a staff. When had it gotten there?

"Huh?" Kaguya blinked. "You're not using your katana today, Sakura?"

A hush immediately fell over the hall. As soon as Kaguya said *katana*, she felt bewildered. No one at Charon used a katana. Why would she say something like that?

"Kaguya, are you sure you're not still dreaming?" Koyuki asked.

"We've never had anyone here who uses a katana. Just who in the heck are you confusing me with?" said Sakura.

Kaguya looked down, embarrassed, while Koyuki and Sakura laughed. Who *had* she been thinking of? Why a katana? Kaguya was just as confused as they were.

"N-never mind... Ha-ha-ha, maybe I am still dreaming."

"Honestly..."

Amused smirks appeared on all their faces. The other girls were staring at Kaguya like someone might stare at their goofball younger sister.

A part of Kaguya's heart grew warm. No one was relying on her anymore; she didn't have to shoulder all that responsibility now.

I hope things can last like this forever, she thought.

• • •

"It has been one week today since Lieutenant Kaguya Shinohara fell unconscious."

Over in Extermination Bureau Headquarters, several members of Charon had gathered in a hospital room in the specialized medical ward under Azuma's command. Lying in the bed by the window was a young woman in a coma.

A young woman with scarlet hair—Kaguya Shinohara.

"Since falling unconscious during the hero battle that occurred one week ago, Kaguya has been like an empty shell, with steady vitals but no signs of awareness. As for the hero in question, there were no obvious differences between it and any other hero that has appeared before now," explained Captain Azuma as he stood next to the bed. He looked tired. "In short, her condition remains unchanged."

The air in the room seemed to deflate like a balloon. Disappointment filled the space. A week had already passed; at this point, the chance of her waking up again appeared slim. They were all beginning to fear the same thing.

Haru spoke up timidly, a frown on her face. "She's not…dead, is she?"

"Her vitals are fine. And she's receiving nutrition via an IV drip."

Kaguya was hooked up to an IV, just as Azuma said.

"What do you think is happening to her…to Lieutenant Shinohara…right now?"

"As for details…I don't know, but I suspect it's not fundamentally different from the fatigue and health problems she was experiencing before from hopping into the heroes' minds."

In Azuma's opinion, this was likely an extreme version of those earlier symptoms. Although to be honest, that was simply the only possibility he could think of.

"The bigger problem facing us right now…"

Azuma glanced toward a corner of the room. A girl was sitting there—Mari Ezakura. Mari was assigned to Technical. She sat on the chair with her knees up, watching Kaguya intently.

"…is the death of Technical's director."

It happened last week.

Azuma and the others had returned in a panic, carrying Kaguya, who still had not woken up, only to be greeted by news of the Director's death. The official cause of death was blood loss. She had been stabbed through her throat and between her eyebrows by what appeared to have been a bladed weapon.

Given the blood-soaked, katana-shaped Chronos that had been found next to her body, her death was being treated as a suicide. Mari Ezakura had been the first to cry foul play. *"The Director would never do anything so stupid,"* she insisted.

Azuma agreed. Moreover, suicide via a katana would have been no easy task. They weren't even talking about across the stomach, like some form of seppuku. In order to stab yourself in the throat with a katana, you would need to hold the sword by the blade since it would be impossible to reach the hilt even with your arms extended as far as they could go. However, there were no injuries on the Director's hands.

The Director's death—and Kaguya's coma—had both come as a great shock for Mari.

Considering the state Mari was in, Charon had taken her under emergency protection. Whoever had killed the Director—if they had done it because of the Director's research, then Mari was in more danger now than anyone.

Due to the Director's death, the Bureau was shutting Technical No. 2 down indefinitely. Unless Kaguya returned, Technical would likely be dissolved.

The entire situation was hopeless.

"A whole week…," Azuma said, staring at Kaguya's sleeping face and scowling as if he had just bitten down on something sour.

He had been worried that something like this might happen.

Diving into another person's psyche was inherently dangerous. Azuma had once entered someone else's mind himself, so he understood. But he still hadn't been able to stop Kaguya.

"Does she have any family…?" Koyuki asked softly to no one in particular.

"No," Azuma answered. "She was an orphan, just like us."

Kaguya had no family. Both of her parents had passed away, and her brother had been missing ever since the day that Kaguya had almost transformed into a hero.

About her brother, though…

Kaguya had tried looking into where he had gone, but all traces of him had disappeared seven years ago. It was a dead end. It was unclear whether he was even alive, although he probably wouldn't have abandoned Kaguya if that were the case; therefore, it was more likely that he was already gone.

"She could still wake up, though…," said Koyuki, her hollow voice diffusing into the quiet of the hospital room.

The atmosphere was indescribable. Although no one said so out loud, they all knew how unlikely it was that she would awaken.

"It's still only been a week, right?" said Haru, as if to argue with the silence filling the room. Her voice sounded troubled. "Maybe we're being too pessimistic. She could open her eyes all of a sudden. That's how it's always worked up until now, right?"

"Yes. Up until now."

Including when they had faced that fog hero.

Speaking of which…, thought Azuma.

While it had only taken a few dozen seconds, Kaguya hadn't woken up immediately after that fight, either. Perhaps that delay had been a precursor to what they were seeing now.

"I don't think we need to worry too much, but…," Azuma said, turning to look at Kaguya, an uneasy expression on his face. She was unable to breathe on her own and had been hooked up to a ventilator. It was difficult to see her like that. "What if…something happens, and she turns into a hero?"

"I don't want to think about that, but you're right. If something like that were to occur…"

Haru lowered her gaze. Azuma didn't need her to finish the sentence. If Kaguya turned, who would be able to save her?

"No one."

Azuma cast a pained glance toward Kaguya, who continued to sleep just as before.

"No one would be able to save her if that occurred…"

・・・

Mari Ezakura had first met Kaguya around when Technical No. 2 had lost most of its staff. Like almost everyone else in the Bureau, Mari and Kaguya were orphans. Mari couldn't even remember her parents' faces anymore.

Maybe that had something to do with why—even after learning

the truth about the creatures that had stolen her parents from her—Mari had felt nothing in particular toward them. She had never been particularly prone to strong fits of passion since she was more the lukewarm type.

Despite this, Kaguya had never given up on forging a connection with her. Kaguya had even once covered for Mari when Mari, due to her own carelessness, had committed an irreparable blunder.

Something about the way Kaguya treated her reminded Mari of the older sister she had lost. It was around that time when Mari started growing attached to Kaguya.

"…"

Whatever else happened, Kaguya was Mari's mentor and hers alone.

Kaguya was already seventeen. In a few more years, she would lose the ability to see heroes and be taken off the front lines. Once that happened, Mari figured she would probably quit soon after as well. There would be no reason to stay at Technical if Kaguya wasn't there. Mari didn't really care about heroes one way or the other.

"…"

She sat in total silence. Elegant silence. No one spoke to her now.

Garbled static. She tilted her eyes upward at the sound.

The members of Charon seemed to be listening to something on their comms. Someone must have been contacting them.

"Major Mirai," Azuma said softly, causing Mari to realize he was speaking with Combat Support. "Have things calmed down on your end…?" He made it sound as if the person he was talking to had a lot on their plate. "I see… Lieutenant Shinohara…still shows no change…"

At those words, Mari finally lifted her head. She could see the exhaustion on Captain Yuuri Azuma's face, even from a sideways glance.

"There's been a hero sighting…?" Azuma asked. "Understood. In a shopping complex? All members are prepared to mobilize immediately."

The words barely registered in Mari's mind. It was as if they were coming from somewhere far away. Who knew that words were such a meaningless string of sounds when you paid no attention to them?

Once the request came in, the looks on everyone's faces changed.

They immediately moved to depart. As Mari watched them go, she couldn't help but feel the distance between herself and them. How could they just leave Kaguya like this, given the state that she was in?

Alone now, Mari stared intently at Kaguya's bed.

"Kaguya..."

She still hadn't woken up.

It was too painful to see her like this. Mari could feel a weight settling in her chest. But not all of this heaviness was related to Kaguya.

The truth about the Chronoses—the Director's theory that the Chronoses were sentient. Should she tell the others? Should Charon know whose suffering they relied on?

"But...if I tell them..."

It was obvious what would happen next. The members of Charon would not want to use the Chronoses anymore. Then who would be left to oppose the heroes?

This decision had been dropped into Mari's lap. She was the only one who knew that the Chronoses were sentient now. If she just kept her mouth shut, it would be as if none of it were true.

Should she speak up, or should she stay silent? For whose sake? Obviously, for Charon's.

"What does Charon have to do with me...?" she muttered, sulking. No one answered her.

The members of Charon were the only people who could use Chronoses without suffering rebounds. The reason for this still wasn't clear.

But there was one thing that Mari knew for certain: It was their fault that this had happened to Kaguya. They had placed too much responsibility on her shoulders, and the weight had broken her.

First, Charon had stolen Kaguya from Mari, and now, they had left her like this. That was exactly why Mari hated Tactical Infantry.

CHAPTER TWO
Regression

Azuma had responded to the call and was now facing off against a hero at a shopping complex near the train station.

The hero was on the second floor of the mall. Azuma had heard the sound before even spotting the creature. Its screech sounded like a screaming child.

"SKREEEEEE!"

It was shaped like a wheel, spinning around a single axle at its center. At a diameter of around only twenty centimeters, it was unusually small. However, this size meant it was also extremely hard to hit. It had other advantages as well.

"SKREEE, SKRRREEEEEE!!"

That din was unbelievable.

The blaring shriek had caused most bystanders in the vicinity to fall immediately unconscious. Even Azuma and his team were forced to cover their ears. Its shrill, piercing cry was too much.

"Tsk, this isn't good."

Azuma tried to echolocate the heroes' eggs. Although the sound of the eggs was a different frequency, all this noise was making it hard for Azuma to locate them.

"If we could just shut it up for a little while…"

The sound seemed to be resonating from inside the wheel, which was empty—nothing connected the axle to the rim.

A mantle of darkness protruded from the axle's tip.

"Erk—"

Azuma could see it with only his right eye. Buried within the darkness was its face.

He felt a shiver run down his spine. The smile he saw beneath its black shroud was painted on a face of madness.

The face belonged to a young girl—a child. But its smile was completely unlike that of an innocent child's. Azuma reflexively covered his right eye, still not yet used to seeing these faces.

It didn't make his job any easier, observing the humans inside. Even though they weren't actually human anymore, it felt like he was taking the life of the person within, assisting them in their act of suicide.

But it's just a hallucination... Right, Lieutenant?

He drew the katana smoothly from his waist.

A *living weapon*—beautiful and grotesque. Traced with coiling veins, the blade appeared neither man-made nor organic. For some reason, the blade felt comfortable in Azuma's hand.

This katana...

The katana that was believed to have been used to stab the Director—through her throat.

I wonder if that's really true...

If it were, he doubted it would have wound up in his hands so easily. The Chronoses might be valuable weapons, but they would have still qualified as evidence. Azuma had accepted the weapon once it was offered, seeing as he did not have a good enough reason to refuse.

"SKRRREEEEE!!!"

The hero howled again. The force of its scream, which threatened to rupture Azuma's eardrums, caused cracks to appear in the building's walls.

"It sounds almost like a child crying," muttered Haru, having weathered the wave of sound, seemingly unperturbed.

"Then I guess we'll just have to hush it..."

Azuma dropped down into a loose stance. This new Chronos was longer than his original katana, and at first, the weight had been difficult for him to handle. But he had quickly gotten used to it once he learned how to swing it properly.

For some reason, it didn't feel like it was his first time handling this blade. Not that he was concerned, seeing as that feeling didn't get in the way of its use. Still, though.

"Azuma," Rindou said quietly over the comms. "Where's the egg?"

Azuma strained his ears.

Ever since the hero attack six years ago, Azuma's ears had been special. Every member of Charon was a survivor from that attack, but as the person who had been exposed at closest range to the hero factor, only Azuma was able to hear the sound given off by the eggs.

It was of a much higher frequency than normal sound, meaning that even with all this noise he should have been able to isolate its source—*should have*.

"…?!"

Azuma's eyes went wide. He couldn't hear the egg.

Or perhaps it would be more accurate to say that something was *preventing* him from hearing it.

The sound of the egg was lost in a sea of static that was being emitted at the same frequency. No matter how hard Azuma strained his ears, he couldn't seem to isolate the egg's sound.

"Azuma?! Where is it, man?!" Rindou asked.

But Azuma couldn't answer. This was a new type of hero, one that was able to prevent him from locating its egg.

"I—I can't hear it."

"What?!"

Just then, the hero started to make a strange new sound, like a whirring *twang*. It began to spin.

"Ah?!"

Azuma braced himself, but nothing else happened. The wheel simply continued to spin indiscriminately. It didn't look as if it was trying to come any closer.

I wonder...

If Kaguya were there, maybe this hero would have been among the ones she was able to save. Now he was even relying on her in his thoughts; he felt pathetic. Without Kaguya's help—

"Azuma."

Rindou spoke sharply, snapping Azuma out of his thoughts. Indeed, this was not the time for soul-searching.

"What do you mean you can't hear it?"

"I can't hear it. Something's preventing me...I think. It's like there's too much static."

Rindou couldn't stop from clicking his tongue loudly.

"Sorry... It's just that's gonna make dealing with this thing a real pain in the ass."

The hero they were facing was small, making it difficult to aim. If they tried to slash from outside the rim, the spinning of the wheel would simply deflect their blows. Trying to decimate the entire creature with a single high-powered strike might be a good idea, considering how small it was, but in that case, its speed was going to make actually hitting it a problem.

"First thing's first, we need to stop it from moving. What's the plan, Captain?"

Azuma was silent for a moment. The hero, however, was not about to give them even a second to think.

There was a sharp *whoosh* as the hero swooped toward Azuma.

If Azuma wanted to avoid the rim and hit the center, he was going to have to thrust. But the wheel was so small; if he missed, his Chronos blade might get caught and break.

Unless...

Azuma broke his stance, stepping forward with his left foot instead. He took a large step toward the hero and then, with his next step, kicked the hero as hard as he could.

The creature was flung far, far away, howling like the wind as it was knocked back—or so it seemed at first. But the hero suddenly pivoted.

Spinning even faster and more frantically than before, bolting straight toward the person who had kicked it. Straight toward Azuma.

Azuma could not make out the spinning clearly, but he didn't need to.

What he could see, however, was the hero's face. Its expression. The young child's smile, spinning insanely. He felt simultaneously terrified and nauseous. It was horrifying—something he never wished to see again.

The moment the smiling face was pointed his way, Azuma lifted his blade with unerring speed and accuracy—

—but the hero changed trajectory.

"What?!"

It dodged the blade, evading with absolute efficiency before diving straight at Azuma's face. There was a metallic *clang* as Azuma blocked with his sword.

The contact was brief but effective. It was now Azuma's turn to be flung backward, although he was only knocked back by a few steps. He righted himself immediately, none the worse for wear.

Azuma made a series of snap decisions.

"Koyuki, I need a favor," said Azuma, letting Koyuki know his plan over the comms. "I need you to fire off six shots. Once the hero stops, I'll move in."

"That's…not the worst idea, Azuma, but it's too dangerous." Koyuki argued. "You want me to do a preemptive strike, right? So that you can lunge in once its defenses are open? It's spinning too fast, though. It's like a barrier at this point. The bullets will just ricochet. Not even Rindou could get close at this rate—"

"Don't worry… I know what I'm doing."

The hero continued to scream and spin about. Its behavior was baffling.

Azuma held his katana in one hand and pointed it out in front of himself with the flat of the blade laid across his forearm, ready to thrust. He had wanted to finish this fight with a single strike. Ever since he began seeing their faces, Azuma had started to feel a vague sense of pity for the creatures—a desire to put them out of their misery quickly.

"What are you planning to do, Captain?" Haru asked. "You don't even know where the egg is, right? You might as well be going in blind."

Azuma didn't really need to be told that right now. He tried to think. What would the old Azuma have done? The Azuma from before he had met Kaguya? Right. He would have probably rushed in headlong, throwing safety to the wind.

That seems like a bad idea...

Azuma immediately abandoned that train of thought. He turned his distinctively stubborn stare toward the hero—and toward the little girl inside.

This was a homicidal monster. That was all. Nothing more, nothing less.

"Going in blind or not...it's time to stop that thing," he said, his clear and quiet voice resonating in his comrades' ears.

What was the best way to stop a rampaging wheel? Simply shove something in its spokes. Not his Chronos, of course. That was irreplaceable. Instead, something with inhuman powers of regeneration—a piece of his own body.

"Once its defenses are open, one of you needs to take the kill."

"...?! Captain Azuma, wait!!"

Out of the corner of his eye, he saw Haru, who seemed to realize what he was about to do, turn pale. But he couldn't spare any more time for her right now.

Without another word, Azuma dashed ahead. As he drew close to the wheel, which was spinning faster than the eye could process, he thrust his right arm forward.

"Argghhh!!"

Azuma's small scream went unheard, lost in the cacophony of the wheel.

His hand was not torn off, but it was badly mangled and bent. It would probably heal quickly, but the sight was still none too pleasant to see.

As soon as the wheel came to a stop, Koyuki took her shot. Gunfire echoed as the bullet hit its mark, blasting the hero to smithereens, egg and all—wherever the egg had been. There was the sound of an explosion, so small it was almost a letdown, and then all of the previous noise instantly stopped.

"..."

The person beneath the hero had been a young girl. As the blackness covering the creature cleared, her innocent face peeked into sight for a moment and then began to collapse. A gloomy undertone of madness and despair lurked behind her smile, but otherwise, it was now the same smile you might see on any young girl. It took but a few seconds for it to gently drift away.

After watching the hero crumble…

"What the hell were you thinking, flying off the handle like that?!" Rindou bellowed. He rushed forward in a panic and was speaking to Azuma face-to-face instead of over the comms. "I don't care if you heal faster than normal people—"

"Sorry…"

Haru rushed forward as well. "What are you, stupid?!" she shouted before deftly beginning first aid. Azuma watched her blankly as the comms crackled to life.

"Azuma…" This time it was Koyuki. She sounded concerned. "Does it hurt?"

"Not really…"

Although she had phrased it as a question, her tone implied that she knew how he felt.

Koyuki was Kaguya's roommate. Ever since Sakura passed, she and Kaguya had become particularly close. They ate lunch together almost every day. The only time Azuma got to eat lunch with Kaguya instead of Koyuki was when Koyuki was already busy. They had grown practically inseparable.

Koyuki tended to mask her own pain. But she never managed to hide it completely.

"I'm fine," Azuma insisted. "You don't need to make such a fuss."

Knowing that Koyuki was in pain, too, there was no way he could just unload his feelings on her. It was better to keep it inside.

"Everything is just back to the way it used to be...," Azuma told himself.

But deep down, he didn't really mean it.

CHAPTER THREE
Resolve

That night, Rindou sat in the meeting hall and reflected on that day's fight against the hero.

Azuma's ability to hear the eggs had been unexpectedly neutralized. That was all it had taken to place them at a disadvantage. The thought made Rindou's skin crawl. Fortunately, today's opponent happened to be small. But there was no guarantee the same would be true next time.

If anything, heroes were often too big to slay with a single strike. What would they do then? Rindou wasn't sure.

"Although I guess this is just what everyone has to go through..."

The ability to locate the heroes' eggs was unique. Azuma was the only one who possessed it, and Charon had been relying on his ability up until now. Now that Rindou had given it some thought, he realized things had been pretty easy for them. Azuma pointed, and they attacked. It was as simple as that.

"Except...once Kaguya showed up, even that much was no longer necessary."

With Kaguya on their side, they had been able to eliminate any opponent, no matter how aggressive and powerful. Rindou would be lying if he said they hadn't started to use her as a crutch.

"We really started relying on her at some point..."

At first, they had rejected her. But at this moment, even Rindou found himself wishing she were there.

"I suppose you could say we got too dependent—"

"Too dependent…? Who do you mean?"

A voice spoke up from the entrance to the hall, interrupting Rindou's thoughts. He lifted his head. Not that he needed to look to see, but it was Koyuki. She was leaning against the wall.

"Kaguya or Azuma? Which one are we too dependent on?"

"Who said you could eavesdrop? Mind your business."

"I just got here."

Koyuki plopped herself down on the sofa without bothering to ask first. The cushion springs beneath her sagged, though not nearly as much as they did for Rindou.

"Both," he said, answering Koyuki's question. "The truth is Azuma and Kaguya have been carrying us… Actually, once Kaguya arrived, even the carrying was just for show. At the end of the day, the two of them would be more than capable of handling things on their own."

"That's true." Koyuki glanced down at her hands. Smooth and pale, yet calloused. "I've been fighting against heroes all this time, but even though it's only been six months since Kaguya got here, I've started to wonder: What if we could save them instead?"

Rindou did not reply.

"Heroes are just monsters, nothing more and nothing less—that was what I used to think."

Rindou had felt the same way. He was probably even more staunch about it than Koyuki was. It wasn't that he held any strong grudge against the heroes or anything. It was just, having thrown his life away once, fighting them had now become his reason for going on.

But something felt different now.

"Things go smoother when she's here, at least. Being able to immobilize them like that has saved our butts plenty of times," said Rindou.

"Is that all you care about? Really…?"

Rindou frowned, not liking what Koyuki was getting at. "What's that supposed to mean...?"

"Why don't you just admit you like saving the heroes, too?"

"Come on, don't give me that shit—"

"How long have we known each other, Rindou? You can't fool me."

"Get off my nuts, geez...," Rindou grumbled, scowling. But he didn't disagree.

Koyuki chuckled. "You've been trying to act like some kind of tough guy ever since you met her. It's fine by me, but you're gonna give people the wrong impression, you know?"

"Just so long as you guys get me," Rindou said before suddenly catching himself.

"Hmm?" Koyuki hummed with a devilish grin.

Rindou realized instinctively that he had just put his foot in his mouth.

"You're gonna make me blush, big guy."

"Quit acting dumb," he said, doing his best to come off as intimidating, but it was useless against Koyuki.

The two were stuck with each other by this point. They knew each other inside and out—in a way that was completely different from the kind of awkward relationship that Azuma and Kaguya had. They were used to not holding back with one another.

"Anyway, putting that aside," Rindou said, forcefully changing the subject, "it's not good that we're so dependent on them. Maybe we should rethink the way we do things."

"You're right. They've been supporting us up until now. It's our turn to return the favor."

To pay Azuma and Kaguya back for taking them for granted, Rindou and Kaguya needed to learn how to defeat heroes on their own. If they couldn't do that, then there was no point in them being there in the first place.

"It's time we stepped up to the plate, Rindou," Koyuki said, making a fist and thrusting it out toward him.

Rindou nodded, realizing immediately what she was saying.

Obviously, he was on board. He made a fist and bumped it against Koyuki's smaller one.

Koyuki was his comrade, the best word to describe their relationship. It was different from what he had with Azuma or Kaguya, even a little different from what he had once had with Sakura. Something unique and difficult to describe.

Koyuki's catlike vermilion eyes and Rindou's auburn brown ones needed to meet only briefly for the two comrades to know that they were in total agreement. This was a connection that was rare for someone like Rindou.

"Anyway, I'm going to bed," Koyuki announced, standing up from the sofa. She smiled at Rindou as he glanced up at her questioningly. "I feel a little tired today…"

"Just today?"

This time it was Rindou's turn to see right through Koyuki. She laughed, her eyes widening slightly.

"I'm tired, too," Rindou said.

"Ha-ha, I'm sure you are. You should get some sleep as well. Takanashi will get pissed if you stay up too late."

Rindou stared off into the distance as if the mention of Takanashi's name had caused him to remember something. Specifically, he stared in the direction of the kitchen.

"Takanashi, huh? Just what the hell has she been up to lately anyway?"

"Apparently, she's been poking her nose into things at the Bureau. She's originally from Inspection, after all."

There was no need to ask *what* she was poking her nose into. The Director's death, of course…as well as other matters.

As a former Inspection officer, uncovering answers was what Takanashi did best. It was her bread and butter. Rindou hadn't had many opportunities to speak with her lately, seeing as she had been so busy with her investigations. Not that he spoke with her much to begin with. Still, though…

"Just what the heck does she get up to all day?"
It was hard not to be at least a little curious.

After Rindou left, Koyuki leaned back on the sofa and let out a huge sigh. The sound, as it settled into the quiet of the deserted meeting hall, seemed a little sad.

"I told her, didn't I?"

That there was no need for a girl from Technical to try so hard to prove herself with Tactical Infantry.

"Or did I never say that out loud…?"

How could any of them have said it out loud?

Kaguya had completely changed the way that Charon fought. She had shown them a new way forward. It was easy to see what Rindou was getting at.

Charon had grown complacent in the end—despite knowing how dangerous that could be.

There hadn't been anything different about the hero they had fought last week. Meaning that whatever had occurred, it must have been on Kaguya's side. But it was their own fault. They were the ones who had pushed Kaguya to the breaking point like this.

"Everything is just back to the way it used to be…"

Like Azuma said, things were just back to the way they once were from Charon's point of view. Back to their original way of doing things.

Kaguya probably would have been livid had she known.

"As for that other girl…"

From Koyuki's point of view, Mari Ezakura was practically a stranger. But thinking about how she must be feeling now caused even Koyuki's heart to ache. Ezakura's boss was gone, and her mentor, Kaguya, was stuck in a coma.

The door squeaked on its hinges, and Koyuki lifted her head. Due to shoddy installation, even the slightest movement caused the door to protest.

"Oh... Azuma," she said.

Azuma entered the room, seemingly lost in thought, as usual. There were thick worry lines between his eyebrows. He always had a tendency to brood, but that tendency had become even more pronounced since losing Kaguya.

"You look like you've got one foot in the grave...," Koyuki said, causing Azuma to finally notice her presence. "What's gotten into you? You sure you're getting enough sleep?"

"You're hardly one to talk...," Azuma said with a smile of uncharacteristic chagrin as he sat down opposite Koyuki. "You don't seem very eager to go to bed yourself."

"Hey, don't change the subject... But no, I can't sleep. It's too quiet."

Kaguya had always been working on something late into the night. Now that the room was quiet again, Koyuki found it surprisingly difficult to sleep. The fact that there was nothing actually keeping her awake made her insomnia all the more aggravating.

The same had happened after Sakura left.

"Come to think of it, Azuma, there was something I wanted to discuss with you."

She'd just remembered what it was and decided it took priority. She patted the seat next to her, causing Azuma to look blatantly annoyed. He probably expected she was going to nag him about something—not that he was wrong.

"Well? What is it...?"

"It's about today. I know it's always been your tendency, but aren't you getting a little too reckless lately? You're not immortal, you know."

"I didn't mean to fly off the handle or anything—"

"It doesn't matter if you meant to or not. I'm telling you that you did."

Koyuki knew Azuma was probably wrestling with his own demons. When you got down to it, it was their fault that Kaguya was in a coma right now, after all.

"I was just trying to... Never mind. I don't think there's really a difference now from how I used to do things." As expected, Azuma was deflecting. "But I'm sorry if I worried you. I'll try to rein it in going forward."

"That's all I ask."

Koyuki settled back into her seat on the other side of the sofa while Azuma frowned. She had a feeling there was more to whatever was making Azuma behave this way. Even despair wouldn't drive a person to such lengths.

"You don't need to get so carried away. We're all in the same boat, Azuma."

"..."

Azuma was silent for a moment, seeming to understand what she meant. A moment later he turned away.

"Even if Kaguya wakes up tomorrow, we can't go on like this. The same thing will just happen again because she won't stop. We need to find a way other than just defeating the heroes."

"Yes, you're probably right..."

So that was what was behind all of this.

Azuma had tried sending Kaguya away once before out of concern for her mental and physical health. At the time, they had all agreed—Azuma included—that they would just defeat the heroes like they used to. No more saving them.

But then Kaguya returned—and she showed them. They were forced to realize that they couldn't go on just killing the heroes.

"We were doing just fine before she came along. We can be fine again, so long as we just keep defeating them."

"Yes, so long as we *just* defeat them... You can see them now, right? The human faces inside the heroes."

Azuma had told her about it a little while ago. As an aftereffect of temporarily turning into a hero, he could now see into the shadows that covered the heroes' faces.

"Yes... Not that I want to."

"That's tough..." Not only could he hear the heroes' eggs, but now he could see the heroes' faces as well. "Is that why you're always in such a hurry to take them out so quickly?"

"Maybe… It's not a very pleasant thing to see. It would be hard to scrub their faces from my memory, no matter how hard I tried."

Unlike Kaguya, Azuma couldn't speak with the heroes. He could only see them. The stress, Koyuki imagined, had to be tremendous.

"But not so much that you want to stop going on missions, I'm guessing? What if you just covered your right eye while you fought?"

"No… I mean, Kaguya's not here right now," Azuma said, a faint smile playing on his lips as if he was embarrassed. "If I don't look… there will be no one to remember their last moments. They really will die as just monsters."

"So you're looking at them on purpose…"

The captain can be a real softie in the most unexpected of ways sometimes, Koyuki mused. The creatures they fought had already transformed into heroes; it was too late to save them. And yet he was purposely putting himself through the pain of looking at them just so that there would be someone who would remember their faces.

"You used to say they were just monsters, nothing more and nothing less."

"Yes, but the past is the past… Speaking of heroes," Azuma said, annoyed and purposefully changing the subject. "Today's hero gave us some trouble. I couldn't tell where the egg was. We got lucky earlier, but…"

Today's hero had been small, meaning they had been able to destroy it with a single strike—egg and all. But if it had been as massive as some of the heroes they had faced in the past?

"Things won't always go as easy as they went today," Azuma added. "We need to come up with a better plan."

"You're right… Maybe we should try asking Second Lieutenant Takanashi. She's used to fighting heroes without knowing where their eggs are located, after all."

There was another slight squeak as the door opened, and Koyuki and Azuma turned to see who was there.

Speak of the devil—it was Haru Takanashi. Her eyes widened slightly in surprise.

"What are you doing here at this late hour…?" she asked Koyuki.

"You're one to talk."

It was already past one AM. Haru would have usually been fast asleep.

"I had business with Captain Azuma," said Haru. "Since he wasn't in his room, I figured he might be here. But I didn't expect *you* to be up as well."

"Well, excuse me for wasting space."

"That's not what I… Never mind. You can be really high-maintenance sometimes, you know that?"

Haru looked overtly annoyed. While her reaction was a little aggravating, even annoyance was far more emotion than she had originally been willing to give them. Now her reaction was almost charming in a way.

"You wanted to speak to me?" asked Azuma. "If it's not too urgent, maybe it would be better to wait until tomorrow…"

"No… It's not an emergency, but I do think it's something that qualifies as fairly urgent."

"What is it?"

At the word *urgent*, Azuma tensed involuntarily. He leaned forward slightly so that he could better listen to what she had to say.

"You don't need to be so formal about it. But…well, it's something that feels a bit heavy for me to handle on my own." Haru spoke to both Koyuki and Azuma. "I have a favor to ask…"

A favor?

Koyuki and Azuma glanced at each other.

• • •

The two looked puzzled. Haru sat herself down on the sofa in front of them, their four eyes boring into her.

"What do you mean?" Koyuki said, the first to speak. "What kind of favor?"

"I want to look into why Inspection was so interested in Kaguya."

"You think they're up to something? Something to do with Lieutenant Shinohara?"

"Before I can answer that, there's something I need to explain…"

And she did. Haru explained what had first brought her to Charon and the things she had done after she arrived. It was actually her first time confessing all of this, but Azuma and Koyuki did not seem very surprised by what she said. They remained fairly levelheaded as she spoke.

"Because I was transferred from Inspection so suddenly, I still have access to the database. Someone will probably notice before long, but in the meantime, I've been extracting all of the data that I can."

"E-extracting…? Isn't that a problem?"

"Oh, it's a big problem. But this is no time to be sticklers for the rules. The Director was just murdered, after all. But here, look at this," Haru said, pulling a photograph from her inner breast pocket.

"Is this…a photo? On paper? I didn't know stuff like this still existed," Koyuki mused.

"Warrant Officer Ezakura discovered it with Lieutenant Shinohara in the archives at Headquarters."

Azuma and Koyuki were barely listening, however. They were too shocked by what the photograph showed.

"Judging by this picture," Haru began, "the origin of the term 'hero' might be somewhat different from what we were led to believe. But if so, then I wonder why they *are* called heroes."

And why was it kept hidden?

"Obviously, the Director was murdered. There's no doubt about that. And I think it is somehow related to their interest in Lieutenant Shinohara."

Azuma lifted his head slowly, fixing his eyes on Haru.

"That means…," he said.

Haru could see the panic in his face. He looked like a wild animal that had been spooked.

"What if—what if Kaguya is in danger, too? Just like the Director?!" Azuma demanded.

"Calm down. None of this is for certain. But…yes, it could be dangerous to leave her alone."

"C-could be…?"

"There's no need to panic. Warrant Officer Ezakura is almost always in the room with her. However, that does have something to do with the favor I wanted to ask you."

Azuma stared at Haru dubiously.

"I wanted to talk to you about taking me off mission duty for a little while," she continued calmly. "I don't make much of a contribution to battles to begin with, so I don't think it will be much of an issue in terms of combat strength."

"But why…?"

"It's not just about Kaguya Shinohara. There's a lot of things I need to dig into, and I need to do so as quickly as possible."

Azuma furrowed his brow ever so slightly. In that brief moment, a million thoughts ran through his head. But his expression immediately returned to normal. He nodded, giving his approval.

"I'm interested in knowing the truth myself. Fine. You're off missions for the time being."

"Thank you." Haru's eyes relaxed with her warm smile before immediately taking on their usual hard glint. "The Bureau is hiding something…"

And whatever it was, she had a feeling it was big.

INTERLUDE ONE
Delirium

Kaguya cocked her head to the side. She had the feeling that she had forgotten something very important.

She was currently watching the other members of Charon as they returned from battle.

Sakura, Koyuki, Haru, and Rindou. The battle had ended without any serious injuries, and no one had been lost. They were just as they had been when they'd left.

This time Haru had been the one to enter the hero's psyche. Exhausted, she was pressing a hand to her temple as if her head hurt.

"Just my luck. Why did I have to wind up being the closest…?"

"You did a great job out there, Haru," said Sakura, patting her on the shoulder. "It took you a while, though, didn't it? Did you have trouble persuading them?"

"Yeah… To be honest, I'm not too cut out for that part."

Kaguya giggled slightly. It sounded like Haru had worried for nothing.

The door to the hall opened, and several young men and women continued to file in, making small talk as they entered. Kaguya, who had been left to look after things while they were gone, went to greet them. The first face she spotted was Sakura's.

"Oh hey, Kaguya. We're home," said Sakura.

"Sakura, everyone, welcome back."

Kaguya greeted the other members as they settled into the room, but she was overcome by a feeling that something wasn't right. As if there was something bizarrely missing. Something that *should* have been there but sadly was not.

No, it's more than that...

This wasn't just an inkling. She felt certain. There was definitely something wrong about this image, something that was missing. But she had no idea what it could be. She scoured her hazy mind—trying manually to connect the dots—but nothing came to her.

Something abnormal—indistinct and indescribable. A feeling that couldn't be explained, like something was off. An oppressive malaise that was constantly weighing down on her.

"Hey, what's that?" said Koyuki. She had just noticed what was on the table—what Kaguya had put there. "Oh wow! Is that…cake?!"

"Y-yes, I just made it."

Since she was staying behind anyway, Kaguya figured that the least she could do was bake. Everyone was delighted, just as she had hoped.

"A homecoming cake? Kaguya, you're the best. Nothing beats something sweet after battle."

"I don't think you're using that word right, Sakura," Koyuki remarked. "We were just away on a short mission."

"Oh… Well, then it's a welcome-home cake."

"A welcome-home cake"? What a goofy thing to say. Everyone burst out laughing, charmed by Sakura's cute turn of phrase. Even Kaguya.

"There are more cakes in the refrigerator, too," she told everyone. "I made a bunch."

The team members were visibly excited. Haru immediately went to the refrigerator, opened it up, and peered inside. She cocked her head in surprise.

"It looks like there are ten in total. Isn't that a bit too much?"

"Too much? Is that a joke? If anything, I was worried I hadn't made enough," Kaguya said in her defense.

Koyuki rolled her eyes. "Kaguya, I hope you don't mind me saying this, but the weird one in this situation is you and your stomach."

"Really? Maybe you all just eat like birds. You need to eat if you're going to keep up your strength, you know?"

"Yes, but only *enough*! It's amazing you're able to pack so much away without making yourself sick…"

Kaguya cocked her head to the side. She didn't really eat *that* much, did she?

"Oh, what's the harm? We're not that tired today anyway. Might as well stay up and eat some cake," said Sakura, coming to Kaguya's rescue.

The squad disbanded temporarily. Sakura and Koyuki, who stayed behind, began chowing down on the cakes. Kaguya took a piece for herself as well.

Everything has been so great these days, thought Kaguya. Nobody was dying. Nobody was turning into a hero. It felt like she had been waiting for something like this forever. Her eyes began to well up with tears.

What's wrong with me, crying at a time like this…?

Kaguya wiped her cheek surreptitiously so that no one else would see. She could feel the wetness on the back of her hand. Even that trail of warmth on her cheek felt precious.

CHAPTER FOUR
Strife

Azuma and the rest of Charon were in Ikebukuro. They had just received a report of a hero sighting.

"SKREEE!!"

An insect-like screech rose into the air. The hero looked like what might be described as an amalgamation of books. Its body was shrouded in numerous volumes that functioned almost like appendages.

A hero comprised of countless books forming a single creature. It was shaped almost like a snake—its belly looking like an accordion's bellows with how the alternating books connected. They could hear the pages fluttering with the creature's every move, which made their hair stand on end.

"Azuma, do you have a read on the egg?"

"No…"

Azuma strained his ears, but once again, he couldn't hear it. There was a kind of static scream that interfered with his ability to hear the egg.

Unfortunately, the hero was much larger this time. It was about as thick around as a child's trunk and looked as if it could swallow at least a smaller human without trouble.

The mouth, however, was not visible due to the dark shadow that blotted out the space around its face.

Inside that void, Azuma had a clear view of the face of the young girl who had turned. It was like a hallucination that was only visible to his right eye. Bleakness, like heavy lead, spread throughout Azuma's body as he witnessed the sight.

They just had to defeat a hero—same as always. This had once seemed like the most natural thing in the world to Azuma, but no longer.

Now he could see them—their faces. And he had chosen to look so that he could remember their final moments for them.

"...Hah..."

The mental strain it caused was extreme. Koyuki had warned him not to get too reckless, so he was making an effort to tone things down. But sometimes, when he saw those faces, it took a moment for his emotions to catch up with his thoughts.

I thought...I would be able to get over it, but...

A hideous grin of madness confronted him with each swing of his katana. And there he was, like a reaper delivering quietus. A merciful executioner.

Before, against the fog hero, he thought he would get over it eventually.

But ever since Kaguya wound up in a coma, I've been stuck. At the end of the day, all I can really do is defeat heroes.

Every time he saw one of the heroes' shattered smiles, he was reminded of the fact that he, too, had once been in their shoes. The thought was like agony.

"Azuma, are you okay?" Koyuki said, sounding concerned.

"Don't worry. It's nothing. Right now, we need to focus on trying to find the egg."

"Y-yes, you're right. And it doesn't look like this hero is going to make it easy for us."

She could say that again. The members of Charon had relied on Azuma's ability for so long that they didn't know how to fight properly once they were forced to go in blind.

The hero began to make its move.

"Ah…!"

The snake hero suddenly reared up, baring its belly to Azuma and the others. The countless thick, mismatched books on the creature's underside opened up, exposing their contents to the other squad members. But there were no words or pictures inside, only darkness. It was a blinding dark, as if every page had been doused in blackness.

"Don't look at it!" Azuma shouted. He knew his voice was trembling. "It's the same as the darkness around its head. It's all the same!"

The hero's face awaited within the blackness of the books. An illusion, of course. A glimpse into the depths of the hero and the shadows inside.

The girl was approaching adolescence but still younger than Azuma and the others. Her childish face—distorted in a hideous smile—repeated infinitely in each of the open books.

Her visage bore a twisted cackle, but there was no time for panic. Azuma heard someone click their tongue over the comms. It was Rindou.

"I hate when they go for quantity over quality. We'll just have to cut a path open by force. Isn't that right, Koyuki?"

"I guess, but you're making it sound so easy. Each of those books might be weak on their own, but it's always the heroes that try to overwhelm you with numbers that turn out to be the worst."

All the many books began moving independently, like butterflies, each taking on their own twisted forms to attack. They morphed into birds, insects, trees, and other shapes and began harassing the members of Charon.

A hero could not move without an egg. Parts that were sliced off from a hero's body, apart from the egg, became mere meat. There was always an egg. But Azuma could no longer hear it.

"SKRRREEEEE!!"

The hero's scream caused Azuma to snap out of his thoughts. No amount of confusion was enough to put a damper on his fighting instincts. It was almost laughable in a way.

The books flocked to attack. These books that colored the girl's interior world were all different sizes and thicknesses.

The first book to enter Azuma's field of vision resembled a dictionary.

Blotted out in darkness and transformed into a blunt weapon, the book flew toward Azuma. He slashed through it as easily as silk and then prepared for the next attack. A novel, a picture book, a comic—he chopped through each with a single slice of his blade.

They were like ordinary books. All it took to cut through them was to connect.

"However...," Azuma said, hesitating for a moment.

He had once started to turn into a hero himself. He could no longer remember it clearly, but immediately before turning, he had seen things.

Images of his younger sister completely transformed into a hero. A girl scattering into pink. Many other visions. So many humans who had become heroes—the ones he couldn't save. The images were still burned into his eyes.

Don't think about that now.

Azuma shook his head. A trip down memory lane could wait until later.

"Azuma, maybe you haven't noticed the way you're just standing around...but things are starting to look pretty bad here."

Apologizing briefly, Azuma turned to face the hero again. He took it all in—the mad smile resting within the darkness around its face.

If Kaguya were here...

...What would she do? What choice would Kaguya want him to make? What was it she expected from him?

"Captain Azuma, please."

A memory of her voice, lingering in the evening light, suddenly passed through Azuma's mind. He remembered what he had said to her in response. That he would do what he could, when it came to the heroes.

More books attacked. This time it was some sort of illustrated encyclopedia series. There must have been dozens of them lined up in impressive spectacle. They formed a clump as if the cover of one were glued to the back of the next. Azuma stood in their way.

Koyuki had fired her rifle several times by now, causing relatively serious damage with each shot. She seemed to have realized something.

"There, it's protecting that area over there...." she muttered. "Rindou, look!"

Rindou did as he was told. Azuma also turned his attention in the direction that Koyuki was indicating with her eyes.

The area corresponded to what would have been the snake's eye. A thin book was placed there. It was an extremely small notepad, noticeably different from the swarm of books currently causing havoc all around them.

Encyclopedias, comics, and other thick books were rotating in the air around the notepad as if to protect it.

"That's it! Koyuki, cover me!"

"Leave it to me!!" Koyuki hollered, readying her weapon.

The hero realized that the jig was up, and its main body, which was made up of countless books in the shape of a snake, suddenly began to rampage. The chaos prevented Azuma from getting close.

Koyuki, however, did not back down. She kept her gun at the ready, paying the commotion no mind.

She had made plans with Rindou in advance.

Their first priority had been locating the egg. The egg was the core of the hero. It was like the heart of a living creature. If heroes were in fact living creatures, then surely heroes would also attempt to protect their hearts.

"So the plan is, I attack with everything I've got," Rindou had said, *"and you stay back and keep your eyes peeled. Try to figure out if there's an area it's trying to protect."*

While Rindou served as bait, Koyuki would watch how the hero moved and countered and try to identify where its defenses lied. Once she identified the spot, she would shoot.

Despite the sheer volume of matter rampaging about her, Koyuki never broke her stance. She was waiting for an opportunity. A single moment was all it would take. One moment when nothing interfered with her line of sight toward the egg.

It was a delicate task, like threading the eye of a needle. Several of the rampaging books seemed to recognize Koyuki as a new threat as she took aim. They moved to attack.

With enough of them together, even books made for fairly dangerous weapons. Koyuki, however, held her ground. A hardcover illustrated encyclopedia flew her way. It was sure to hurt if it made direct contact, but just as a corner of the heavy tome was about to connect with her face, Rindou kicked it out of the air.

The two functioned like a well-oiled machine while Azuma stared in amazement from the side. Each time Rindou found himself in a pinch, Koyuki came to his rescue. Likewise, whenever Koyuki was in danger, Rindou swooped in to her aid.

Up until now, they had relied on Azuma's power and then later Kaguya's power at the end of the day. But now that neither Azuma nor Kaguya could use those powers, it was up to them instead.

"Duck!"

Rindou dropped down immediately. There it was, just above his head.

Koyuki had her line of sight. She could see the notebook, which formed the creature's red eye, clearly in the middle of her scope. Although she could neither see nor sense them, she also spared a thought for the original human who must be resting inside. Whoever they were, they, too, must have had a reason for ending up like this.

"What kind of dream are you dreaming, I wonder?"

She pulled the trigger.

Instantly, the bullet launched from the barrel and hit its mark—easily destroying the snake's face, along with the egg inside, and causing the book to catch fire and explode. As the crimson flare seared itself into her eyes, Koyuki offered up a solitary prayer.

Whatever frustrated wish, whatever dream this hero might have been dreaming—may it end gently, at least.

CHAPTER FIVE
Steel

"…"

Kaguya, of course, continued to sleep. Haru felt indescribably sad.

She was sitting in the hospital room, staring at a single photograph. She had gotten her hands on it after Mari had told her about it.

This photograph was exactly what she had been seeking for so long. However, she had too many questions now to feel happy that she had found it.

The date displayed in the photograph was April 6, 2030. Thirty years ago—it was a marvel that a paper photograph from that time still remained. But the real issue was with what the photograph displayed.

"A hero…"

A hero, one of those creatures that Haru knew so well, standing majestically in the middle of an urban neighborhood, just existing. As if it *belonged there*. There was no sign in the photograph of the hostility and destructive behavior she was used to seeing in heroes.

She flipped the photograph over. The words *Technical Research Lab No. 1* were written on the back. Meaning this photograph had likely been in Technical No. 1's possession.

Then what was it doing in the archives at Headquarters of all places? Since Mari had found it, it must have been somewhere fairly easy to discover. That was just one of the questions Haru now harbored.

"Hmm... It seems like answers only bring more questions..."

The whole reason that Haru had gone rogue, operating separately from the other members of Charon, was to uncover the truth. Both because she was originally from Inspection and because she felt like she was in Charon's debt. She had originally come to Charon to betray Kaguya, after all.

"Based on this thirty-year-old photograph, however, something clearly must have occurred to change things over the following twenty-five years."

There were no documents or records from that period, unfortunately.

Haru decided to start by investigating the katana that had been left behind at the scene of the Director's murder instead. With a little bit of scavenging, it hadn't taken her long to uncover more details about the sword.

She had also learned a certain piece of information about the Chronoses. Something she wanted to let everyone know.

Just then, the sliding door rattled opened. Haru, whose back had been facing the door, turned around in surprise.

"Umm...?"

"You're...Warrant Officer Mari Ezakura, correct?"

The girl's golden eyes widened as if she hadn't expected anyone to be there. This was Haru's first time finding herself alone, one-on-one, with Warrant Officer Ezakura. Haru could not help but feel awkward. Warrant Officer Ezakura was hardly someone she would have gone out of her way to spend time with.

"U-umm... What are you doing here...? Isn't Charon on a mission...?"

"Yes... I had something else to deal with. Did you come to visit Kaguya?"

Mari didn't answer. Like a wary cat, she kept her distant eyes fixed on Haru.

"What are you so afraid of? It's not like I'm going to bite."

"Who said I was afraid…? I'm not. And I don't have anything against you personally."

Mari slowly settled into the other chair in the room. She had a clear view of Kaguya from her new position.

"So why are you keeping at arm's length like that?" Haru asked.

Mari, who barely took up a corner of her chair, answered curtly in a voice that could barely be heard.

"Because I hate you…"

Haru Takanashi. The young woman who had only just recently joined Charon. Mari knew she was being harsh, but she didn't apologize.

Naturally, Mari had barely ever interacted with her before. Never, really, unless you counted simply being in the same room together.

Haru seemed more than a little offended by Mari's words.

"You hate me? I don't see what I've done to deserve being spoken to like that, considering as I've barely said two words to you before."

"Not you, specifically… Charon."

Mari's voice came out surprisingly barbed. She knew she was just lashing out at this point.

"I've been by Kaguya's side since the beginning. It was Charon. They're the ones who put her in this state. That's why…that's why I hate them all."

"Oh, is that all?" Haru said, sounding surprisingly indifferent. Or even as if she was laughing at Mari a little. "In other words, you just want someone to blame so that you don't have to face up to how unfair reality is."

"…!"

"If you really need someone to blame, it should be the heroes, not us. But I suspect you already know that."

Mari did. She understood it very well. Which is why she remained silent now. She wasn't about to apologize, though. She was still simmering quietly when…

"I'm sorry. I shouldn't have said it like that."

Haru apologized first, taking Mari by surprise.

"We all understand how you feel. We just haven't said anything about it... It was obvious you never approved of Lieutenant Shinohara working at Charon."

"Well...I didn't exactly hide it."

In fact, she had consciously chosen not to hide it. She thought that if she made her feelings obvious, there was a slim chance Kaguya might have changed her mind. Although that didn't pay off in the end.

"So if you hate us, I guess that's just the way things are. Although you should probably keep that information to yourself."

Mari wasn't sure if Haru was being philosophical or just didn't care. It was hard to get a read on someone like her. But Mari could tell that Haru wasn't a bad person.

"Umm...," Mari ventured timidly. "Second Lieutenant Takanashi? What are you actually here for?"

"I learned something about the Chronoses and wanted to let everyone else know."

"Something about the Chronoses...?"

Mari was also harboring a secret about the Chronoses. She braced herself, worried about what might be coming.

"I uncovered some records at Inspection... Records related to Technical."

"Records related to Technical...?! What kind of records?"

"I learned some details about how Chronoses are created."

Haru visibly hesitated for a moment. It didn't seem like she was hesitating over whether or not to tell Mari what she had learned, so much as she was actually afraid to put the truth into words.

"It's related to the Director's death as well."

"What?" Mari leaned forward impulsively. "Wh-what do you mean, related? What does this have to do with the Director?"

"There was something that was bothering me. That Chronos that was apparently found by the Director's body? It shouldn't have existed, but there it was after the Director died, just lying there. I think the Director's death may have been the trigger for it."

Mari could only open and shut her mouth reflexively. This was too much to hear.

"And…you're going to tell them that? You're going to tell the other members of Charon?"

"Yes… Is there a problem with that?"

"But if you tell them the truth, won't they stop fighting?"

Haru looked Mari straight in the eyes for the first time since arriving.

"What do you mean?"

"Well, that would mean that someone needs to die in order for a Chronos to be made. If Charon were to hear about that, they might not be able to bring themselves to wield the things anymore."

Haru stared at Mari silently. The lack of expression on her face made it impossible to tell what she was thinking. Mari felt more and more uncomfortable with each passing second.

"S-so wouldn't it be better, maybe, not to say anything?"

"Warrant Officer Ezakura," Haru said, a reprimand in her voice. "Don't you think that's being disrespectful to them?"

"Disrespectful…?"

"Charon have kept fighting all this time, regardless of whatever obstacles they had to face. They're hardly soft enough to throw in the towel over something like this."

"H-how?" Mari rose to her feet involuntarily. "How can you be so sure?! If…if Captain Azuma decided he couldn't bring himself to use that sword anymore…"

"If he did decide something like that, then he was obviously never cut out to be the squad's captain in the first place."

Cold—Haru seemed as cold as ice to Mari at that moment. But beneath that coldness, Mari also sensed burning passion. Mari wasn't sure how to respond.

"You've got a secret of your own, don't you?" Haru asked as if she could see straight through Mari. "Something you're keeping to yourself.

Whatever that secret is, I'm guessing that it's something that would be difficult for Charon to hear."

Mari was mortified that Haru had caught on to her so easily. But Haru was right. Regardless of the outcome, Mari was fairly sure that her secret would hit Charon like a ton of bricks.

"I don't know what your secret is. It's up to you to decide whether or not to share it in the end. However..."

The only other sound in the hospital room was the measured noise of Kaguya's breathing. Haru's voice hung deliberately in the air as if she had a point that needed to be made.

"In my opinion, they have a right to know."

"A...right to know?"

Mari considered this. What Haru was preparing to tell everyone was indeed shocking news, but it was hardly crucial information. Mari doubted that anyone would get hurt if Haru just kept that information to herself.

Mari's secret, however, was like a lit grenade. Something inside Mari was screaming at her not to let it out.

"B-but—"

"What do you think she would do?" Haru said, directing her eyes toward Kaguya. Mari followed her gaze. "What would Lieutenant Shinohara think about all this? Do you think she would choose to stay quiet out of consideration for Captain Azuma's feelings?"

Mari's thoughts ran to Kaguya and to everything she knew about her.

Kaguya would tell them.

The answer came to Mari more quickly than she had expected.

Kaguya would never act so fainthearted. Even if that meant causing Azuma pain. Even if that meant Charon would stop fighting. She would just laugh and say, "We'll cross that bridge when we get there."

Kaguya was Mari's mentor, an object of love and respect. And whether Mari liked it or not, Kaguya believed in the other members of Charon. Mari doubted Kaguya could be so wrong about something like that.

"Kaguya would tell them..."

Mari made up her mind. She decided to follow her heart.

"I know she would. She would do it for Charon's sake... You're right. She would consider it disrespectful not to tell them the truth, just because it might hurt them."

"I agree. But what about you?" Haru asked, turning her gaze toward Mari in expectation. Mari answered her gaze head-on.

"I'm going to tell them. I'm going to tell them what I know."

"Good. Then we can both tell everyone what we know once they get back."

Although Mari couldn't see it, she could sense Haru's bemused smile.

"So do you still hate me now?"

"Absolutely."

That remained the same, but...

"However...Kaguya trusted you."

"You really do think the world of Lieutenant Shinohara, don't you?" Haru said, shrugging her shoulders in an exaggerated fashion like a character from a movie.

Watching her out of the corners of her eyes, Mari steeled her nerves. Charon was ready—ready to hear the awful truth.

CHAPTER SIX
Awakening

Once the battle ended, Azuma noticed he had a message on his terminal.

However, it was just one sentence long: *I'm waiting in Kaguya's hospital room.*

Haru must have learned something. There would be no need to message him if she was only visiting Kaguya. He hurried toward Kaguya's hospital room.

"Warrant Officer Ezakura…?"

Upon arriving, he saw that Mari was there as well.

She had probably just come to pay Kaguya a visit. But the expression on her face was a complete turnaround from the gloomy look she usually wore. It seemed as if she had made up her mind about something important.

Her presence, however, was slightly inconvenient right now. Azuma had come to speak with Haru.

"I'm sorry, but would you mind leaving the room for a little while? Takanashi and I—"

"No, Captain Azuma. Mari should stay."

The expression that appeared on Haru's face was difficult to describe. Like someone staring ruefully at a cup of spilled coffee.

"Oh? I suppose that's fine."

Azuma gave Haru a questioning look. The only people in the room were Haru, Mari, Koyuki, Rindou, and Kaguya, who was unconscious.

Haru began without further ado.

"I've learned more about how Chronoses are created."

"You've what…?"

"I was able to access Inspection's database and get my hands on some data connected to the Chronoses. There were a lot of things about the Director's death that didn't seem to add up…"

Haru began explaining in a soft voice. She spoke about how the final stage of creating Chronoses involved bathing the weapons in human blood and how this was also part of the reason the Director was killed—that it wasn't just to keep her quiet.

"How sinister…," Koyuki said in disgust. "In other words, that means that the Chronoses we use every day were created out of blood and death."

They had left their weapons in the transport truck, so there were no Chronoses in the room with them at the moment. Azuma's thoughts ran briefly to his katana, which had been found at the scene of the Director's death. It must have absorbed the Director's blood.

Azuma, however, was not too affected by the news. He was used to such revelations by this point and was not about to lose his head over every new surprise.

"This may just be my own opinion, but I would rather prioritize those who are still alive over those who are no longer with us," he said. "I'm sorry, but choosing not to use these weapons out of some compunction just doesn't seem like an option to me."

"Good… I'm glad to hear it." Haru looked toward the corner of the room. "That's all I had to say. But Warrant Officer Ezakura apparently has something to share as well."

Azuma's gaze settled on Mari, and he tried not to show surprise. A mixed expression appeared on the warrant officer's face. Determination rippled with fear.

Mari began speaking somewhat timidly.

"What I wanted to speak about is related in a way—well, possibly, I think. But I need to ask you all something. Are you willing to keep fighting, no matter what you learn?"

"…? What do you mean, no matter what?"

"Well, if something even more awful were to occur, for instance. If something were to come to light that was completely untenable. Are you sure you could keep going on, just like before?"

"I don't know what it is you're suggesting…," Azuma answered calmly. "But it wouldn't change anything about what we need to do. We all know how important it is to defeat the heroes—"

Azuma paused mid-sentence. If defeating the heroes was all they cared about, there would have been no need for all this handwringing in the first place.

"No, not just defeat heroes. To save people as well. To prevent any more people from dying whenever possible, including even the heroes."

"Okay… Then my mind is made up. The Director confided something in me before she died… Something about the Chronoses."

Mari's voice commanded the room. Azuma and the others simply listened in silence.

"According to what she told me, they can think. These Chronoses… They have minds of their own."

"Minds…?"

Azuma misheard her at first. He thought she had said *mines*. As if there was some sort of secret metal that was used. But obviously, that would not merit such a fuss.

"Sentience, I suppose you could say."

"Sentience…?"

Azuma was still confused. What was she trying to say? Sentience was something found in humans, not in inanimate weapons. How would anyone even confirm something like that?

"They retain their awareness and are still conscious, even now, of what happens in the world around them."

"…? What do you mean?"

"It's, um, sort of like locked-in syndrome," Mari explained, scrambling to remember what the Director had told her.

Mari explained how Chronoses contained the consciousnesses of the original humans they were created from, still sealed inside. She also told them about the rebounds—how they were the consciousnesses' manic attempts to resist.

Azuma was speechless. As were Rindou and Koyuki.

"Is that—?" Azuma's mouth felt unpleasantly dry. "Is all of that true?"

"It is. I learned it firsthand when I visited the Director's lab...," Mari explained, almost as if she was trying to defend herself. But they weren't worried about that right now.

"Is there any proof?"

"Nothing that could rise to the level of conclusive evidence. But I witnessed some of the Director's experiments in person."

Mari elaborated on what she had seen in detail: Yuuji Sakigaya and the stress response tests. And the tubes of liquid, red like blood.

"Sorry, but I'm not buying it," Rindou said, looking uneasy. "This is probably all just speculation on your part."

"You're right; it is. I can't deny that. But I'm telling you, you have to believe me. What reason would I have to lie about something like this deliberately?"

"Tsk. So what are you telling us for?" There was something dangerous in Rindou's voice, wild like an animal's. "It doesn't change anything, does it? Whether we know the truth or not? So then why even tell us?! What possible reason—?"

"Rindou, stop."

Azuma held up a hand to restrain Rindou, just in case. He almost looked like he was about to strike Mari. After managing to get his own breathing under control, Azuma turned to face Mari.

"When you say they are conscious of the outside world...does that mean they can feel pain as well?"

"Th-that's what the Director said."

"Weapons that can feel pain...?" Koyuki was starting to grow belligerent. Perhaps it was her fatigue speaking. "What kind of nonsense is that? Do you even hear yourself? What makes you think we would ever believe something like that?"

"Well... I don't...I guess..."

Mari cowered in response. However.

"Permission," Haru said, softly, as if coming to Mari's aid. Everyone turned their eyes toward her. "She said that the weapon had given her *permission*."

"She? You mean Kaguya?"

Haru nodded. She seemed to be working out her thoughts as she spoke.

"If Chronoses really do have minds of their own, that word choice would make a lot more sense."

"B-but that was just Kaguya speaking off the cuff, wasn't it?! The idea that Chronoses could be conscious and feel pain is ridiculous. They're just weapons—"

"Living weapons. And the rebounds, which only those of you in Charon are immune to, may in fact be an expression of that will."

But to what end?

"In other words, the rebounds may be their method of communicating that they do not want to be used as weapons."

The room fell quiet. It felt like something cold and silent was pressing down on them from above.

"So what makes us different, then...?" Azuma asked, his voice shaking slightly.

The idea that these Chronoses, which they swung around like tools without a second thought, might in fact have minds of their own—he didn't want to admit it might be true.

He briefly remembered his katana, now tossed haphazardly into the armory. Was there someone in there? A person inside?

Someone who had witnessed the Director's death?

"I've never felt any kind of resistance. Yes, there's physical recoil with the guns, but as for what everyone else experiences..."

Azuma trailed off. He wanted to insist that Mari was wrong, but it was difficult to do so with much confidence.

"That's just speculation, though, right…?"

"It's speculation, yes, but everything adds up." Haru had never handled a Chronos and was able to consider the matter with more detachment than the others present. "The reason that none of you experience rebounds is because you were altered by the hero six years ago, correct?"

"Yes. At least, that's what I've been told," Azuma said, answering for all of them.

It was Kaguya's theory. That also fell into the realm of speculation, but even to a layman like Azuma, her explanation seemed reasonable enough.

"Everyone in Charon contains a hero factor due to your contact with the hero from six years ago. It's why the weapons are unable to resist you. Either that or their resistance just has no effect on you."

"What do you mean…?"

"The reason is unclear. But even if we speculate that Chronoses are sentient and are able to reject being used by humans, it may simply be that this pushback has no effect on people who contain the so-called hero factor. Remember, even though Lieutenant Shinohara once started to turn into a hero herself, she does not actually contain the hero factor, so—"

"Stop it." Koyuki's voice, like a soft cry, interrupted Haru's train of thought. "Stop talking about us like we're monsters."

"I'm sorry…"

Haru averted her eyes uncomfortably. No one spoke. Unable to bring themselves to agree with what she was saying, yet unable to refute her. Not even Azuma could think of anything to say that might lighten the mood.

This was all so much to process. The notion that Chronoses could contain a hero's consciousness was already mind-boggling enough. Add to that the idea that rebounds could be an intentional manic act of resistance on the part of sentient creatures? One that was only ineffective against them because they had been, in essence, bred by the heroes?

The silence was petrifying.

As difficult as it all was to believe, there was no indication that any of it was a lie. First and foremost, why would Mari make up such a thing in the first place? And as for the Director? Well, the Director had been killed. If this were all just unhinged paranoia on her part, constructed from whole cloth, then there would have been no reason for her to meet such a fate.

"So Chronoses are sentient and can feel pain. If that's true...," Rindou said at last. "Could that have something to do with the fact that heroes also possess psyches of their own? The two things can't be completely unconnected, right? That would have to be a pretty wild coincidence..."

"Well..."

Mari fell silent, seemingly uncomfortable. It wasn't that the question had been unexpected. Rather, it seemed as if she had anticipated they would ask that but had no answer. At least, that was what her expression seemed to say.

"I don't really know..."

"In my opinion," Azuma continued, "this must have something to do with why the Director was killed. The Director must have learned something that was inconvenient for someone. It's the only explanation I can think of. And that something is almost certainly what Warrant Officer Ezakura has just informed us of."

"But why?" Mari asked, lowering her eyes in thought. "Obviously, I can understand why they wouldn't want to let the soldiers who use Chronoses know something like this, but would that really be enough of a reason to take things this far...?"

"There's probably something more. Something else they want to keep hidden."

No one disagreed with that assessment.

• • •

After the others had dispersed, Azuma remained behind, leaving just himself and Kaguya.

She lay upon her hospital bed like Sleeping Beauty, the hero's egg still in her throat.

Azuma was used to the sound. He could hear it clearly right now. Apparently, the only reason he couldn't hear the eggs during battle was because of the static that was getting in his way, not because he had actually lost the ability.

Azuma hesitated and then stroked Kaguya's throat lightly as she continued to slumber wearily. Of course, she did not stir.

Azuma obviously wasn't going to do any more than that.

"I...I hope this really is just fatigue."

Hypothetically, Kaguya had fallen into a coma from all the mental stress she had been under. However, no one knew for sure.

"It turns out the Chronoses might be sentient...," Azuma said, taking a step away from Kaguya. "And apparently, it takes every drop of blood in a person's body to create one. It's hard to believe, isn't it...?"

Azuma no longer felt very comfortable using his katana. Not to the point that he was actually going to stop. But he didn't like it.

"You can talk to the heroes, right? I wonder if you can talk to the Chronoses as well."

Kaguya could hear the heroes' voices.

"How would you feel about all this if you knew, Kaguya? I mean, it's not like we can just stop fighting at this point..."

Kaguya had attempted to use a Chronos herself several times in the past. She would probably be as shocked by this news as they were.

Azuma leaned over Kaguya as he spoke, peering down into her face. He stood up straight again. As he did so, he caught a flash of silver light out of the left-hand corner of his eye.

It was his earring. The cross-shaped accessory his sister had left for him. He took a moment now to remove it. He only took the earring off once a day before he went to sleep. But he had been so busy lately that he had been forgetting to do that. He went to stuff it into his pocket casually.

"Ah!"

Instead, he dropped it. It landed on Kaguya's throat.

The earring was pure silver, but fortunately, it wasn't very large and didn't land with much weight. Kaguya's eyes remained closed.

Apologizing to her internally, Azuma scooped up the earring and tucked it safely into his pocket.

No one said a word. It was as if time had stopped, but only within this one hospital room.

If Kaguya were to wake up now—Azuma had spoken about this with Koyuki earlier—would they finally be able to get her to stop what she had been doing?

"No. I doubt I could, at least… It's not so easy to change a person's heart."

Azuma turned his back toward Kaguya. His thoughts were on today's fight with the hero now.

He walked toward the room's sliding door without turning around. Just as it began to rattle open beneath his hand—he heard the sound of cloth shifting behind him.

"?!"

Azuma spun around in shock. What now? What was happening?

And then he froze. Every previous thought had flown from his head.

"…Kagu…ya…"

Kaguya Shinohara had woken up.

CHAPTER SEVEN
Transition

It took the girl a moment to realize she had no idea where she was.

A white ceiling. Her eyes settled on the thin blanket, almost as white, draped over her where she lay in bed. An astringent smell, like disinfectant, filled the room. There was also a young man in the room wearing a turquoise uniform.

Huh…?

Upon waking up, Kaguya Shinohara promptly cocked her head, confused. She could have sworn she had been somewhere fun, somewhere amazing. What was she doing in this bed?

Wait, where am I…?

She took a slow, careful look around. The young man in the turquoise uniform was staring at her in shock. He seemed astonished. Kaguya wasn't sure how to respond.

After all, she had only just woken up. Her thoughts were still in a jumble. It felt like there was a fog hanging over her head.

Part of Kaguya realized she must have still been half asleep. She felt like you do when you wake up in the morning after sleeping for too long and the blood won't circulate fully to your head.

But those bluish eyes were staring straight at her. Kaguya was still trying to shake the dust out of her mind when the young man with the silver hair spoke hesitantly.

"Kaguya…?"

It took her a moment to realize that this was her own name. She then remembered the name of the young man as well.

"Captain…Azuma…?"

Her lips felt like they were operating separately from the rest of her body. After saying his name, Kaguya finally registered the situation she was in.

She was in a hospital room. At Headquarters. And the young man standing before her was one of her colleagues from Charon. Yuuri Azuma.

The boy suddenly skyrocketed in resolution, eventually materializing into a solid concept in her mind. From a theoretical sign to a flesh-and-blood comrade. One whom she had fought with, side by side.

"What…what in the world is going on? Why are you staring at me like that?" she asked him.

"Y-you don't remember what happened to you?"

Before she could ask what he meant, it all started to come back to her. The last thing she could remember was fighting a hero. And then she had lost consciousness. She had collapsed after fighting heroes before. Perhaps this had been something similar.

Satisfied with that explanation for now, Kaguya put on her biggest smile and said nothing.

"Kaguya… Do you know what day it is?"

"What day?" Kaguya cocked her head to the side. It was early July, wasn't it? The fifth, maybe? "July fifth, right? But why are you asking me that?"

Azuma furrowed his brow uneasily. "Kaguya…," he said gently. "It's already August. It's the first week of August. It's been nearly a month."

"What?"

That didn't make any sense. Did he just say August?

"It's August…? Today? Now?"

"Do you remember the last thing that you were doing?"

"Th-the last thing that I was doing was fighting a hero, wasn't it…? If I remember right, you pinned the hero down for me, like you always do. And then I entered the hero's psyche...," Kaguya said, listing the events as they occurred to her.

But that was where she hit a wall. She couldn't remember anything after connecting with the hero. No, that wasn't entirely true—there was something she could still recall.

"And then...I think I entered some kind of darkness..."

Kaguya recoiled slightly in fear. After that, there was nothing. Apparently, she had lost consciousness. There were no further memories to be found.

But what about the hero?

"H-how long have I—?!"

"A whole month. You've, um...been unconscious."

Azuma explained how she had been in a coma.

But why...?

Not just unconscious but fully comatose. Kaguya didn't think she had been in poor health beforehand, physically or mentally.

"I'm sorry for worrying you...," she told Azuma.

"It's fine. More importantly, how do you feel? It will probably be hard to move at first, but other than that?"

Kaguya shook her head, indicating she was okay. He was right—she could barely move her body. But that was natural, considering how long it had been since she had used any of her muscles.

"What about the others?" Kaguya managed to croak out. Where were they? Koyuki, Rindou, Haru, Mari, and the Director? For some reason, she wanted them there right now. "Where is everyone?"

She had barely managed to get the words out when the door to the hospital room slid open.

"Speaking of which, I forgot to mention—," Koyuki said, already mid-sentence as she entered the room.

"What...?" Koyuki froze in obvious shock, the door still half open. Kaguya waved. "Kaguya...?!?!"

Koyuki's voice was so loud it bounced off the walls. Kaguya didn't even have enough time to register the shock before the other members of Charon came rushing back into the room.

Kaguya gasped as their familiar faces became real once again—she could physically feel the change.

"G-good morning, every—"

"Waaahhh!!"

"?!"

Kaguya was thrust backward into her bed as Mari catapulted into her arms. She clung to Kaguya, crying in a way that Kaguya had never seen her cry before. Mari could be a little childish at times but never so impetuous as this. Kaguya was flabbergasted.

"M-Mari, what's gotten into you?"

"Into *me*?!" Mari cried unreasonably. "There was no one left... I was all alone..."

"No one left? What do you mean?"

Kaguya glanced toward Azuma for help. Azuma moved with a start, forcibly detaching Mari from her. Mari meekly allowed herself to be pulled away. Kaguya could see tears welling up in Mari's eyes.

Azuma took Mari's place, stepping in front of Kaguya.

"Warrant Officer Ezakura, Kaguya has only just come out of her coma."

"O-of course. I'm sorry..."

Mari reluctantly gave Kaguya breathing room. Before she could get away, however, Kaguya spoke up to stop her.

"Mari, what did you mean earlier, when you said you were all alone?"

"Oh...!" Mari covered her mouth as if realizing she had said something she shouldn't have.

An uncomfortable silence ensued. Something was wrong. Kaguya could feel some sort of tightness building in her chest.

There was only Mari and her colleagues from Charon in the room right now. Someone was missing. Not that Kaguya would expect the Director to come visit her in the hospital, Kaguya knew she could be standoffish about such things. But still...

"Where is the Director...?"

Once the words left Kaguya's mouth, the air in the hospital room seemed to freeze.

Something was clearly amiss. At the mention of the Director's name, several of the others averted their eyes, unsure of where to look. The expression on Azuma's face as he stood in front of her was visibly pained.

"Kaguya, the truth is...," Azuma said, his voice soft with concern. His face was contorted in pain, and he seemed worried about what effect his words would have on her. "The Director is already..."

Kaguya stopped hearing what he was saying halfway through. The Director was dead—not only that but she had been stabbed through the throat with a Chronos and was found with a gaping hole in the middle of her forehead.

"B-but...," Kaguya said, finally managing to string together her words. "How could something like that happen? An accident? It was an accident, right? What did the Bureau say?"

"They're calling it a suicide."

"That's not possi—*hurk*!"

Kaguya wretched harshly, the sudden strain on her vocal cords having apparently been too great.

There was no way the Director could have wounded herself twice if it had just been an accident. As for suicide, regardless of which wound she caused first, the throat or the forehead, she would not have had enough strength left to cause the second.

It had obviously been murder.

Kaguya was in so much shock that she didn't even cry. Maybe it just didn't feel real yet; Kaguya's boss, someone she had spent the last two years with, was suddenly gone.

"In any case," Koyuki said gently as she rubbed Kaguya's back, "now isn't the time for this conversation. You're probably going to need a lot of rehabilitation. You should take your time."

"You're right... I'm sorry."

Azuma looked uncomfortable. The atmosphere in the hospital room felt strange and dour. Kaguya was still having trouble accepting the situation.

Ah...speaking of which...

Suddenly remembering something, Kaguya began scribbling across a notepad as she pressed a hand to her throat. The battles with the heroes. These were very important. What had they been doing while she was gone?

"Wh-what about the battles with the heroes?"

"..."

There were many things that question could mean, and Azuma registered them all.

"Things have returned to normal," he said, keeping his face neutral, as if they were just making small talk. "Back to how they were before you came here. We're back to just defeating the heroes again. I know you must not be happy to hear that."

Kaguya looked disappointed, as expected. "No, I'm sorry. I know it's the only way."

There was nothing Azuma could say in response. It was the truth, after all.

Kaguya's eyes were downcast. She lifted her face again and turned toward Azuma, cocking her head slightly. "You know, it's kind of funny... Seeing that expression on your face."

"This expression? What do you mean?"

"I guess you've changed. You used to insist that heroes were nothing but monsters."

"Oh..." Azuma felt oddly wistful. Come to think of it, there had been a time when he had thought that way. "You must have rubbed off on me, I guess."

"I have? On you?"

"Is that so hard to believe?"

There was a mischievous twinkle in Kaguya's eye. Azuma waved his hand in the air dismissively.

"You can be very adorable when you want to be, you know that, Captain Azuma?"

"You've just woken up. Stop babbling and get some rest."

"Rest is the last thing I need. I've been asleep for a whole month. If anything, it's about time I got out of bed and got some work done."

Her attitude made Azuma uneasy.

"There's no need to overdo things…"

"Overdo things? Who's overdoing things?" Kaguya said, smiling like normal. "I'm just trying to get back in the saddle. When have I ever not tried to save one of the people inside the heroes?"

Never. Not as far as Azuma knew. Even when it was impossible, she had still given it a try. Which was precisely what was making Azuma feel so uneasy right now.

Someone who didn't know when to quit was sure to break eventually. Break into so many pieces that there would be no coming back.

CHAPTER EIGHT
Discord

"Her full workup came back fine. There's some physical atrophy, but she should recover from that quickly," Azuma said, summarizing the results briefly.

For some reason, Koyuki felt a little depressed. Kaguya was almost back to where she was before entering the coma.

"Two weeks," Kaguya said, explaining what she had been told about her condition. "I'm supposed to get some rest and a little rehabilitation before getting back to work, but supposedly, two weeks should be enough."

"Hmph…" Koyuki felt a complicated mix of emotions. "That seems pretty short. Wouldn't it be better if you rested a little longer?"

"Short? I actually thought it seemed a bit long."

"Kaguya. You've been unconscious for a whole month, and not just from normal exhaustion. There was contact with a hero. Two weeks is hardly enough time to recuperate from that."

"I don't know," Kaguya said, cocking her head. As far as she was concerned, two weeks was overkill.

"Look at it this way, Kaguya, what would you say if it were me? If, after being in a coma for a whole month, I said I only wanted to take two weeks to recover…?"

"Hmm… I suppose I wouldn't like it."

"There, you see? That's exactly what I mean. That's how I feel. I'm worried you're taking things too fast." Koyuki slipped into the chair on her left. "Listen, Kaguya, I was talking with Azuma and... Hey, are you even listening to me?"

Kaguya had glanced at the bottom bunk, where a sheet of paper of some sort was placed. She snatched it up suddenly. A document. It looked like it had been ripped out of some kind of report.

"What was I thinking, leaving something like this just lying around...?" she muttered.

"What is it?"

"This? No, it's nothing..."

"Huh...?" Koyuki said softly, rising from her chair. She stood in front of Kaguya and peeked over the top of the page that Kaguya was holding in her hands. "A document? Is this...a personnel report?"

Based on the format and what she could see from this angle, the piece of paper seemed to be from a physical of some sort. There were two types of handwriting on the page. One was Kaguya's. Looking more closely, she realized that the other handwriting was Azuma's.

"Is this report...about Azuma?"

"It is..."

Kaguya reluctantly handed the piece of paper to Koyuki. It was indeed a self-assessment on Azuma's physical condition, written in his own handwriting. Kaguya's additions only seemed to be notes and addenda. At a glance, the paper didn't appear to be anything particularly special, certainly not worth holding onto.

Koyuki cocked her head as she read the words written on the page.

"Elevated pulse, increased body temperature, sweating, redness in the face. And hold on... It says these symptoms only occur when he's in your presence, Kaguya."

Koyuki wasn't sure if these symptoms qualified as a *disorder* per se—but they certainly occurred in response to some *very* specific stimuli.

"Kaguya? Did you have any reason for saving this?"

"I... Um, I wasn't really sure what it all meant..."

"You weren't? I thought you couldn't stand not to get to the bottom of things?"

"Y-yes, that's true..." For some reason, Kaguya blushed slightly and turned away. "But I mean, it's very unusual, isn't it...? What if Captain Azuma is experiencing some sort of issue with his nervous system? What would we do then?"

"Yes, what would we do then? But as far as I can tell, it seems like Azuma's heart only races when he's near you, Kaguya."

A certain possible—okay, completely obvious—interpretation had occurred to Koyuki by this point.

"Are you really sure you don't understand what this means, Kaguya?"

"N-no... Is it something I should know about? Please...tell me, Koyuki."

"Well, if you need to be told..."

It felt a little tasteless to just spell things out. And a little embarrassing, to be honest. Not that Koyuki was completely inexperienced in such matters, but who wouldn't get a little tongue-tied when it came to talking about stuff like this out loud?

If she didn't say something, though, Kaguya would probably go her whole life without ever noticing. Maybe Kaguya just needed a push. A little one.

"Kaguya, do you know what a 'crush' is...?"

"Huh?" Kaguya was taken aback. She made a sound Koyuki had never heard from her before. "Crush? What do you mean, crush? What kind of crush?"

"I mean *love*," Koyuki said. She took the paper from Kaguya's hand, laid it on the desk, and began writing it out in pen. *L. O. V. E.* "Of the romantic variety."

"Romantic love... Yes, I'm aware of the general concept. But why bring something like that up right now...?"

"If not now, when? This seems like the perfect time."

Koyuki peered into Kaguya's face. As far as Koyuki could tell, Kaguya looked perfectly cool and collected. There were no signs of even the slightest hint of self-consciousness in her face.

"What about you, Kaguya? Have you ever had a crush on anyone?"

"Me? You've got to be kidding," Kaguya laughed in exasperation, as if Koyuki had just said something hilarious. "First of all, the emotion of love is just a temporary glitch in the brain. What more proof do you need than the fact that the feeling lasts no more than three years at most? Just the amount of time that is needed for smooth procreation and some basic initial rearing of offspring…"

"Maybe, but I have a feeling Azuma probably likes you."

"Huh…?"

"Elevated pulse, increased body temperature, sweating, redness in the face. His heart might as well be doing backflips. And it only happens when he catches sight of you."

Several long seconds passed as Kaguya gave the idea some thought.

"And this is what love feels like?" she asked.

"Yes. I'm glad you're so quick to catch on. I was worried I was going to have to explain the birds and bees to you next."

"But that doesn't make any sense… These sound like aftereffects or some kind of arrhythmia. Or possibly a disorder of the autonomous nervous system—"

"Think again, Kaguya," Koyuki said, cutting her off. Kaguya was just being silly now. "What kind of syndrome would it be if his heart only races when he's in your presence? There is no way the effects of turning into a hero would be so arbitrary and ridiculous."

"R-ridiculous…?"

"Poor Azuma. I really think you would have never noticed without someone telling you."

Everyone knew how Azuma felt about Kaguya. They just didn't talk about it. Even Haru seemed to have picked up on it, meaning it was practically an open secret.

And yet Kaguya herself seemed completely clueless. On top of that, even Azuma seemed to be ignorant of his own feelings. Without a helping hand, these two were never going to get anywhere.

"H-he likes me? Captain Azuma…?"

"Well, the only one who knows for certain is Azuma himself. What if you tried just asking him?"

"Asking him? I mean... I mean...," Kaguya repeated herself, continuing to say *I mean* several more times in a row. "Imagine how embarrassing it would be if you were wrong."

"Then what about you, Kaguya?" Koyuki asked, deciding to tease her friend a little. "How do you feel about Azuma? Is he just a colleague? A friend? Or is it *love*?"

Kaguya must not have been used to conversations like this. She seemed absorbed in her own thoughts, but in an awkward way. Like these new thoughts were quicksand, pulling her deeper and deeper within.

"No, I don't think I'm in love...," Kaguya said, carefully tidying away the document in a drawer. "I'm pretty I'm just experiencing a disorder of some sort."

"The only one who can know your feelings for sure is you, Kaguya. I think it might be a good idea to sit down with your feelings and really work them out."

"My feelings...?"

"I get the impression it's something you haven't taken the time to do before. With so much going on all the time, it's important to rest and take stock of yourself."

They had now found their way back to the original topic.

Apparently, after being in a coma for a month, a rehabilitation period of around two months was usually called for. Two weeks would barely be enough time to just get back into the swing of daily life.

"I understand the importance of rest," Kaguya said, nestling back into the darkness of her bunk. "I heard about the Chronoses from Mari. Finding all that out... It's shocking, isn't it?"

"Yes... I suppose it is."

Kaguya's face was hidden in the shadows of the lower bunk, making it impossible for Koyuki to discern her expression. The height of the chair made it easy for her to hide her face in the shadows. For a moment, it reminded Koyuki of the darkness that clung to the heroes, but she quickly chased that thought away.

"I know there's no clear proof, but if the Director said this was true, then I think it probably is," Kaguya said, speaking frankly. Kaguya had full faith in the Director's abilities.

"Koyuki." Kaguya lifted her face again. "What do you plan to do, now that we believe the Chronoses are sentient?"

"I haven't decided yet," Koyuki said honestly. "We can't defeat the heroes without using them…at least once."

Haru had explained how the soldiers who were unable to use Chronoses safely made do with other weapons for the most part—utilizing explosions, traps, and other tricks to immobilize the heroes and only resorting to the Chronoses once they had a guaranteed shot.

"You're not sure how you feel yet, then?"

"Can you blame me?"

Mari had given Koyuki and Kaguya more details. Major Mirai had managed to get her hands on a report that she then backed up to an information terminal for safekeeping. Honestly, Koyuki barely understood most of it, but Mari summarized the contents for them in an easy-to-understand manner.

Every time Koyuki fired a gun—a Chronos—a bullet traveled through its interior cavities at 250 meters per second, exiting the barrel with proportionate pressure and heat. The impact from being fired was equivalent to being dropped from a height of several hundred meters.

Koyuki only had to move her finger by a few centimeters to fire a gun, but that small gesture was all it took to create so much pain. She still found it hard to believe.

"Just because I'm not sure doesn't change anything about what we've done in our battles up until now." Koyuki was proud of herself on that front. By killing heroes, they had saved many, many people along the way. "But if possible…going forward, I would rather avoid using the Chronoses whenever we can."

"That's understandable." Kaguya lowered her eyes, apparently having thoughts of her own. "In any case, we're going to have to change the way we fight."

"The style Takanashi explained might be a good idea," Koyuki suggested. "Where everyone works together to corner the hero before delivering a final blow with a Chronos."

A look of pain crossed Kaguya's face, but Koyuki pressed on.

"I know you don't like it, but it's the only way. We can't just leave the heroes to run amok, can we?"

Kaguya nodded reluctantly. She was probably feeling sorry for the young men and women stuck inside the Chronoses. *Some things never change*, thought Koyuki, amused.

"You're just as sweet as always, Kaguya. You feel sympathy for the people inside the weapons, even though we can't even sense them."

"Of course I do. It's just so sad, the way they're trapped in there."

"Yes, I guess it is…"

When a human transformed into a hero, a Chronos was manufactured using a piece of the detached flesh of that hero. But the consciousness of the original human remained within the new Chronos.

The young men and women who became heroes did so out of a craving for solace and dreams. Instead, they only became Goddesses or Chronoses in the end. It was more like a nightmare than a dream.

"It's not exactly pleasant to hear, is it? There were probably people like that inside the heroes we've faced up until now. And in the weapons we use."

"Don't, Koyuki. None of us knew any better. If Mari hadn't remembered what the Director had told her, all of this might have stayed a secret forever."

"I know…"

Koyuki understood what Kaguya was saying. And regardless of the truth, nothing could be done about it now, one way or another. Koyuki knew better than to blame herself for her ignorance, but that didn't mean she didn't feel a sense of responsibility anyway.

Rebounds didn't exist for the members of Special Ops Squad Charon. Meaning that they had essentially denied the people trapped within the Chronoses that one manic cry of resistance. Koyuki decided not to pursue that train of thought any further.

"I'm probably just overthinking things... No one did any of this on purpose, after all." Upon calmer reflection, maybe things weren't so complicated. "Besides, as long as we keep defeating the heroes, that will mean fewer boys and girls winding up in that same situation in the end. All we can do is keep the faith."

"No...I don't think that's all we can do."

Kaguya's and Koyuki's expressions were like night and day. Kaguya looked troubled. Koyuki may have wanted to keep things simple, but something was obviously weighing on Kaguya. Enough so to cause Koyuki to worry.

"What do you mean...?"

"Chronoses are created from pieces of flesh cut loose from heroes. But what if we could prevent that from happening?"

"Prevent it...? I think I understand what you're trying to say, but how would that be possible? We would have to defeat them without attacking at all, wouldn't we?"

Consider Azuma's slashing attacks, for example. No matter how carefully he chose to swing his sword, a blade was still a blade. It was going to cut.

"And not just Azuma's sword, either. My guns and Rindou's blows cause damage. The heroes' bodies are going to be affected by that."

"No... Theoretically, it's perfectly possible. Assuming I participate, that is. We just do things like we did before—Captain Azuma, yourself, or Rindou takes the lead while I make a beeline for the hero. That way, no one has to wind up as a Chronos."

"That's...easily said, but..." Koyuki's anxiety was beginning to spiral. "You're still not going to stop, are you? That's what you're saying, isn't it?"

"Stop? You know me better than that—"

"Don't you see? No one wants that." Koyuki's voice suddenly

grew pointed. "I'm not mad, but...why are you so dead set on acting this way...?"

"I just don't want to give up, and I don't see any other choice. This has to be what I'm here for."

"Kaguya..."

Koyuki was already speaking before she even realized she had opened her mouth. This was something she hadn't been able to say until now. Because of how indebted they all were to Kaguya.

"...I don't like that," said Koyuki. "That's something I don't like about you."

"Huh?"

"The way you don't give up. It's one of the best things about you, but honestly, sometimes, I absolutely hate it."

Never give up. Never quit. The words had such a cruel ring to them. How could a person ever run when they had already convinced themselves that *never giving up* was a virtue?

As soon as a person decides they won't give up, they are trapped by those words. Every individual has their limits, and properly understanding those limits and stepping back when necessary is the most natural thing in the world. And yet Kaguya was allowing herself to be ground down beneath the curse of *never giving up*.

"Maybe *hate* is too strong a word. But it certainly doesn't make me happy."

"I guess I can see how you would be a little upset with me. I'm sorry, Koyuki."

Koyuki lifted her face suddenly, not having expected to hear that. Was Kaguya beginning to see reason?

But no—Koyuki's faint hopes were dashed to pieces as soon as she looked into Kaguya's eyes. Nothing had changed. It was that same expression that Kaguya held in her eyes the day they had first met. Koyuki sensed, intuitively, that she was already too late.

"Kaguya."

Koyuki took a step closer. There was something she wanted, no, needed to say to Kaguya. But Kaguya smoothly evaded her, striding toward the door. She must have already known what Koyuki was about to say. Koyuki shouted after her from behind.

"Kaguya!!"

Something took hold of Koyuki. A feeling that she had to stop Kaguya now while she still could.

"I'm not saying you need to quit. Of course not! That side of you is something that I love. But try to understand how I feel…! Can't you see what I have to go through every time I'm forced to watch you collapse?!"

Kaguya looked like a deer caught in headlights. Koyuki continued.

"I shared this room with her—with Sakura—for so long. And then, after she was gone, it was just you and me. Me on the top bunk, you on the bottom."

Kaguya nodded silently, overwhelmed, but Koyuki wasn't finished. She had needed to let Kaguya know how she felt for so very long.

"Every time I climbed that ladder to the second bunk, I caught sight of you asleep down there. I saw you from up close, closer than anyone, even closer than Azuma. Saw what you were going through each and every time."

Koyuki was the one who had been there. Who knew better than anyone the way Kaguya had been suffering. No one could tell her otherwise. They had shared the same room every single day before and after battle. They had lived their lives together. So Koyuki knew full well what Kaguya's reckless behavior was doing to her. She had seen it intimately, whether she wanted to or not.

"It's why I eventually came around and opened up to you."

At first, Koyuki had not wanted to accept Kaguya. It was only after seeing what Kaguya was going through that Koyuki slowly began to change her mind. She knew that someone had to keep an eye out for her.

"But the way you're acting now… It's not like before. You're not just trying to save the heroes anymore. You've let Sakura's words—no, your own words—paint you into a corner."

"Wh-what is that supposed to mean?"

"You keep saying you *won't give up*, and now that promise has trapped you. But you're worth more than just that. No one is going to be upset with you for not keeping your word!"

"I'm not trapped! And, of course, I know no one would be upset with me. I don't care. I'm not doing this for respect."

"You know that's not true."

Koyuki could see through her. They may have only known each other for half a year, but Koyuki understood what went on in Kaguya's sharp mind. A kind of intuition, girl to girl, that Azuma couldn't see.

"You're afraid of letting someone down. I know it. But it's not *us* you're worried about letting down, Kaguya. It's yourself."

Kaguya couldn't see outside herself. No, not *couldn't*. Wouldn't. That stubbornness had saved them countless times in the past. For instance, when Kaguya had come back to them after Azuma had begun to turn. That was part of the reason why Koyuki felt like she didn't have a right to press Kaguya on this issue.

But she had a duty. An obligation as a friend.

"Don't you see?! You were in a coma for a whole month. The next time you enter a hero's psyche, you might never wake up! And even if you do, what if it's two months this time? What if it's years? Don't you even care?"

Kaguya seemed too overwhelmed to respond. Maybe she cared, maybe she didn't. Who knew? She was just standing there, saying nothing. Like a coward.

"Well, I'm not okay with it..." Koyuki just barely managed to get the words out, probably too quiet for Kaguya to hear. "I'm not okay with the possibility of you never waking up again."

Tears suddenly began to well up in Koyuki's eyes.

"This room...is too quiet for just one person, Kaguya."

With that, Koyuki fell silent. If she said any more, she was worried she would begin crying for real.

"Koyuki...," Kaguya said, concern in her voice.

Instead of leaving the room, Kaguya walked back toward where Koyuki stood. Koyuki reflexively looked up, and they were face-to-face.

A little above her own eye level—but nowhere near as high as Sakura's—Kaguya's beautiful violet eyes were fixed on her.

Kaguya hugged her gently. Koyuki meekly accepted, unable to stop her.

Koyuki already knew what Kaguya was going to say next. *Don't,* she prayed softly. *Please don't say it.*

"I'm not going to stop. But…I am sorry," Kaguya whispered, her voice like a sigh.

Koyuki swallowed, her eyes widening. But she had known what was coming, and she didn't cry.

Kaguya gently separated herself from Koyuki and turned to leave once more.

Now alone, Koyuki sank to her knees. It wasn't that Kaguya hadn't understood. It was that she hadn't even tried.

CHAPTER NINE
Exposure

The next battle happened several days later.

This hero had an aquatic theme, and just as expected, it was able to manipulate water. It resembled an enemy out of a comic book, but fighting a creature like that in real life was much more difficult than in the comics. It had appeared in the locker room of a swimming school. Next to it lay a red swimsuit and swimming cap.

Of course, water couldn't be cut or punched. This battle was mostly on Koyuki.

"It's so cold...!" she moaned.

The hero activated almost as soon as the fight began. With its ability to gradually fill the locker room with water, their work seemed cut out for them.

Koyuki took up position on top of a row of lockers as the sound of trickling water filled the room. So far, the water level was only up to their knees, but it was enough to sap the heat from their bodies subtly.

The hero's egg was visible, ensconced deep within the creature's liquid body. On the one hand, that made life simple, seeing as they didn't have to search for it this time. But on the other, it seemed the egg was only visible because the hero didn't need to hide it in the first place.

Azuma firmly gripped the hilt of his katana, which felt fairly familiar to his hand by this point, as he withdrew the blade in one smooth and silent motion, steady against the scabbard. He knew even this motion would cause a fair amount of pain.

But he wasn't so weak that he would hesitate to draw his weapon in combat.

"What do you think, Koyuki? How many shots will it take?" Azuma asked.

"Ten might be enough to reach it... It seems pretty viscous."

Koyuki had just fired off one shot earlier to check the creature's viscosity. The bullet had penetrated the hero's body with a quiet *thwump*, stopping just a few centimeters in.

"But if its body is thick and viscous...," Azuma said, taking a step forward—he was both the captain and the point man. "That also means it will be slow to recover. I'll secure a trajectory. You just shoot once I've opened up a path."

"Fine by me, but try not to get hit. I only have so many bullets." Koyuki said coldly before turning her attention back to finalizing her position.

Azuma took several steps toward the hero. Keeping his movements as economical as possible, he carried through with the momentum and struck at the creature in a flash.

The water split open. There was no blood. No screaming. It felt like cutting through slime. Almost immediately—before the cleft had a chance to close again—the sound of gunfire filled the air. The bullet, shot from behind by Koyuki, whistled past Azuma's ear and buried itself into the hero's body. Azuma quickly struck again, widening the gap.

They repeated this operation several times.

"We've gotten pretty deep."

"Yes. This next shot should finish it."

Azuma heard her quickly reload—the sound of metal dropping and bouncing and then splashing into the water. *That's going to be hell to clean later*, Azuma thought, slashing as deep as he could this time before leaping back quickly. As he moved, he caught sight of Koyuki out of the corner of his eye, hunkering down into position, her eyes like steel. She had swapped Chronoses and now had a rifle suited for indoors but still capable of powerful impact.

She rose up slightly to redirect the fearsome weapon's recoil, allowing Azuma to see her finger as it moved clearly. Then she fired.

Bam! Almost immediately, the air echoed with the sound of gunfire, and a hole split open in the hero's body. There, inside that opening, was the egg.

Kaguya was not with them at the moment.

After learning of Koyuki and Kaguya's conversation, Azuma had initially wanted to ban Kaguya from participating in missions for the time being. Koyuki had pleaded for him to do so as well. It wasn't like they could rely on Kaguya all the time.

But there was always the possibility that being too heavy-handed could backfire and make things worse. Unable to ignore that possibility, he gave Kaguya permission to join them but only on the proviso that she keep her distance from the heroes. As a result, Kaguya was currently stationed farther back, on standby.

"Koyuki, I need to match your timing. How many more seconds?"

Koyuki didn't answer.

"Koyuki," he added more strongly. That seemed to snap her out of it.

"Sorry. Two and a half seconds."

"Got it… Koyuki, I understand how you're feeling, but right now—"

"Yeah. I got it. I said I was sorry." she repeated, sulking slightly.

Azuma sighed inaudibly. He understood that Kaguya and Koyuki were fighting, but Kaguya wasn't even here. Why was Koyuki letting it bother her so much?

The door to the locker room was closed. The only ones who were inside now were Azuma, Koyuki, and Rindou. Participation had been limited to those who could use Chronoses. Because the hero had appeared inside a pool locker room, the situation was more cramped than they were used to.

It looks like we're going to wrap this up faster than I had thought.

Azuma opened another gash in the hero's body, acquiring visual confirmation of the egg. Ignoring the unpleasantly gummy water that clung to his body, Azuma swung his katana as the creature continued to heal rapidly and aimed to slice the egg in two.

He felt the blow make contact. It was over. Now all they had to do was retrieve Kaguya and the others, head back to base...and think about how they would handle things the next time.

That was when Azuma noticed something was off.

The hero hadn't dissolved.

There was no collapse. No dispersal. No breaking down. No fall.

Was this some new type of hero that didn't die even once its egg was destroyed? Impossible! No organism could evolve to survive the destruction of its heart.

But the hero was still alive, despite the fact that Azuma had destroyed its egg. That could only mean one thing.

"A decoy!!"

There was a cracking sound, and then the egg broke. The hero's body vanished, and a flood of water began pouring into the room, equal in volume to the size of the creature's body.

"The real hero must be—"

Somewhere else? Outside—probably. Outside, where Kaguya was waiting.

Azuma tried to open the door, but the water pressure was too strong. He screamed, his voice lost in the sound of rushing water.

"Kaguya!!"

"...!!"

Kaguya froze, staring at the creature in front of her.

It appeared as soon as the locker room door was closed. It looked like a doll made of craggy stone.

"T-two heroes at once...?! Or is this some kind of clone...?!"

Kaguya fought back as hard as she could. She was essentially facing a boulder. She could see weaker chinks of flesh between the stone, but Kaguya was clearly outmatched, forced onto the defensive with her tiny little pistol.

Clone or not, it didn't make much difference. This fight was all one-sided. She was doing what she could with her pistol, but the deficit in strength was too much. She was stuck on the back foot the entire time.

"Ah…!"

Before she knew it, the creature's stone arm was coming straight for her face. Kaguya was trapped with nowhere to run.

But there was still hope. She wasn't done yet.

Kaguya was holding her pistol, a Chronos, in her hand—and she was in the perfect position to shoot and enter this hero's mental world. If she could get inside the hero, she could stop it.

Kaguya readied her weapon, just like always. She held it up to shoot, as she had done a thousand times before. All she had to do was squeeze the trigger, and the person inside the hero was sure to—

"Huh?"

She couldn't do it. And it wasn't because she had been attacked first. No, for some reason, her legs wouldn't move. Her hands. All she had to do was pull the trigger, but…

"Wh-why?"

She froze. This wasn't some ability the hero was using against her. She had been fine just a moment earlier.

"Lieutenant Shinohara!!" someone shouted.

The hero's arm was moving straight toward Kaguya. Unless she did something now, she was going to die.

From out of the corner of her eye, she could see that someone was trying to force open the door. But it was obvious they were never going to do it in time.

In time…?

Since when did Kaguya need anyone to save her?!

"…!"

Just as the stone arm was about to connect, Kaguya dodged it by a hairsbreadth, pointed her gun at the hero, and pulled the trigger. Instantly, as if her consciousness were being funneled down, she disappeared within her target.

CHAPTER TEN
Enough

"Oh..."

She was standing in the middle of an exquisite beach that spread as far as the eye could see. The white sands were deserted. The waves approached and receded at regular intervals, creating a constant cadence of beautiful sound.

Looking up, she saw the clear sky, which was just as blue as the ocean. Not a single cloud in sight. Just steady, unbroken blue, as if filled in by the hands of an untalented painter.

The sand crunched beneath her feet. She hesitated for a moment and then removed her sandals. They would just get stuck in the sand anyway.

After standing aimlessly for a moment, Kaguya began walking with no particular direction in mind.

They had to be here somewhere. The young man or woman who had turned into the hero.

Kaguya had a sneaking suspicion it was a girl. Not that she had any particular proof—it was just something about the appearance and scent of this world.

After walking for a little while across the sand, she reached a place where the sound of the waves changed. A figure was waiting there, wearing a white, wide-brimmed hat and a dress of the same color. She stood still, like a subject in a painting.

Kaguya had been right; it was a girl, after all. She was a little bit younger than Kaguya.

"It's chilly today, isn't it…?"

Kaguya stood next to the girl on the white-sand beach as the sound of the waves filled the air.

The girl showed absolutely no response. Kaguya continued to stand beside her silently, like a pebble.

The water ebbed three times before the girl finally turned around. She fixed her eyes on Kaguya, almost as if she had only just realized that Kaguya was there.

"Yes, it is," the girl agreed. "It's almost as if the warmth has vanished from this world."

What a poetic way to put it. But the girl's words were on point. It wasn't cold per se, but it wasn't hot, either. It all depended on your own interpretation. Kaguya, in her turquoise uniform, felt a chill coming off the ocean as it swelled and receded. Something cold.

"What…are you doing here?" she asked the girl.

"I'm watching the ocean. Can't you tell?"

But what Kaguya wanted to know was why the girl was just standing there, staring at the water. Following the girl's gaze, Kaguya made a small exclamation of recognition. It wasn't the ocean the girl was watching, but a boy swimming inside it. He looked a bit younger than the girl.

"Tell me… Are you happy?" Kaguya said to the girl.

"What?"

The girl turned her eyes toward Kaguya suspiciously. Kaguya met her gaze head-on.

"What do you mean, happy? Why would you ask me that all of a sudden…? What are you up to?"

"Nothing. I just wanted to know more about you. What your hopes are… Your wishes," Kaguya replied, phrasing herself in a roundabout way.

The girl turned to face her. **"What did you come here for? In fact, how did you even get—?"**

"I came here to stop you."

The girl reacted as if she had no idea what Kaguya was talking about. Just as Kaguya had expected.

"Stop me? What do you mean, stop me? I'm sorry, but… this is private property. I'd appreciate it if you would just leave."

"You're right that this is a private place. We are actually inside your mind."

"Are we…? Well, perhaps you should hurry up and get lost. Now, before he gets back."

Kaguya glanced toward the ocean. The boy was coming their way, having apparently realized that something was off.

He was probably the Goddess. As Kaguya watched him with this thought in mind, she suddenly narrowed her eyes, realizing that something was amiss. He rushed toward them in a hurry, the distress on his face plain to see.

He wasn't behaving very much like a Goddess. Goddesses always acted aloof, as if they believed they were calling all the shots. Just like the girl in white was behaving, actually.

"Oh, of course." Kaguya finally put two and two together. "You're the Goddess."

The younger boy playing alone in the water—he was the real master of this world. The girl did not deny it, flashing Kaguya a pretty smile instead. Kaguya could see the insectoid shadow deep in her eyes.

"Don't get in the way," the Goddess said just as the boy raced toward them. He eyed Kaguya with obvious hostility. **"You can see how happy he is, can't you? What right do you have to rob other people of their happiness?"**

"Maybe…"

The boy did seem extremely content.

Was the Goddess supposed to be his older sister? Some sibling whose presence the boy found indispensable in his life? If so, this might be happiness of a sort. Just leaving things the way they were. But Kaguya knew she could never do that.

"This is my mission. It doesn't matter what anyone else thinks, it doesn't even matter how I feel about it myself."

"**You could have fooled me. That look on your face isn't very persuasive,**" the Goddess said as if she could read Kaguya like a book. Goddesses were highly skilled at manipulating human hearts.

"What do you mean? What kind of look...?"

"**Maybe you should stay in here as well. Nothing is painful or difficult in this place.**"

What was she saying?

"I'm not interested in intruding in someone else's private thoughts," Kaguya said, although technically that was exactly what she was doing.

The Goddess's eyes grew colder in response. She stared at Kaguya with a fake smile plastered across her face as if she were taking measure of something formlessly simmering inside Kaguya.

"**Oh? And just what are you going to do about it?**" the Goddess asked bewitchingly.

Kaguya responded with action rather than words.

"I'm going to do *this*."

There was a splash as something heavy fell into the water. Kaguya had shoved the Goddess just as the boy drew near, causing the Goddess to fall into the ocean.

This wasn't a cliff but merely a sandy beach. The Goddess's hat fell off, and she got soaked, but it wasn't like she was injured. The boy, however, realizing that his sister had been attacked, angrily thrust himself into Kaguya's face.

"**What the fuck is wrong with you?!**"

Kaguya turned to the foulmouthed boy. That was hardly the kind of language expected from a child who didn't even look to be ten years old.

She wasn't used to interacting with small children, but something seemed off. Kaguya was having trouble putting her finger on exactly what it was, but perhaps it had something to do with the way the boy carried himself.

She remembered encountering a similar phenomenon before.

Yes, that's right. This is like that time with the sand creature.

The sand hero. When she first made contact with him, he had been a young boy, but it later became clear that he was actually an adolescent. He had been in a coma for the past ten years.

Maybe something similar was happening here. Kaguya bent down and made eye contact with the boy.

"How old are you?"

"…?"

The boy narrowed his eyes at the strange question. He was just about to answer when there was another loud splash as the Goddess rose up out of the water. Surprisingly, not a single drop of water clung to her body. As if she had been shoved into an illusory sea.

The boy rushed to his big sister's side. She embraced him, smiling beautifully as if she were a saint. She directed a gaze of kindness his way, so profound that it was difficult not to believe that it was sincere.

The boy seemed truly happy. Kaguya found herself oddly loath to ruin that happiness.

But I have to see this through.

That was Kaguya's role. It was her mission.

She would never give up, no matter how much resistance or animosity she faced. But that didn't mean she didn't sometimes want to give up.

"Can we…talk for a little while?" she asked.

The Goddess was resisting more stubbornly than Kaguya had expected. Kaguya tried to get the boy away from the Goddess. She also repeatedly shoved the Goddess into the illusory sea or openly insulted her to her face, not even caring that she was doing so in front of what was supposedly her younger brother.

At first, of course, the boy reacted to Kaguya angrily, but he slowly grew intimidated by her unusual ferocity. The Goddess, after all, was only imposing on the boy's mind. All she had were flimsy illusions, whereas Kaguya was flesh and blood—real.

"Wait..."

Kaguya peered at the boy closely. His eyelashes fluttered in surprise, and he took a step backward. He quickly recovered, however, and squared off, facing her. He held a water pistol full of seawater in his right hand, which he pointed toward her now. The way he held it told Kaguya everything that she needed to know.

"You're with the Extermination Bureau, aren't you?"

Even though it was just a water pistol and thus completely harmless, he kept his finger off the trigger. It was common sense to keep your finger off the trigger of a gun when not in battle, but that wasn't something that a child would have any way of knowing. And even if they did know better, that knowledge wouldn't apply in this case, seeing as this was just a water pistol.

Which meant this must have been an ingrained habit.

The only people this young who could have formed such a habit were the soldiers of the Extermination Bureau.

"The ex...termination bureau...?"

"Yes. It's the organization I belong to. And which you belong to as well. It was created to save people from the heroes. Don't you remember?"

"I don't know anything about that!" the boy shouted, sounding suddenly like a petulant child. **"I don't know what you're talking about. I'm just playing with my big sister today! But if you don't—"**

"Listen to me," Kaguya said, kneeling down. She was certain now. "You remember, don't you? Who you are, and what you were doing. And what you've become now. You caught on to who I was as soon as you saw me, didn't you? You weren't angry because I had hurt your 'sister.' That look on your face doesn't lie."

Kaguya spoke coldly and without leniency. Speculation or not, she was giving the boy no room for denial. There was no real reasoning behind what she said; all he had to do to end this matter was insist she had no idea what she was talking about. However, the boy did no such thing.

Instead, the sound of the waves began to grow louder. As if they were coming from inside her own ears.

A voice mingled with the sound of the waves. A grating sound, like scraping glass.

"Aaaggghhhhh!!"

It was a scream. A man's scream.

The scene suddenly changed.

Two blood-soaked humans were standing before Kaguya. A young boy cradling a young girl. It looked like it was already too late for the girl.

"Of course I didn't forget."

The boy's voice was deep. He was almost old enough to be called a young man now. He stood next to Kaguya and stared at the scene before them. He didn't reach out, however, because he knew it was already too late.

"How could I ever forget? My sister was killed by a hero."

"I see… Of course."

At some point, the boy's clothing had changed to a turquoise uniform. He glanced toward Kaguya and sighed, sounding tired.

"If you're wearing that uniform, you should understand. All this fighting is pointless. There's no way for us to know if it will ever end, and there's no reward for us in the end. It's all so damned awful, so why do we keep doing it? What are we even here for? It's like we're trapped in some tiny sandbox garden with no escape," he said plaintively.

What could Kaguya possibly say in response to that?

"Will you remember for me? Remember what I wished for?"

"I will. I won't forget. Both the way you died and the way you lived will remain etched in my heart. So long as I remember, it means you didn't die as a monster in the end."

"I'm sorry..." The boy looked genuinely apologetic. **"Your being here saved me. Now I can die as a human being..."**

"I...hope so."

The scene around her suddenly vanished. In the blankness, total whiteout, a smile of surrender formed on the boy's lips.

"Don't forget us."

There was a loneliness to his words. Kaguya felt uncomfortable. It felt like a piece of herself, something inside her, had once again been shaved away.

Unaware of what Kaguya was feeling, the boy trembled and disappeared, much as a wave dissipated into foam.

• • •

"...guya! Kaguya!"

She could hear a voice coming from somewhere far away.

People were staring down at her, half-destroyed building walls visible behind them. Azuma and Koyuki stood at the front of the crowd.

Kaguya gasped and sat up. She felt something like dirt scattered across her palm. Several small stones had embedded themselves lightly into her skin. It was this pain that finally pulled her entirely awake.

She took a look around. They were watching her with trepidation. She could feel the heat and humidity against her skin. Kaguya breathed a sigh of relief, realizing the world was just as it had been before she had entered the hero. She had not been asleep for another month like last time.

"Are you okay...?" someone asked, their voice gentle.

It wasn't just a perfunctory question—the person sounded genuinely concerned. Kaguya had heard that same voice, been subject to that same look of pity, countless times before. It was Azuma who had actually spoken this time, but she knew they all felt the same way.

Kaguya tried to tell them she was fine. She sat up without trouble, her usual smile upon her face, and—

Wait, what's wrong with my voice?

I'm fine, she tried to say again, but something rose up in her throat, clogging her mouth like a dam clogs a stream. The words wouldn't come out.

"Kaguya...?"

Kaguya remained silent. Azuma looked worried. She needed to let him know that she was all right, that she wasn't injured.

"Ah..." It took every drop of willpower she had to squeeze out the words. "Fine. I-I'm...fine..."

Why did she sound so strange? Every time she tried to speak, she felt that lump in her throat threatening to overflow. She needed to tell them. The others stared at her, speechless, as she tried to form words.

This didn't make any sense; she wasn't injured, was she? She felt something hot streaming down her cheek—tears.

It was only then that Kaguya realized she was crying.

CHAPTER ELEVEN
Teardrops

Fortunately, the fight ended with only minor injuries.

By the time Azuma arrived, everything was already finished. The hero crumbled before his eyes, leaving only Kaguya behind.

Before Azuma could take even a step closer, Kaguya opened her eyes. He asked her if she was all right, but Kaguya remained silent, making him worry even more.

With some trouble, she eventually managed to say that she was okay. However, Azuma and the others weren't focused on her words. Instead, they were focused on her tears, and she even didn't seem to be aware of them herself.

"Are you feeling better now?" Azuma asked Kaguya.

"Yes…I'm sorry. I don't know what came over me… I feel like a child."

"It's fine. You're probably just tired."

They practically had to force her into one of the barrack's infirmary beds. She was sitting up at the moment, smiling in embarrassment.

"Tired…? Yes, maybe I am."

"Of course you're tired. It's been less than a week since you came out of your coma and barely over a month since you first entered it."

Although she'd been awake for only a few days, it felt like years already.

"What were they like…? The hero?" Azuma asked hesitantly. "Male? Female? How old were they? What did they look like? What were their last words? Can you remember?"

"He was male. A little older than me. I think probably around eighteen. His face was…pretty normal. As for his final words, well…"

Azuma regretted asking. He hadn't been trying to stress her out by asking about what had happened in the hero's mental world. He was hoping it might help to lighten the burden for her instead, if only by a little. But her face grew darker as she spoke. He watched as she struggled to find the words, her long eyelashes downcast.

"'Don't forget us.' That's what he said. His wish was…not to be forgotten."

"That was a pretty cruel thing for him to ask…"

"Cruel?"

"Yes. Cruel, arrogant, and cowardly."

He meant it. Asking someone not to forget you was brazen and conceited. And trapping someone emotionally like that, even if you were about to die, was just craven.

But no one was forcing Kaguya to do this. She had accepted all of this of her own free will.

"What are you going to do? Are you going to remember him?"

"Of course. That's what I'm here for, isn't it…? The whole reason I intervene in their minds, even when it's already too late, is so that there will be someone to remember their last moments as humans."

"Are you sure that's all there is to it…?" Azuma said.

Kaguya lifted her head in response.

What Azuma saw there was a face on the verge of collapse. There was something pleading in her pale violet eyes, something which perhaps she herself was unaware of. Although Kaguya was attempting to keep up a calm facade, it was apparent at a glance that she was anything but.

"Is that really what you want? I can't help but feel it's not and that you're just forcing yourself to continue at this point."

"I'm not forcing anything!" Kaguya said, scowling. "The entire reason I'm out there fighting is to save people who have become heroes.

Sure, I was a little tired and needed to rest for a bit, but I can hardly just ignore a hero when I come face-to-face with one."

"Why not? I don't see how you're under any obligations."

Azuma stood and whipped open the curtains. Sunlight suddenly streamed into the room, causing Kaguya to close her eyes and hold up her hand to block the light.

"Captain! If you wanted to open the curtains, you could have at least told me before you—"

"You're too hard on yourself."

Azuma stepped toward the window, likely leaving him backlit from Kaguya's point of view. He was standing there on purpose because he didn't want her to see his face.

"All of the heroes we've encountered so far, today's included, had absolutely nothing to do with you. How much do you really know about them? You don't even know their names or where they come from."

"Yes, that's true, but—"

"Kaguya, you've got a goodness that is almost blinding. It's hard not to appreciate that. I've always felt that way about you, and I even look up to you for it."

"Y-you look up to me...?"

"Yes, because you have something I don't. We used to take it for granted that heroes were just monsters, nothing more and nothing less. You're the one who changed that for us, and I am always going to think highly of you for that," Azuma said, explaining calmly and honestly how he had felt for so long. At times like this, he believed it was important to be honest about your feelings.

"Y-you're not acting like your usual self, Captain Azuma... You didn't eat something you found lying around on the ground, did you?"

"Do I look like someone who goes around eating food off the ground?"

"What if I said yes?"

"I guess I would feel pretty bad about myself," he replied.

Kaguya gave a little laugh, dry and forced. Even on the surface, Azuma could tell her heart wasn't in it.

"In any case," she began, "I can't agree with what you're saying, Captain Azuma. I'm the only one who can see them like that, remember? If I don't remember them, who will?"

"I'm telling you that you need to take better care of yourself. I probably shouldn't say this, but who cares if they are remembered? It's not like you're getting a gold star for it or anything."

Kaguya scowled even harder. Maybe because what Azuma was saying made sense. He pressed further.

"Why are you even being so stubborn about all this?"

Azuma didn't understand why she was so determined to stick to her guns on this issue. What was holding her back?

There was, of course, an obvious answer.

"Is it Sakura…?" he asked.

Kaguya's eyes wavered for a moment. She didn't say anything. Azuma sensed intuitively that he had just hit the nail on the head.

Still, he doubted that was all. After all, that didn't explain why she had been so zealous about this even before coming to Charon. If there was another reason, it could only be one thing.

"Or is it your brother?"

Her older brother, who had vanished before Kaguya's very eyes, and was now quite possibly dead.

This, too, seemed to have hit the mark. Kaguya's eyes remained closed as if in defeat. She looked like a criminal, wrestling with her own guilt. Azuma had a sudden flash of insight.

"It's that you want to be forgiven, isn't it?"

This wasn't justice or even obsession. She may not have been aware of it herself, but she was seeking salvation. Salvation for herself.

"You still want to be forgiven. By Sakura for not being able to save her. By your brother, who became a hero. All because you couldn't help them."

Azuma was finally beginning to understand the motivation behind Kaguya's self-destructive behavior.

"This is about saving yourself, not the heroes. About absolving yourself of what happened seven years ago and of what happened a few months ago. I'm right, aren't I, Kaguya? You've been fixated on your own past shortcomings, haven't you? Not on others, after all."

"I..."

Kaguya's voice sounded feeble. She pursed her lips and grew quiet. A look of fear surfaced in her violet eyes. As if, until Azuma said those words, she had never realized that about herself.

Azuma had just poked at something at Kaguya's center—deep at her core—which had left her unable to speak.

Obviously, Sakura's words were a motivating factor for Kaguya. Every time she felt unsure or like she wanted to quit, she found herself remembering the last words Sakura had said to her.

However, it would not be incorrect to say that Kaguya's focus had shifted. When she started, her feelings had been pure, but at some point, those feelings had festered into a kind of compulsion, a conviction that this was just something she *had to do*.

Kaguya did not want to admit that her own feelings had turned into a curse inside herself. Because if she did, then she would have to reject even Sakura's final wish.

"I just...thought that this was my mission..."

"Your mission? Don't kid yourself."

Azuma sneered. His attitude had grown ruthless. Did Kaguya really think she was being righteous? No, she could see the truth by now.

It was fixation.

"This has all been for your own self-gratification. Can you tell me I'm wrong? I don't think you can."

"How can you say something like that...?"

"It's the truth. This may be unfair of me to say, but we never forced you. No one forced you to do any of this. And no one would have blamed you if you had chosen not to. There's nothing righteous about being so pigheaded."

"Oh, but you weren't against it, were you...?" Kaguya could hear the accusatory note in her voice, but she couldn't stop herself. "No one would have blamed me if I hadn't handled everything, but none of you really cared if I stopped, did you? At least, not until it put me in a coma. What else was I supposed to do? No one had to force me. I wanted to do what I did, but it seems damned cowardly to me now to pretend that you had nothing to do with it."

Azuma was obviously at a loss for words.

"You were happy to let me be pigheaded because it made things easier for you. If you really thought I was in so much danger, then why did it take you this long to—?"

Kaguya suddenly came to her senses, realizing what she was saying. She felt ashamed.

Azuma had in fact protested her behavior, on one occasion at least. Kaguya was the one who had steamrolled over all his objections.

"I'm...I'm sorry. That isn't what I meant to say." She was acting like a spoiled child. It didn't matter how the others around her felt or reacted. Only she could take responsibility for her own words and actions. "I'm trying to shift the blame for what I did onto others. I shouldn't have—"

"No, you're right," Azuma said, surprising Kaguya. "I'm sorry we let it go on like that. We were cowards."

"Captain Azuma..."

Azuma bowed humbly, which only caused Kaguya to feel more flustered.

"However, there is still something I need to say," he added, not backing down. "I don't want to watch you keep hurting yourself anymore. None of us do. If Sakura's words are what is holding you back..."

Azuma hesitated for a moment. At least, it seemed that way.

"...If that's what's holding you back, then just forget them. You've got no obligation to keep clutching onto that."

"B-but how could I just forget what she said?! Sakura was our friend. She meant so much—"

"Yes, she did. But she's gone."

The simplicity of his words left Kaguya dumbfounded.

"Sakura was important to me, too. I have no intention of forgetting her, even now. But she's already dead, Kaguya. Don't beat yourself up over a few words. You need to live your own life."

"But…," Kaguya whispered. That wouldn't be fair. How could she just allow herself to forget about what Sakura had said to her? Sakura had trusted her.

And what about Koyuki?

"I agree with Azuma…"

Someone else had entered the room.

It was Koyuki herself. She leaned against the door as she spoke and then approached slowly. She was standing on the opposite side of the room from Azuma, who was by the window where the curtain divider stood.

"We're not telling you to forget about Sakura. I think it's good to remember her. But we don't want to see you destroy yourself like this because you've let the past control you," Koyuki said, mirroring Azuma's earlier words.

They stood on either side of Kaguya, leaving her trapped with her feelings.

"There was no choice today. Things just worked out that way. But what about the other heroes we've encountered so far? Did you really need to take everything on all by yourself? Just let it go. All of it. Even Sakura."

Even Azuma lifted his head in surprise at that.

"Sakura…?"

"That doesn't necessarily mean forgetting her. Let me put it a different way. Stop trying to hoard her death all for yourself. Yes, you were the only one able to hear her and speak to her directly in the end. That's true…"

Koyuki crouched down. She made eye contact with Kaguya, her catlike vermilion gaze crossing with Kaguya's distinguished violet hues.

"…but Sakura was our friend and colleague, too. As are you. Don't try to carry all this weight on your own shoulders."

This room is too quiet for just one person.

"That was what I was trying to tell you the other day, Kaguya."

Kaguya finally understood. What Koyuki said was true. Though it may have appeared as if Kaguya was valuing their memories, the truth was that she was hoarding them all to herself, and she had let that get to her head. She meant it when she said she didn't want to shoulder everything by herself but also took some sort of perverse pride in doing so.

"Even Mari Ezakura stepped forward to tell us the truth about the Chronoses," Azuma interjected. "She trusted us, even though that must have been scary for her."

"She did...?"

"People from Technical seem to have a habit of keeping things bottled up inside." Azuma's smile was blatantly uncomfortable rather than accusatory. "Even the Director had apparently failed to mention what she knew to anyone else, despite how important it was."

Come to think of it, Kaguya recalled that was true, too. For someone with so much responsibility for someone so young, the Director had rarely—if ever—shown weakness. But she must have been struggling with a lot of things in her own way.

Kaguya quickly turned to the windowsill, which was adorned with red flowers—the same color as Kaguya's hair. These appeared to be roses, which didn't fit the setting.

Roses had thorns; it seemed unlikely that those would be allowed in a hospital room.

Kaguya stared at the flowers and said softly, "I'm sorry, Koyuki... I finally get it."

The difference between Kaguya and the Director was that Kaguya had someone she could talk to. Someone who was there to stop her before she crossed that final point of no return.

"Thank you for everything. For worrying about me all this time."

Koyuki lowered her gaze slightly and then asked a question.

"What about today's hero? What was it like...?" she asked as if it were a casual discussion topic. Kaguya slowly began to share what she had seen.

The human inside the rocklike hero had originally been a member of the Extermination Bureau. His ideal world had been a gorgeous beach with a young woman who he called his sister and doves—the image of peace. He must have hated fighting, so much so that he had willfully abandoned reality.

Once Kaguya began, it was like a dam had burst. Before she knew it, she was talking about all of them, all of the heroes she had come into contact with so far.

Yuuji Sakigaura. Sakura Arakawa. Even Azuma. Yuki, Shinji Takamura, Suzume. There were fifty-two of them in total—the *people inside* whom she had connected with. And Kaguya remembered each and every last one of them. All fifty-two names, faces, and last words.

"It's amazing that you managed to remember all that," Azuma said, sounding impressed.

Maybe it was. With over fifty people to keep track of, you would expect it to be difficult to match a name to every face. But she even remembered their last words, despite the fact that she had never written anything down. Maybe this really was a curse.

Kaguya told them about all of them, every last one, up to and including today's hero.

No, not all of them. There's still one left.

"That just leaves my brother..."

Her brother, who had turned into a hero long ago.

"I had been afraid all this time. I haven't seen him in seven years, not since that day I turned into a hero."

Of course, she had searched for him. But she had zero information to go on. And then, at some point, a possibility entered her head. One that she couldn't manage to shrug off.

What if she had actually *killed* her brother?

"If he had just gotten sick of me, that was one thing. But I started to worry... What if, when I turned, I actually killed him? How would I ever cope with that?"

Maybe it was self-indulgent, but she truly wanted to believe that she could not have killed her brother. She suddenly found herself confronted with a rush of feelings, however. Things she had always pretended to ignore while Charon's eyes were on her.

Although these feelings were always on the verge of spilling over, she had managed, one way or another, to keep a lid on them until now. But at the moment, she couldn't hold it in any longer. She clamped a hand over her mouth. If she didn't, she was afraid of what might come spilling out.

It was just Azuma and herself in the room now. Koyuki must have quietly stepped out at some point.

"Should I leave, too…?"

"What…?"

"You want to cry, don't you? I can tell from your face and your voice."

Who was he to tell her how she felt? Kaguya was about to insist he was wrong, but as she opened her mouth to speak, she finally recognized the strange agitation she had been feeling for the past several moments for what it really was.

She just wanted to cry.

Loneliness, toil, hatred, burden, despair, regret, and fear—they all pointed inward, forming a sluggish mass in her chest. Eating away at her from the inside, whether she knew it or not. Well, she certainly knew it now.

It was all in front of her, and the rest followed quickly. The feelings rose up into her throat, and she couldn't push them back down, try as she might. Azuma turned his head away, unable to bear seeing her like that.

"I should probably go after all. You can come join us again once you've settled down."

"Wait." Kaguya clutched at his sleeve. "Please…stay with me."

Azuma hesitated, frozen in place. He could hardly just brush Kaguya's hand away. But even Azuma likely understood that no one liked to be watched while they cried. Certainly not Kaguya, of all people.

But this is about trust.

She trusted him enough to let him see her at her weakest. Before long, the sound of steady sobbing filled the hospital room. The sound was measured, as if she was trying to hold her breath or to hold back slightly.

Azuma didn't try to comfort her or urge her to stop. He just stood there quietly while Kaguya gripped his sleeve. That was all. But in that moment, it was the greatest redemption Kaguya could have hoped for.

"Are you feeling better now?" Azuma asked once more.

"Y-yes, thank you…"

Eyes red, Kaguya hugged her pillow and cast her eyes downward, seemingly embarrassed. She had pressed the pillow to her face partway through, leaving clear streaks behind. Her hair was slightly disheveled as well.

"I'm sorry. I didn't mean to… I got tear stains everywhere…"

"It's fine. I can wash it later."

"I know. But I got so carried away I used you as a handkerchief. I'm sorry."

Before Azuma had pressed the pillow into Kaguya's hands, she had been crying into his sleeve instead.

Azuma started to wonder if that was the real reason she had asked him to stay but decided not to assume the worst. After all, learning he had just been used as a substitute handkerchief was not going to do any favors for his self-esteem.

"To be honest, I feel relieved. It's good to know you're capable of crying like everybody else."

"Why…? You've got a thing for crying faces? That's a pretty niche fetish, Captain."

"No," Azuma said. He didn't want people to peg him as some sort of pervert. "I just don't think you've cried even once since meeting us. Out of sympathy for the heroes, sure, but I can't remember you ever crying just for yourself. Even when Sakura died. Or the Director. Particularly the Director. You knew her for a long time. Or over the stuff with your brother, for that matter."

"Now that you mention it…I guess I hadn't. But it's not that I didn't feel sad, you know. There were just too many other things demanding my attention."

"That's what we meant about taking on too much by yourself." A pained smile played on Azuma's lips. It obviously wasn't Kaguya's responsibility to solve all their problems for them. "After Sakura died, it was the heroes. And now it's whoever killed the Director. There's always something else to worry about… You need to rely on us more. You don't have to keep everything bottled up. You can believe in us a little more."

"Okay. Then that's what I'll do going forward."

This time it was Kaguya's turn to smile uncomfortably. Azuma knew he was being a little pedantic, but he also knew that was what it would take to get through to Kaguya.

In any case, she no longer seemed convinced that she could solve everything all on her own. In particular, when it came to the current commotion surrounding the Director's death.

"Regarding the situation we're in right now, I doubt I'd be able to do anything about it on my own." Kaguya turned her eyes upward toward the ceiling. "Seriously, what is happening around here? To us?"

"I know. It's been one crazy thing after the next ever since you came to us."

No, even before Kaguya arrived. It all began six years ago. Even earlier than that, actually. This whole thing started thirty years ago. And it continued ever since.

But it was true that something about the situation had changed recently.

"I don't think these changes would have happened without you being here… This whole idea that the Chronoses are sentient. The Director only reached that conclusion after you made her aware of the heroes' interior worlds. Which…is why she was killed, I suppose."

"But why…?" Kaguya placed a hand on her chin, lost in thought. "I understand that the Director was killed because she learned something that someone didn't want her to know. But *why* didn't they want her to know?" she pondered aloud, the light dancing in her violet eyes. No sign of her previous sadness remained there now.

* * *

Why didn't they want the Director to know this?

Kaguya gave the question some thought. If the information that Chronoses were intelligent was to be shared with Chronos users, it might negatively affect battle. That was one possibility, of course. But if that was all, then why hadn't this information been shared with even Technical?

"It doesn't seem like sharing the information with those who don't use Chronoses should have been such an issue. All they really needed to do was to keep it a secret from Charon. With that in mind, it seems odd that they kept Technical in the dark."

An uneasy lump had settled in Kaguya's chest. A mystery that she was absolutely determined to solve.

Why? Why hadn't Technical been allowed to know the truth?

"Chronoses are sentient…and the heroes possess mental worlds…"

As shocking as it would be to some to learn that Chronoses are sentient, there had to be more to it than just that. Something else. Something important, just out of reach.

Chronoses and heroes. They both possessed awareness…

"Of course…!"

Kaguya's brain may not have been as brilliant as the Director's, but it was still of very high caliber indeed. With a flash of inspiration, Kaguya's brain now made a sudden beeline toward the answer. Although she could not check her work, she was almost certain she had discovered the solution.

"It's the other way around," she said.

"The other way around?"

"Chronoses weren't derived from heroes. Heroes exist for the sake of Chronoses."

What were Chronoses? Were they sentient weapons randomly created from pieces of flesh taken from the heroes, who just so happened to possess a similar mental world…? Or were the heroes created so that the Chronoses could be made?

"Chronos… It's right there in the name."

"Chronos? The god of time…?"

"No, I don't think that's it. I don't think it has anything to do with time. There is another meaning to the name."

A portion of heroes didn't just happen to become weapons randomly. This must have been what the heroes were intended for from the start. The entire reason they were created.

"Chronoses possess—or rather, have been instilled with—human consciousness."

In other words...

Kaguya quickly rifled through her thoughts. She remembered once looking into how Chronoses had received their name. She had found something interesting in the documents she had uncovered, though it hadn't made much sense to her at the time.

"Chronos is often associated with Chronus as well, the Greek god of agriculture..."

Chronus, the god who had eaten his own children. Who had *instilled* himself with his own children. Kaguya hadn't understood what it meant at the time, but she could see it now—the true nature of Chronoses had been there in the name all along.

"It's why they both have consciousness. The heroes and the Chronoses."

It was no coincidence. It was what they were created for from the start.

Someone had created these sentient monsters in order to create sentient weapons. It all fit. Or at least it fit more than the notion that it was all a coincidence that heroes possessed mental worlds and Chronoses happened to be conscious.

"The heroes exist so that Chronoses can be created. No, let me rephrase that. The Extermination Bureau created heroes so that they could create Chronoses."

Kaguya got out of bed swiftly, already forgetting that she had been in tears just a moment before.

"I think, maybe, the Director must have realized this. When you look at things this way, it changes everything."

The lump in her chest began to loosen, growing lighter the more she spoke.

"It's why the hero in that photograph seemed harmless. Heroes originally existed for humanity's sake. They weren't our enemies at first."

"But then...why?" Azuma asked. It was the most obvious question. "Why have things turned out the way they have...?! With us always teetering on the verge of death...?"

"Something must have happened. Something from which there was no coming back."

Maybe a simple miscalculation, some kind of accident. But once heroes grew dangerous and began to cause carnage, that had been the start of it all.

"What about the Extermination Bureau?" Azuma asked shakily. "Do they only exist to hide their own mistake? Just an organization dedicated to keeping all of this a secret...?"

"No, I think there must be more to them. Covering their own tracks doesn't seem like enough of a motivation for what they've done."

If the truth came out, people in the Bureau might lose positions of power, but that alone wasn't enough of a secret to require murder. There must have been some other reason.

Something more was at stake beyond the mere fact of the Chronoses' sentience.

Just then, one of their comms chimed. It was Azuma's device.

It seemed to be a message, not a telephone call.

"What is it? Who is it from?" Kaguya asked.

"It's Takanashi..."

"Second Lieutenant Takanashi? What could she want?"

Azuma did not answer. Kaguya looked away, not wanting to pry. Finally, Azuma whispered softly.

"Design specs...," he said.

Kaguya looked up at him. "Design specs?"

"Takanashi sent data. We intentionally caused a crash, and she was asked to handle recovery."

Before Kaguya could ask him to explain, Azuma showed her a photograph.

"This is..." Kaguya stared at the photograph and gulped.

It did indeed seem to be design specs. But that wasn't what Haru wanted them to see—what she thought they needed to see.

A single word was written beneath the photograph.

"'Hero.'"

It looked as if both the word written underneath the photograph and—more importantly—the photograph itself, which had apparently been included for reference purposes, were from an important section of the document.

"This is how it looked, the first hero."

A hero—someone who saves the innocent and protects the world. The creature in the photograph fit that image perfectly. Of course, there were aberrations, but it still resembled a hero from out of a children's show. The explanation that the first hero had resembled something from an anime had apparently been true after all. This was the starting point.

They had finally found it. The reason the creatures were named heroes. Kaguya was only starting to figure it out now. The Director must have arrived at the same answer, only with far less information to go on.

"What...what does it mean? What is this?"

Azuma looked confused. Kaguya considered the possibilities as she stood beside him.

Heroes were clearly created by human beings. And so much about the Extermination Bureau just didn't add up. Not least of which was the fact that they had been willing to kill to keep all this a secret.

Kaguya suddenly remembered what the hero from earlier in the day had said—about being trapped in a sandbox garden.

A box, isolated from the outside. So that those inside were unable to see the truth of the situation they were in.

Didn't that describe the state of the very Bureau itself? Of the mystery of the heroes? And, of course, of the Bureau's test subjects—the Bureau soldiers, who were treated as practically disposable?

That was why things were the way they were.

"It's a closed diorama...," Kaguya said, her voice sounding distracted as she arrived at an answer. "This place...is all an experiment."

CHAPTER TWELVE
Deceit

"A diorama? What do you mean?" Azuma asked Kaguya.

"It didn't exist at first. This so-called Extermination Bureau."

"What…?"

"There was no organization dedicated to defeating heroes at first. This whole place is just the setting for an experiment."

The hypothesis had only just occurred to Kaguya. She began to mull over her thoughts, confirming her suspicions in order. The Extermination Bureau had been their entire youth. But what was its true identity?

Kaguya had experienced a lot. She had joined Charon, been at loggerheads with Azuma, and lost Sakura. She had fought battles, and as she fought, she had begun to shoulder the tragedy of these heroes all on her own. She had met Haru, learned that there were some people who didn't want to be saved, and then made up her mind to try to save these people anyway.

But what was the truth behind the Extermination Bureau?

"It's all a sandbox designed to help perfect the weapons known as Chronoses. That's what this fighting has been for."

The existence of the heroes. The existence of the Bureau. All of it. It really was to defeat the heroes. But not for humanity's sake. Just for their own.

A million thoughts ran through Kaguya's head, which she tried to corral together.

"Thirty years ago, heroes were created by the Extermination Bureau in order to make Chronoses. But twenty-five years ago, they made some kind of mistake. So what did they do next…? Naturally, they would have begun investigating the cause and implementing countermeasures. That is almost the most fundamental process in clinical research."

And the Extermination Bureau likely carried out this process *correctly*. Clinical research into the Chronoses, investigation of the causes, and application of countermeasures. They did it all.

And they did it within the closed sandbox known as the Bureau.

For instance, their fights with the heroes. Every fight with each of the many heroes they had encountered to date must have provided the Bureau with extremely valuable data. Data as to why the heroes had suddenly turned dangerous and aggressive. Those many long years of research were all for a single end.

"B-but…who's doing all of this…? What did you call it…? 'Clinical research'?"

"I suppose it must have been Technical No. 1. The group wiped out by that hero that appeared six years ago."

Appeared? No, that probably wasn't quite right, either.

Were they really supposed to believe that every member of Technical No. 1 just happened to be present where the hero appeared? That didn't add up. The Bureau must have been involved in the hero incident six years ago as well.

"But so then why was the Director killed? Wasn't she carrying out their work? It wouldn't make sense for them to kill her."

"I think she must have caught onto something. Something inconvenient for them. Such as the fact that the Chronoses were sentient, or maybe the organization's real goals."

The fact that the Chronoses were sentient would have been very inconvenient for the Bureau. A spark that could lead to the complete destruction of their sandbox. Already, the cracks were beginning to show.

Why had the sleeping dogs been left to lie for twenty-five years? There must not have been anyone capable until now of putting the pieces together. After all, who would ever imagine that a weapon could possess a mind and awareness?

But the Director had figured it out. And the reason she had been able to do so…

"Of course… It was me."

It was because Kaguya had discovered that the heroes had mental worlds. The introduction of an outsider, the external element Kaguya Shinohara, had caused the sandbox to break.

This had clearly been a major miscalculation on the Extermination Bureau's part. Enough to make them eager to collect Kaguya. But they had made an even bigger miscalculation along the way. Mari knew the truth. And—according to Mari—the reason she had decided to tell Azuma and the others what she knew was because of the strong will displayed by the members of Charon.

It was their powerful will to save people. That was what had led to the sandbox becoming broken. It was almost ironic in a way.

"But what about the Bureau's real motive? What in the hell are they after?"

"They want to reengineer Chronoses. Without the rebounds, I suspect. To perfect them… That was what the Director was trying to do. It was the same thing."

The same thing, but their methods had been as different as night and day. As had been their motivations.

The Director was so idealistic and direct that she sometimes came across as mad. Everything she had done, however, had been for the sake of humanity. That was why Kaguya had stayed by her side.

But the Extermination Bureau's motives—this experimental sandbox's motives—were not the same as hers. The Bureau did not hesitate to sacrifice people for their own ends. Why were they so desperate to develop new Chronoses?

"What in the world are Chronoses…?" Azuma muttered, voicing Kaguya's exact thoughts. "Who are they for? *What* are they for?"

"I don't know. Maybe we don't need to know. This all dates back to something from thirty years ago. Something they failed at."

Kaguya gave the matter some thought. How did the people attempting to reengineer the Chronoses view Charon? Charon's members were the only people capable of using Chronoses without rebounds, which was exactly what the Bureau had been hoping for.

Hence why they had brought them all together into a single squad and forced them to fight heroes. The data collected from Charon's battles would have made it evident that Charon's members possessed extraordinary physical attributes. But just having them fight heroes may not have been enough to answer the question as to why they didn't suffer rebounds.

That explained why they had sent in a *technological liaison*.

At least, it accounted for why they had suddenly transferred Kaguya—someone who was researching how to turn heroes back into humans—to Charon and why they had gone so far as to approve of her participation in battles.

"But things didn't go quite as they had expected."

Because Kaguya had discovered the interior mental worlds that existed within the heroes. According to what Azuma told her, his decision to temporarily remove her from the squad had been precipitated by panic from someone higher up.

After she had returned to Charon, they had sent Haru in another failed attempt to detach Kaguya from Charon.

But Kaguya had stayed. And then, just as they were running out of options for how to deal with her, the Director had sent that report. And they knew, of course, that the Director and Kaguya were in close contact with one another.

I was on a mission at the time. She would have told me once I got back. And then—just like now…

The sandbox was starting to come apart at the seams. That was why they had her killed.

That explains their behavior, but there's probably still more that needs answering.

"Kaguya?" Azuma's voice snapped Kaguya out of her reverie. "Are you all right?"

"Oh… I'm sorry. There's just a lot to think about."

"You're telling me. It's not only the Chroneses or the heroes. There's a lot about the Extermination Bureau that doesn't make sense."

Azuma had summed it up perfectly. Kaguya guessed, from the lack of deliberation in his tone, that this wasn't his first time giving the matter thought.

"But it makes you wonder who they are…"

"They?"

"The people inside my sword and in Koyuki's and Rindou's weapons. I can't help but wonder…who are they?"

"Good point… Not to mention that pistol…"

Whose consciousness was it that was sealed inside the pistol that Kaguya sometimes used?

"Do you think…this is something we should share with Koyuki and the others?"

"Of course. They have the obligation and the right to know, Kaguya. If you don't tell them, I will."

The members of Charon held strong attachments to the Extermination Bureau. As did Kaguya, to be honest. They had spent their whole lives fighting for the Bureau, on the front lines, after all.

"I don't believe any of us are so weak as to run away over something like this. Do you?"

"No, of course not. They're all strong… You're right. We should tell them."

Their faith in the members of Charon was unshakable. If this was what it took to cause them to lose their will to fight, they would just have to cross that bridge when they got there.

• • •

It wasn't until several hours after Haru's message that Kaguya told them.

The reason she waited was because both she and Azuma were in agreement that Haru needed to be there to hear this as well. Once Haru finally returned, everyone gathered in the meeting hall to hear what Kaguya had to say.

That the Extermination Bureau was no more than a testing ground for the research and improvement of Chronoses, the weapons refined from heroes.

That heroes existed for the creation of Chronoses and had not originally been hostile. That something happened that had caused the heroes to run amok—and that the Extermination Bureau existed in order to clean up that mess and to collect data.

Once Kaguya finished explaining, the room fell silent. No one knew what to say.

The silence was uncomfortable. They all kept their mouths shut, aware of what the others were thinking. But after a bombshell like that, they couldn't just trudge back to their separate rooms as if nothing had happened.

Azuma was Charon's captain. If anyone was going to break the silence, it was up to him.

"Everyone." Azuma's voice diffused softly throughout the room, his tone gentle but sharp. They all turned to stare. "I understand how you must feel... I still haven't fully accepted this myself."

The truth behind the Extermination Bureau—that it was no more than a facility for lab rats.

"However, that doesn't change what we need to do, does it?"

"Maybe not...," Rindou said, scratching his head reluctantly. "But I don't understand how you can be so okay with all of this." He glared at Azuma. "You're saying everything we've done up until now has all been some faceless jerk's experiment. That it was all for shits and giggles. How are you not losing it right now? That would mean that what happened to Sakura when she became a hero, to all of them... They were all just somebody's guinea pigs."

Rindou was right; there was nothing Azuma could say to that.

"And you're fine with this?! With letting something like that go unpunished...?!" Rindou demanded.

"Of course I'm not fine with it."

Azuma's voice was hard as steel, as if he was barely containing his anger.

Azuma's reaction seemed to have spooked Rindou. Azuma, however, ignored him and let out a loud sigh. This was a ridiculous amount of information to unload on them all at once. It was too much to expect them to process it all immediately.

Koyuki was the next to speak. "I can't do this. I can't do this right now."

For Koyuki, the Extermination Bureau was both her youth and her curse. It was all she had ever known. She couldn't bear it—the idea that it had all been fake.

She jumped to her feet, knocking her chair back with a clatter, and rushed toward the stairs. Kaguya knew exactly where she was heading.

Toward their room to bury herself under the covers on the top bunk.

Azuma stared at Kaguya, who made no attempt to follow, slightly surprised.

"Shouldn't you go after her?" he asked.

"No, it's better this way." Kaguya wasn't going to chase her. Koyuki had just learned something earth-shattering and was probably at her lowest. "Charon's members aren't weaklings. You're the one who taught me that, Captain Azuma."

"Of course..."

Behind them, they could hear Rindou and Haru squabbling among themselves. It sounded like Haru was trying to soothe Rindou, who was having difficulty keeping his rage in check. Haru's voice also sounded like it was on the verge of tears. It seemed even Haru was tempted to cry over what they had just learned.

Haru had gone out in search of information on her own and had found what she was looking for. Kaguya could only imagine how she must have looked when she had sent the photograph of those design specs to Azuma. And then she had trudged all the way back to the barracks only to hear what she must have already known.

She was likely experiencing as much turmoil as the rest of them.

Kaguya, for her part, was taking it all in stride. Maybe the information wasn't as great of a shock for her in the first place as it was for Charon. But more importantly, she had already faintly suspected something like this.

She had been carrying a sneaking suspicion for some time now that something wasn't quite right with the Bureau. That feeling had now simply been given form.

But while she might have been calmer than the others, she was far from fine.

"I...I have to..."

After a moment of hesitation, Kaguya headed up the stairs toward their rooms without saying anything. Not to comfort Koyuki, who had already left. No—Kaguya needed a moment to herself as well. Now that she had put all of this out into the open, she felt a clamor building in her chest. Something she had to work her way through...

As Kaguya reached for the door to their room, Koyuki stepped out from inside, her eyes slightly puffy.

"Ah..."

"..."

They stared at each other for a few seconds.

And then, at the same time, they both broke into smiles. The tension finally broke. Koyuki was the first to speak.

"What? Don't tell me you were worried about me. Or were you running off to cry again yourself?"

"N-no, I was just, um..." Kaguya was too embarrassed to admit that was exactly what she was about to do. "I was just wondering what was for dinner. I left today's menu in our room."

"Relax. I'm only teasing you. And I'm not such a baby that I need anyone to make a fuss over me."

They spoke almost as if they were exchanging friendly banter.

Somewhere along the way, the relationship between them had developed to the point where they no longer needed to hold back with one another.

"Hmph…"

However, it probably wasn't so easy to switch tracks on a dime like that. Koyuki turned her head upward, likely holding back tears.

"Geez. I had kind of suspected something like this, but to be confronted with it out of the blue like this…"

"Wait, you suspected?"

"Of course," Koyuki said, turning to face Kaguya once more. She put on a brave smile. "There were too many red flags. The Chronoses, the heroes… I knew the Bureau was no normal organization. It's bizarre, after all, the way they purposely hide themselves from the world… I knew something was wrong. I just didn't want to think about it too deeply."

Because if she had let herself think, and had realized the truth, it would have overturned everything she knew and had believed in.

"This organization is a kind of dreamworld of its own. In a way, Kaguya, I think you came here to lead us out of these lies."

"That's—"

"I don't mean anything bad by that. Instead of not knowing, not seeing, not thinking, I would rather see the reality for what it is. Even if that reality is almost entirely painful. What I'm trying to say is I don't regret learning the truth."

Koyuki smiled a genuine smile before shifting her face into an expression of concern for Kaguya.

"But what about you, Kaguya? Are you all right? This place was important to you, too, wasn't it?"

"Well, it would be hard to say that I'm completely fine… My brother, Sakura, the Director. They're all gone. I don't want to believe this could have all been some sort of make-believe any more than the rest of you do." Kaguya wasn't looking to garner sympathy, though. "However, the truth is the truth."

And accepting cold, hard truths without letting emotion get in the way was what the Director—what the members of Technical—did best.

"The people of Technical, like Mari and the Director, have a habit of bottling everything up inside. Until it gets to be too much, and we explode."

But Mari had made the right choice in the end. Even if the Director had not been able to entrust what she was doing to anybody else.

"And what about you?" Koyuki asked, seeming like her normal self once again. "Are you finally starting to rely on the others around you?"

"...Yes." Kaguya wasn't putting on a show; she meant it. "Koyuki, I'm not going to take you for granted or make you worry anymore. I'm not going to leave you in this room all on your own again."

"Good..." Koyuki smiled mischievously, and it didn't look forced. "And here I thought you were gonna start crying on me."

"Not a chance. I've got appearances to keep up, after all."

"You mean like when you bawled your eyes out?" Koyuki teased, her own voice still a little weepy.

Kaguya turned beet red. "What? How do you know that?!"

"Azuma told me."

"What?" Of course—how else would Koyuki have known? But that wasn't what Kaguya expected to hear. "Is that...is that the sort of thing you usually tell other people about?!" she shouted, her cheeks flushed. "It kind of seems to me like something you should keep to yourself..."

"Well...I guess I kind of dragged it out of him. He did linger in your room for a while, after all. He said something about being forced to serve as a handkerchief, I believe...?"

"What?!" Kaguya said, recoiling in embarrassment. "But he knows I didn't mean to..." She suddenly turned on her heel as if to escape the conversation. "C-come to think of it, I think I left that menu downstairs in the meeting hall."

With that, Kaguya raced down the stairs.

Along the way...
Kaguya passed Azuma. She noticed that his eyes were moist.

He must have noticed that she had seen. But he pretended to be oblivious as he continued past her. Neither his bravado nor his true feelings, however, were lost on Kaguya.

"..."

She thought about saying something but chose not to in the end. Azuma wasn't weak. He didn't need someone to check on him and hold his hand.

They had just learned a harsh truth, but Azuma would likely come to grips with it in his own way and turn his thoughts to the future once again. He wouldn't have been cut out to be their captain in the first place if he needed to be coddled instead.

"Now then… Let's see what's for dinner."

In the end, Kaguya said nothing.
She already knew she could trust in him.

CHAPTER THIRTEEN
Promise

It had only been two days since Charon had learned the truth.

Just two days. That was all it had taken for them to get back onto their feet.

From Kaguya's perspective, that about-face seemed staggeringly fast. They had just learned that their whole lives had been lived as someone's lab rats. Under the circumstances, it would not have been strange for one or more of them to announce they were leaving the Bureau.

"I mean, it's not like dwelling on things is going to get me anywhere," Rindou said. "And if I left now, where would I go? The Bureau's recruits are all in the same boat, after all."

"That's true, I guess. Only people with no relatives wind up in here."

Neither Koyuki nor Rindou nor, least of all, Azuma were about to sit around feeling sorry for themselves, wasting their energy thinking about a past they had already lost. In Kaguya's opinion they could afford to be a little more ambivalent about things than they were being, but that probably just came down to their different personalities. And perhaps to their experiences.

"Actually, this might have something to do with why the Bureau only hires children orphaned by the hero attacks."

"I think so. Children can see the heroes, after all. The Bureau could have run some sort of application process if they wanted one, but they don't."

That was always an option—the Extermination Bureau could have made their existence public and fielded willing applicants. The reason they hadn't must have been because, at the end of the day, the Bureau was just the setting for an experiment. The organization's personal playground, so to speak.

"It seems as if they needed to keep the Chronoses a secret to some degree."

"That makes sense. These weapons were originally human. Not only that, they still have awareness and can feel pain. It's diabolical."

True. The Extermination Bureau had strayed far from the path of decency.

"What about those design specs, though? I'm impressed you were able to get your hands on something like that. It's hard to believe stuff like that is just sitting around in the Intelligence and Analysis Branch's database."

"It obviously wasn't in the database. This is something they wanted to keep secret so badly that they were willing to kill for it. They wouldn't dare keep something like that in the database, not even in the hidden files."

"So then how did you—?"

"That's my little secret."

Noticing the wicked glint in Haru's eyes, Kaguya suspected there might have been some form of blackmail involved.

"Well, I'm impressed you were able to *convince* people like that," Kaguya said. By convince, she meant strong-arm, of course. "But couldn't something like that come back to bite you later on?"

"I doubt it would amount to much of a bite even if it did. The Extermination Bureau will probably *see how things are before too long.*"

"...?"

"They can't just stop sending Charon into the fight, and they must know it's too late to kill any more of us now. I doubt they'd just kill us without a good reason since it takes a lot of nerve to kill another person."

Having once attempted to kill someone she was close to, Haru knew what she was talking about.

"So you're saying that, for all intents and purposes, the Bureau's hands are tied? You certainly know how to play hardball. I'll give you that," Kaguya said, praising her.

A bemused look appeared in Haru's eyes.

"In any case, shouldn't Azuma be here by now? What's taking him so long?"

Koyuki glanced toward the door of the meeting hall.

It was almost lunchtime. Azuma was in charge of today's meal. While his cooking wasn't terrible, the general consensus (?) was that it lacked originality, simply a textbook interpretation of flavor.

They did all agree on one thing, though: It was better than Haru's cooking.

"Does he usually wake up this late?"

It was already eleven thirty. Factoring in the time it would take to prepare the meal, it would be around one by the time they finished eating.

"I guess it can't be helped. Maybe someone else should make lunch in his place today—"

"I can do it," Haru said, speaking up out of the blue. "I haven't really done a proper lunch duty since I got here. The least I can do is—"

"Absolutely not!" the others said in unison.

They had yet to recover from the shock of seeing Haru's first meal—which had been some sort of purplish-red stew.

"Ah! Speaking of which, Kaguya," Koyuki said, changing the topic in a panic. "What happened to what we were talking about from before?"

"Talking about from before? What do you mean?"

"You know. The checkups, with the pulse and everything."

Kaguya's brain stalled temporarily. That was the last subject she had expected Koyuki to bring up at the current moment.

"What are you talking about? What pulse?" Rindou said, being the only one among them in the dark.

Kaguya ignored his question. "Well, nothing happened, I guess. Besides, I told you those are just aftereffects..."

"Hmph... Come on, the cat's out of the bag already." Koyuki seemed thrilled with her new choice of topic. "When are you going to woman up and do something about it already? You're obviously just as keen on Azuma as he is on you!"

"I'm what...?!" Kaguya's eyes nearly popped out of her head. Kaguya? Keen? On Azuma? Absolutely not! "Y-you've got it all wrong. Azuma was just going through something unusual, but that doesn't mean that I—"

"I don't know. You seem pretty interested in him to me, too," Haru said, butting in once more where she wasn't needed. "What do you think?" she asked, passing the ball along to Rindou, of all people.

Rindou, who had been out of the loop, hesitated slightly before speaking.

"W-well...she certainly doesn't seem to hate him. That's for sure. At least, they seem to be getting on better than before."

"Of course we are. We've been around each other for several months now. But that's just friendship. Friendship! I obviously care about him... as a teammate. But that absolutely does not mean that there's anything sexual or romantic between us!"

"Oh? Who said anything about *romantic*?" Koyuki asked. Kaguya froze, realizing she had just dug her own grave. "It sounds like you're aware of some feelings after all."

"That's not fair. You tricked me...," Kaguya grumbled. She did not deny it, however. For all intents and purposes, she had just given her answer. "But don't go nuts or anything. I'm just a tiny bit interested. That's all."

Kaguya stood up to hide her embarrassment. Anything to play off how flustered she was feeling at the moment. She began purposely speaking in a loud voice, making a show of how funny she found this whole situation.

"That doesn't mean I *like* like Captain Azuma or anything, so—"
Click.

With exquisite—or what Kaguya would call *atrocious*—timing, the door to the hall swung open to reveal Azuma, who looked drowsy.

"Sorry I'm late. I'll start making—" Azuma blinked, noticing Kaguya, who had frozen in a bizarre stance. "Kaguya, what are you doing?"

"What? Me? I was just standing up."

Azuma cocked his head in a strangely endearing manner. "Oh? I had no idea you were such a big fan of standing up."

"Standing up? What? I mean, I could take it or leave it...," she babbled. Little did she know what was coming next.

"Hmm? I could have sworn I heard you talking about how much you liked something from outside the door. What was that all about?"

"...?!"

Kaguya's cheeks grew warm. Her face, however, went white. "Well... You see..."

You could hear a pin drop. Despite the silence, everybody's attention was riveted on Azuma and what he was going to do next. Was today the day that something finally happened? Kaguya was painfully conscious of the hushed expectation filling the room.

But she didn't have time to worry about that right now. She needed to come up with an excuse. A good one and quickly. Preferably something of the witty variety.

"I—I was just saying how much I like your cooking, Captain Azuma."

This was not her finest moment.

"Yes, that's right. I was just saying *how much I love Captain Azuma's cooking*! In fact, I was looking forward to it so much that I couldn't stop myself from jumping to my feet."

"Y-you do? Well, I'm glad to hear that, I guess."

Azuma looked confused, but he sounded vaguely pleased. Apparently, he believed her. Although...it was a little worrying that he was so easy to fool.

"Just don't go expecting me to start playing favorites with the menu, Kaguya."

"Absolutely not. I wouldn't dream of it."

"But I bet you're expecting an extra-large portion, right? You're going to have Major Mirai in tears again at this rate."

Charon's food, necessities, and other such needs were provided by the Combat Support Branch. Since Kaguya joined them, the amount of food they were going through had skyrocketed. If they tried to skimp on the portions, however, Kaguya's performance out in the field suffered instead. Mirai was close to tearing her hair out when it came to ordering their supplies.

"Portions are, well… Never mind. Forget about that for now. Why were you sleeping in so late, Captain Azuma? You usually wake up right after Rindou."

Rindou was the barrack's earliest riser.

"Were you up late last night or something? There's a first time for everything, I guess."

"Y-yeah…"

Azuma laughed in a somewhat self-deprecating manner as he headed toward the kitchen, turning his back on the rest of them in the hall.

"I started thinking of everyone…from Charon…"

Kaguya didn't need to be told to know who he meant by *"everyone."*

She plopped herself down on the sofa. The past members of Charon, the ones who had died. That was who, probably. Azuma and the other current members of Charon weren't the only ones who had survived the hero attack six years ago. There had been older members. A whole ragtag pack, at least, of adolescents and children.

And all of their deaths had been for the sake of some experiment being carried out by the Extermination Bureau—or at least by the organization that went by that name.

Kaguya's mind wandered to thoughts of the Director and Sakura. Haru was probably also remembering past friends and colleagues whom she had witnessed die in front of her eyes.

The slightly somber atmosphere that descended upon the room was interrupted by the sound of the refrigerator door opening.

Despite being the one to bring up the subject, Azuma himself seemed fairly nonchalant.

"It looks like summer is finally almost over, doesn't it? It was a long one this year."

"For me, it passed in the blink of an eye…"

"That's not very funny…"

Kaguya knew he was right, but to her, the fact that she had been asleep for a whole month seemed fairly trivial.

"Speaking of which," Kaguya said, completely changing the subject. "You seem tired, Captain Azuma. Instead of making lunch, why don't we all go somewhere instead?"

"Somewhere? You mean like out to eat? What brought that on all of a sudden?"

"Why not? It's good to get out every now and again. We'll just ask Major Mirai to foot the bill."

"The poor major…," Haru said, staring off into the distance. It didn't seem like she was against the idea, however. "Fine, what should we eat, then? What sounds good to you, Kaguya?"

"I mean…I know it was my suggestion, but honestly, I'm having trouble coming up with any good ideas."

"Well, make sure it's something where there's a limit on how much you can eat. We don't want a repeat of last time when we went for bottomless soba, and you finished off one hundred and fifty-three bowls. You put the rest of us off our food."

"That was actually quite low, I'll have you know. I only stopped because Major Mirai begged me to in tears."

"Poor Major Mirai," Haru said once again.

"What do you mean by a place where there's a limit on how much I can eat?"

"Anywhere without free refills or all-you-can-eat options."

"How about Italian? All those carbs should be filling."

The girls began making arrangements among themselves, completely ignoring Azuma and Rindou. One place had good pasta.

Another was too expensive, so it wouldn't be fair to Major Mirai. One also had healthy options. And so on and so forth.

After some chatter, Koyuki finally turned to speak to Azuma and Rindou.

"So it's decided, then. We're having pasta today."

"Don't we get a say in the matter…?"

"Okay, what did you want?"

Azuma gave it some thought, but after ten seconds, he still hadn't said a word. It looked like he couldn't come up with any ideas, either.

"All right, then. Pasta it is—"

"Aren't you gonna ask me what I want?" Rindou said, complaining, although he was probably only doing so for show.

"I already know you're just gonna say protein."

"What kind of a meathead do you take me for? But…yeah, you're right."

He had only interrupted them for the sake of banter.

Pasta it was, then.

"Ah…!" As Rindou began to rise to his feet, Azuma made a little exclamation as if he had just remembered something. "Ice cream parfaits."

Everyone turned to stare. That cute little phrase was not at all what they had expected to come out of his mouth.

"Ice cream…parfaits?"

"Yes… There was this place I saw a little while ago. I kept thinking that I wanted to go, but before I knew it, the time just seemed to slip away."

"Really? I'm curious to see what kind of place would catch your interest, Captain Azuma…but to be honest, my heart is already set on pasta today."

"No, I don't want to make everyone change plans now."

It sounded like Azuma wasn't that dead set on parfaits after all. He just wanted to bring it up.

"Well, how about this, then? The next time we go out to eat, we'll prioritize wherever you want to go," said Kaguya.

"Oh? Is that a promise?" Azuma asked her.

"Of course it is. Have I ever made a promise I didn't keep?"

"Not that I can think of off the top of my head. Honestly, it's hard to picture you breaking a promise."

"You see?"

Kaguya grinned, a little satisfied with herself. A smile made its way to Azuma's lips as well. Maybe her grin had rubbed off on him. Either that, or he was just keeping her smile company.

"All right. I trust you won't break your promise. But don't forget about it, either!"

"Don't you sweat it. If there's one thing I'm good at, it's remembering stuff."

"We'll see about that," Azuma teased, taking the lead and exiting the room first.

Koyuki followed, and then Rindou, and then Haru. Purely by coincidence, Kaguya happened to bring up the rear.

As she watched them from behind, a stray thought floated into her head.

Of course I won't forget.
How could I ever forget a promise that I made to you?

CHAPTER FOURTEEN
Precipitation

That night.

A report of a hero sighting had come in. Charon was already on the scene.

The hero had appeared in Chiba, specifically in an area of reclaimed land along Tokyo Bay. A slime-shaped hero had apparently shown up at a private high school in a section where many schools were located—it covered almost the entire school building.

Fortunately, it showed up overnight at three in the morning when—save for a lone security guard already half asleep—not a single creature was stirring. The members of Charon infiltrated the school grounds, bringing Kaguya with them. She held her pistol low.

"If you start to feel unwell–"

"I told you I'm fine. What about everyone else? Are you guys all right?" Kaguya cut in as she turned to face the hero. The slime hero was a poisonous-looking purple and seemed to have enveloped nearly the whole structure. They could just barely make out the entrance below, lined with rows of shoe lockers, and the windows of the classrooms.

"SKRRREEEEEEEE!!"

A screech.

Reflexively, Kaguya pressed a hand to one ear. The shock made her knees go weak and left her numb to her core. The other squad members seemed to have been affected in the same manner. Koyuki, unfortunately, had both hands full and was forced to take the full, unmitigated impact of the noise.

"Koyuki! Are you okay?!" Kaguya shouted, but she could not even hear her own voice.

The screech had been so loud and powerful that it had caused a crack to appear in the school building and the asphalt to split. It was essentially a sonic attack.

Of course, the hero itself was unfazed, seeing as it had made the sound. It wouldn't have made much sense for it to be damaged by its own cries. It extended a "hand" toward the immobilized members of Charon.

Thin tendrils of slime, like the twigs from a tree, split off from the main purple mass. For the first few seconds after splitting, they traveled at normal speed but then suddenly picked up pace as they charged toward the squad.

Azuma, Kaguya, and Haru had only been able to cover one ear due to the weapons they were holding. Koyuki, meanwhile, had both hands full and had taken the full brunt of the attack. The creature's "arms" closed in on each of them.

The attack had taken no more than the blink of an eye to reach them. However, the tendrils suddenly stopped before making contact.

They weren't about to waste this chance. They all hastily moved back. After creating distance, Kaguya finally realized why the hero had stopped.

"Ah...! Rindou."

As the only one of them with two empty hands, Rindou alone had been able to defend against the sonic attack fully. Doing so had given him enough time to approach the creature's main mass and deliver a powerful blow to it with his fists.

"Rindou!!"

"...!!"

The tendrils were headed toward Rindou now. The individually meager "arms" came together to form a single coil, now as thick as a man's chest, which swung at Rindou. However, the creature's movements were less than precise. The wild whipping motion left the hero wide open, and Rindou was easily able to avoid the blow. However, as soon as he dodged…

"Wha-?!"

A second arm of thick slime was waiting for him, like a trap. Rindou failed to notice it until it had already caught him by the leg and had begun to squeeze, tighter and tighter and tighter.

"Argh!"

The pressure threatened to shred his thigh to ribbons. Just as the "hand" was about to tear Rindou's leg to pieces, a gunshot rang through the air. It was the slime's arm that was shredded instead.

"Ah!" Rindou seized the opportunity. He retreated out of the slime's reach, dragging his leg slightly as he went. "Thanks, Koyuki!"

"I just didn't want to owe you one. That's all." Koyuki said with a wry smile as smoke rose up from the anti-materiel-class rifle in her hands.

The tendril of slime that had captured Rindou, the one that Koyuki had just blasted to ribbons, regenerated immediately.

"You've got to be kidding me!"

She fired again—this time at the clock on the school building, located over the main entrance. There was a loud crash, and the now broken clock, along with a chunk of the school building, fell, massively damaging the slime. Just as she was preparing to take another shot…

"Koyuki, wait!"

There was a pause. As Kaguya followed Azuma's gaze, she thought she caught sight of a furtive shadow in a corner of one of the windows.

"You can't be serious. There's someone in there?!"

The slime was creeping in through the cracks in the building and looked like it might envelop the figure inside at any moment. The person ran through the school, desperately fleeing the slimy menace. They heard a voice, barely audible, from within.

"Help me…!"

Haru was quick to respond. She ran straight toward the school on her naturally fleet legs, planning to make her way inside. Azuma called after her as she went.

"Takanashi, do you know the way?!"

"I've got it!" Haru said, barely stopping to respond as she rushed inside.

She had spied the girl's location and had already worked out the quickest route to get there. Step one, at least for someone with her physical abilities, was to enter through a window along the side of the building.

The hero didn't try to chase her. Likely because there was a more pressing threat facing it at the moment.

Two such threats, in fact.

"Captain Azuma," said Kaguya, who was one of those two threats. "I heard you aren't able to locate the eggs anymore. Are you sure you've got this?"

"It's fine. I noticed a spot it was trying to protect during Rindou's and Koyuki's attacks earlier."

Since the egg was essentially a hero's heart, the creatures naturally tended to defend that spot on their bodies more than elsewhere, even if only unintentionally.

"Kaguya," Azuma said as he stood next to her without turning his head. "Let's go."

"Okay!"

With Azuma in the lead, they rushed into the slime together toward where the egg must be located. It was a strange feeling, like running underwater. And yet it was easy to breathe. If anything, it almost felt pleasant.

"There! The second-story window!"

They had only been running for a few seconds when they spotted it right there in front of them. A spot where the slime was thicker and far less transparent than anywhere else.

It was a desk located next to a window on the school's second floor. Azuma suddenly grabbed Kaguya, and before she knew it, they were leaping through the air. He was able to cling to the windowsill without much difficulty and bust out the window with a single jab of his elbow. The egg was right there...on top of the desk.

The desk, which was visible even through the slime, was covered with all sorts of messages that had been written directly on it. A vase had also been placed on the desk, symbolizing death. The egg was delicately enshrined within that vase.

The resistance of the slime suddenly increased, and both Azuma and Kaguya found themselves unable to move. They couldn't reach the egg—the interior of the slime began to spasm. If anything, it felt like they were being pushed away.

"It's so thick...!"

"It seems like it really doesn't want us to touch that egg."

Rather than allow himself to be ejected, however, Azuma placed a hand on the hilt of his katana and shifted his center of gravity ever so slightly. With his hips low and a finger on the sword's guard, he withdrew the katana with a quick slashing motion—too fast for Kaguya's eye to see. There was a soft ting, like the sound of a tiny bell, as a small section of the slime was sliced open.

It was like Moses parting the sea. Kaguya somehow managed to thrust herself into that opening and point her gun. But even now the slime continued its attempts to reject them.

"I know..."

Whoever it was in there, they didn't want to go back. They wanted to stay. To sacrifice themselves to their ideals. They didn't want to be dragged back to reality.

Kaguya understood exactly how they felt.

There were some things that only she could do—that no one else could take off her shoulders. Things that were necessary if she was going to save the heroes.

But Kaguya wasn't going to carry it all alone and attempt to remember everything anymore. She could pick it up, let it touch her, and then let it go. Without letting herself become bogged down in it. Without letting it become a curse. She had to. And when it came to the memories that truly needed to be remembered, she would remember them, but she would share them so that they could belong to everything. So that she didn't wind up hoarding the burden.

"Let's go back."

They could rest easy now.

"I'll take it on for you. I won't forget. But then—"

There was more. More to it than just remembering.

"—I'll share it. So you can rest easy knowing that you won't have to go alone. We'll all be there."

The final blow came like a gentle touch, a soft embrace. Like the warm mercy of a saint.

• • •

Kaguya will probably attempt to save the hero once we get there...

Azuma swung his sword in a flash, positioning himself so as to protect Kaguya. At the current moment, he was situated next to the window, cutting through the hero's body as it attempted to envelop her from all sides.

...and she'll probably bring the memories back with her...

The slime was difficult to cut through, but Azuma managed to do so easily.

...but...I don't think she's going to try to keep them all to herself anymore.

He sliced through a tentacle as it reached for Kaguya's shoulder.

Kaguya entered the hero's world, and Haru got the schoolgirl outside to safety at almost the exact same moment. The hero—a boy—barely had a second to exhale and register that he was still alive when Kaguya woke up.

"Kaguya!" As Azuma shouted her name, a smile slowly spread across Kaguya's face. "Are you okay?"

"Captain Azuma... I'm perfectly fine," she said, her expression tranquil.

Azuma breathed a sigh of relief. "I see. Well, good then. It looks like we're almost done here."

He could see the hero's body beginning to crumble apart. The school building, which had almost been swallowed completely, was free again beneath the quiet night sky.

Azuma jumped from the window first. It was only the second floor, so he was able to land solidly on both feet. Next, he spread his arms out wide and waited for Kaguya. She jumped with zero hesitation, suspended in the air for just the briefest of moments—seconds, really. Less than that. Not even a single second.

"...Huh?"

However, Azuma had forgotten one thing.

They all had.

When Sakura died, the hero's final attack had come after a delay. Once everyone had already relaxed and let down their guard.

Azuma was waiting to catch Kaguya. Koyuki was eyeing the hero's body. Rindou's eyes were turned toward the schoolgirl. And Haru was busy trying to convince him to follow them. They all saw it at once.

Just as the hero was about to collapse and vanish entirely, it extended a single rapid tentacle, as thin as a branch, straight toward Kaguya.

"Ah—"

Who actually made the noise? Like air escaping a tire.

A sick, fleshy sound split the night.

The hero's tentacle penetrated Kaguya's back and then exited out of the front, straight through her stomach.

The first thing Kaguya felt was discomfort.

There was no pain. No heat. Just the instinctively unpleasant sensation of something foreign worming its way inside her body. The cold and the pressure of suddenly being yanked to a stop mid-fall were immense.

Yes. She felt cold. Even though it was still summer. As cold as if she had suddenly been immersed in solid ice.

A moment later, Kaguya realized she could barely breathe. And then...

"Kaguya!!"

Someone was shouting her name. The despair in the voice told her that something bad had just happened to her. She turned her attention toward her own body.

"Ah…"

There was a hole through her solar plexus.

Her lungs hadn't taken direct damage, at least, but the impact had broken her ribs, which had pierced her lungs and left them half destroyed. She coughed up a spurt of blood. Once that happened, she instinctively knew.

It was already too late.

They said that a person would always realize when they are close to death. That they don't need to be told. There was no scientific reason for this. Animal instinct simply made it known.

Kaguya was now experiencing that firsthand. Her body heat fled through the hole in her chest, and her mind was already so foggy that she was worried she might lose consciousness at any moment. Her vision began to shut down in static patches. She could barely make out the figure of someone running toward her.

But she could no longer discern who.

Her sense of equilibrium suddenly disappeared. She was falling. It seemed to happen so slowly for her—like she was dropping down in slow motion. She barely made out the sight of a silver blade cutting through one of the hero's tentacles.

"Kaguya?!"

There was despair in the voice. The tearful silver calling her name.

The world rapidly began to recede. She couldn't see. From the sounds around her, she realized that somebody was rushing toward her now, but even those sounds seemed to fade into the distance. Something hot was streaming from her chest, and from the dim corners of her failing vision, she discerned the sight of her own scarlet hair, becoming steadily soaked in deep red blood.

"Silver…"

It was the last color she saw as the darkness closed in on her. A glittering flash of silver. And the briefest glimpse of icy blue.

Captain Azuma—

Kaguya's consciousness grew hazy. The silver grew faint, and then a chestnut brown began to fill her field of view as if to blot that silver light from her mind.

Kaguya remembered that color. She knew those eyes.

Ren...

Her brother. She was no longer capable of complicated thought. Wavering on the border between reality and dream, life and death, truth and deception, Kaguya did not realize that the young man who appeared before her was only an illusion. And even if she had, she would not have been capable of understanding what that meant.

And so Kaguya extended her hand toward the dream that appeared to her on the outskirts of death.

Toward the figure of her brother.

Toward the Goddess.

They knew.

No one said it out loud, but everyone knew. Kaguya was beyond help.

The pool of blood beneath her had grown so large it looked ready to swallow her whole. Her wound was too deep, making it ruthlessly clear. Nothing could be done for her now.

But what did it mean that she was dying under these circumstances? They all knew the terrible risk. There was something they had to do. No one said it, but they all knew.

"I'll do it…" Haru drew her knife. She did not have to explain what she meant by *it*. "I tried to do it for someone once before, and I failed. This time—"

"Wait."

Azuma bit his lip, clutching the still-bleeding Kaguya. It took less than a second for him to steel his nerves. He stopped Haru before she could finish what it was she was going to say, reversing the grip on his katana.

He wasn't facing a hero this time, however. He was facing Kaguya. "I should be the one to do it."

This was one thing he couldn't entrust to anyone else. If they had to kill her, it ought to at least be as painless as possible. A single thrust with no hesitation.

It had to be through the neck. Or through the brow. Something that would rob her of life and consciousness in a single instant.

Kaguya seemed to have gone blind now. She stretched her hand out toward empty space. Azuma had a bad feeling about this. It seemed she was seeing something that wasn't there.

Quickly—he had to kill her quickly. He moved without delay, aiming to thrust the point of his sword through her neck...

That was when it happened.

A sharp scent suddenly filled the air, billowing toward them on the wind as if to smother the blood-drenched battlefield.

It was the scent of osmanthus.

"...!!"

Azuma was helpless to respond in time. There was suddenly a man there, standing next to the prone Kaguya. He had brown hair and a face that vaguely resembled Kaguya's. He would have been just the right age to be Kaguya's older brother.

But Kaguya's brother was already gone—meaning this must be the Goddess. It took them no time to realize what was happening.

Azuma swung with his sword. Koyuki laid down gunfire. Rindou dove forward in a rush. Haru brandished her knife.

Azuma's sword was at the Goddess's neck. Koyuki's bullets were millimeters from the Goddess's head. Rindou was already within arm's reach of the Goddess's right side, and Haru's exposed knife was closing in from the left.

In another moment, all four of their attacks would connect at once.

But it was already too late.

All four of them were too late.

"N-no...!"

A vortex of wind rose up. A warm breeze enveloped Kaguya as if wrapping her in a sigh. Azuma tried to reach out for her, but to no avail.

And when the wind died down, the Goddess was gone. In its place appeared a single massive flower with petals of the same scarlet hue as Kaguya's hair.

• • •

"Shit!!"

A giant scarlet rose, as large as a person. Several other flowers were bunched together in a circle around the stems in an artistic display that was familiar to even the average layman. It was just like van Gogh's *Sunflowers*, only with roses instead.

The petals closest to the center were a pale violet. Two stems supported the thing's weight, looming quietly and imparting an aura of sanctity to the flowers. The shadow that carved out the face was exactly where the stamen on a flower would have been and was about the same size as a human face. The most distinctive sign of a hero.

"No...," Azuma whimpered. "Don't smile. Not like that."

He could see it. The smiling face of *Kaguya Shinohara*.

Her eyes lacked focus. The corners of her mouth were raised in a cold grin, an image of something fundamentally broken inside.

This was Kaguya Shinohara's hero—ominous and terrible.

The petals were all so unnecessarily large, blooming in maliciously insistent profusion. Although it was a flower, it seemed to stand untethered, with no visible roots supporting it.

It was a flower hero, essentially. A beautiful rose in appearance, the same color as Kaguya's hair. It did not suit her.

They had already grasped the situation and were ready to do what needed to be done. It was their only choice. It didn't matter if they could. Or even if they wanted to. The hero had already grown to an unnatural size and was only continuing to spread and increase. Its petals had already doubled in just this brief span of time. If left to continue, it would cover the school's grounds entirely in just twenty to thirty minutes.

"Kaguya!!"

"Azuma, calm down. It hasn't started moving."

Someone yanked Azuma backward by his arm, bringing him back to his senses. It was Koyuki. She had stopped him before he could dive headlong into the center of the creature's mass.

"We can still kill it," she said, her face as neutral as her voice. "It hasn't noticed us yet."

"Kill it?!"

Azuma had been through countless battles. He understood perfectly well what Koyuki meant—but he was having trouble hearing it right now.

"You mean…"

"Are you trying to make me say it?"

Although angry, her voice remained cool and composed. It was the complete opposite of her usually blunt manner. This was enough for Azuma to regain some degree of composure. She was right. If they were going to kill her, they had to do it now.

If they were going to kill Kaguya…

Azuma drew his katana and held it at the ready, dropping his hips. He had no qualms about cutting down this monster that stood before him now.

Even if, for instance, he happened to catch sight of the face hiding within its shadows.

That's not the real you. You would never smile like that.

In the back of his mind, he knew that it only looked like Kaguya. It was something different now.

Your real smile was never so crazed.

Azuma could feel Koyuki staring at him with concern. He calmly began to issue orders.

"You're right. It hasn't noticed us yet. If we're going to do this, it has to be now." He followed up with his favorite go-to. "I'll create an opening. You take care of the rest."

As the most skilled of the current group, it was up to Azuma to distract the hero, and that meant heading in first. To kill Kaguya.

Hero
Emergence

Captain Azuma—

...Ran

Kaguya Shinohara

[17]

Location: Tokyo Bay, Chiba Prefecture

Type: Unable to determine; Code Red status

Proceed with immediate subjugation

This girl was intent on saving heroes no matter how much it hurt her, and now that she's become one herself, her smile for her friends will endure. She wants to be with the one she loves forever—something she's yearned for ever since she was a child. Come, Captain Azuma. It's time to go.

HERO SYNDROME

"Wait."

Just as Azuma was about to begin running, someone spoke. Beneath her teal hair, her usual poker face was nowhere to be seen. She stared at Azuma in horror at what he was about to do.

"Do you realize what you're saying? That's her. It's Kaguya. If you break that hero's egg, she'll—"

"Takanashi. I'm sorry, but I don't have time to coax you through this right now."

He couldn't let himself listen to that kind of talk right now. This hero—this monster that was standing before him—was possibly one of the strongest they had ever faced. On par with even the hero from six years ago. If they didn't do something about it, the scale of destruction was going to be immense.

"Kaguya..."

The hero towered in front of the school building with imposing gravity, not yet hostile, its scarlet petals swaying passively in the night. But it would likely not be long before it grew aggressive.

No one could save her now. If there were one person who might have been capable, it would have been Azuma, seeing as he had once begun to turn into a hero himself. But unfortunately...

"The only thing we're capable of now is *defeating* the hero. Just as we've always done."

For several seconds no one spoke. It was the same chilling silence as when Sakura had turned.

"You're right." Koyuki said, at last. "I-I don't want to watch Kaguya turn into a hero. But even if she turns all the way, I won't let her hurt anyone. Ever."

This wasn't her first time killing a team member. Laying them to rest like this was her own act of kindness.

She and Azuma were in agreement. Azuma brandished his newly acquired Chronos. It was a little heavy for him and somewhat difficult to use—the blade now housed Sakura's consciousness.

It was now or never. Before Kaguya could become a murderer.

Before she could become a monster, a destroyer, Azuma held his blade at the ready and shouted her name.

"Kaguya!!"

• • •

"Kaguya—"

Kaguya was suddenly snapped out of her reverie by the sound of someone calling her name.

The place she was in was quiet. As she came to, she took a look around. It was the front entrance to a private residential house. The roof was red.

After several seconds, Kaguya remembered that this was her own home.

"Wait, when did I…?"

She felt as if she had been somewhere else just a moment ago.

"What are you doing out there, silly? Hurry up and come inside," said a voice.

Kaguya turned to see who it was. The person who spoke had brown hair. It was her brother, standing in the entrance, looking exasperated.

Chestnut brown hair and pale violet eyes. After taking in the sight, Kaguya realized she had been standing out there for the past several seconds, almost as if time had stopped.

"That's weird… What am I doing just standing here…?"

"Snap out of it already, sleepyhead. Did you forget we both have the day off today?"

"We do? Oh yes. That's right."

Now that he mentioned it, they did. When she tried to remember, the information suddenly came floating back to the surface of her mind.

That's right… We have today off. How could I have forgotten something like that?

Like her brother said, they were both off duty today, and he was going to make them a nice big meal for a change. Where was her head at, forgetting such a thing?

"You seem a little out of it... Never mind, though. Hurry up, come inside, and have a seat."

"Yes... Of course!"

Her brother disappeared toward the living room. As Kaguya removed her shoes, a feeling of joy suffused her chest. It had been so long since it had been just the two of them.

She lined her shoes up neatly in the entryway and prepared to head into the living room. As soon as she began to take the first step...

"—!!"

"Huh...?"

...her leg froze. She could have sworn she heard a voice. Like someone was calling her name. A man's voice, maybe?

"Hey, Ren...?" she said, quickly chasing after her brother. "Did you just hear somebody call for me?"

"Huh?" Kaguya's brother narrowed his feral eyes in response to this strange question, scoffing in an uncharacteristic fashion. "Yeah, stupid, that was me. Are you sure you're okay?"

Oh, of course, thought Kaguya, realizing her mistake. Now that she thought about it, they were the only ones there. Just Kaguya and her brother. What had she been thinking?

"Ha...ha-ha, I know, right? Maybe I really am sleep-deprived after all."

With that, Kaguya shoved the voice from her mind and followed her brother, her heart leaping with excitement in her chest. Everything smelled so good. Kaguya was sure, instinctively, that whatever waited for her beyond that door was going to be just delightful.

"Wow...! Just wow!"

Kaguya's instincts had been correct. As they entered the living room, a royal feast awaited her. Large platters piled high with dishes of all sorts—Japanese, Western, and Chinese alike. There were also small side dishes as well.

"D-did you make all of this? This is incredible... I had no idea you could cook like this."

"Well, it's my first time cooking for someone else."

"This is too much for just the two of us, though. I think you got a little carried away."

"I'm actually worried it won't be enough..."

"If you say so," Kaguya said as she sat down at the table, unaware of just how prodigious her own appetite truly was.

Up first was the omelet with rice that sat directly in front of her. But as she set eyes on the plate, ready to dig in, she was suddenly hit with the feeling that something wasn't right. She had a strange sense of déjà vu.

Wait a second. Isn't this...?

Kaguya recognized the dish sitting before her.

"...? Isn't this from the cafeteria at Headquarters?"

It was one of the cafeteria's specials. Kaguya was certain that she recognized it.

Wait a second. If all of the food here was cooked by my brother, then...

"What's wrong now, Kaguya? Did you forget how to eat?"

"What?!"

Kaguya snapped out of it and turned toward her brother, who she saw was already chowing down. He flashed a familial grin at Kaguya, who had been just sitting there in a daze.

"N-no, I'm fine."

Kaguya smiled back in turn and picked up her spoon. When she looked back at the plate this time, it was a cutely presented omelet with rice, unlike anything she had ever seen before.

I must be spending too much time at Technical lately, she thought. *I'm starting to see things.*

She lifted her spoon, carrying the first bite toward her mouth.

INTERLUDE TWO
Voice

Rindou had something to say.

Back when Kaguya suddenly asked Rindou to spar, he hadn't been sure about her. True, he had been the one to try to push her into it, but he had never expected her to approach him instead.

But he had sensed something in her serious demeanor and decided to see where things went. He soon learned that his instincts were not mistaken. Kaguya truly was trying to change and bring hope.

"You even managed to get in a good hit against me…!"

The sparring, meant as training, had happened suddenly. But in the end, Kaguya managed to succeed. She rushed him one hundred times and was knocked down ninety-nine, but with each and every attack, she gave it her all. And after ninety-nine bouts, just when Rindou was starting to lose steam, she finally managed to connect with a punch.

"It may have just been just once, by random chance, but you managed to beat me…"

And if she could beat him…

"…Kaguya, don't you fucking lose to that!"

Haru had tried to ask her once.

Why was she trying to save all the heroes? Even those who didn't want to be saved. Even when there was no benefit in it for Kaguya herself.

But Haru knew the answer even before she was told. That was just the kind of person Kaguya was. She had the kind of strength that could lift a person up even after they had started to give up.

Strength came with its own fragility, but not for Kaguya. Kaguya was the type to conquer her own fragility, righteous enough to sweep away everything that got in the way.

Which is exactly why Haru couldn't bear it. For things to end in this way.

"Come back to us, Lieutenant Shinohara!"

Koyuki was afraid.

At this rate, she was going to lose Kaguya. No, Kaguya was already lost.

This was what she had been so afraid of. If Kaguya became a hero, no one would be able to help her. Kaguya had saved so many people and had stood by the side of those she couldn't save up until the end. But there was no one who could see her off in return.

It wasn't fair.

Koyuki hated unfairness. Especially when it struck someone who was important to her.

She didn't want to lose anything, not again. And besides, Kaguya had promised.

"Remember you said we would go get parfaits. You told us you never break your promises!!"

It wasn't just parfaits. There were so many things she still wanted to say to Kaguya. Things she wanted to do together. And now...

"Don't let it end like this, Kaguya!!"

Azuma's head was spinning; he was confused and distraught. Part of him was still in denial, clinging to hope. But his more rational self knew it was too late.

She couldn't be saved. They had failed her. They hadn't allowed her to die as herself.

The hero standing before them was on a completely different level from any they had ever faced. Strong didn't even begin to describe the thing. It transcended every hero they had seen before in every conceivable way.

"Come back. Please come back, Kaguya."

Azuma had his own feelings for Kaguya, different from the others'. Even if she couldn't return to them…

"If you can't make it back, don't worry…"

It may have looked like he was giving up, but this was his own kindness to her.

"…I'll be sure to kill you."

And with that, he thrust toward Kaguya with his katana—as hard as he could.

CHAPTER FIFTEEN
Transfiguration

Kaguya could have sworn she felt a *thud* somewhere.

The meal was mostly finished by this point, the majority of it having disappeared into Kaguya's stomach. Kaguya's brother had been right—between the two of them, they really had managed to work their way through the food.

"I could go for more, to be honest…"

"You're kidding me…"

"I don't understand how that's enough food for you! Don't you get hungry later?"

"Hey, I'm the normal one here. I don't understand how you manage to eat enough for six people."

"Don't ask me."

She didn't know, either; she was just born that way.

Her brother stood up, his chair clattering, and headed toward the refrigerator. Kaguya watched him like a hawk, her eyes glued to his sleepy profile and somewhat tense gaze.

"Ren? What are you doing?"

"Dessert," he answered simply. Kaguya's eyes widened, and she stood up in delight.

"There's dessert, too?!"

The news was enough to make Kaguya's heart leap in her chest.

But it wasn't just the dessert she was excited about. The fact that her brother had gone to such lengths just for her was what made her happiest of all.

He pulled a sky-blue tub of ice cream out of the icebox and served the ice cream into a glass dish, piling the scoops up high. It looked vivid and exciting. It was even sprinkled with eye-catching silver dragées.

"It's so pretty...," Kaguya said reflexively. "It almost feels like a shame to eat it."

Sky blue and silver. Something about the color combination worked so well. But she felt a strange sense of déjà vu, as if she had seen that combination somewhere else before.

"Don't be stupid," her brother laughed. "Eat up before it melts."

Without hesitation, he scooped up a full half of the ice cream with his spoon. Imitating him, Kaguya did the same and was just about to place the spoon into her mouth.

The air suddenly smelled like sakura.

Kaguya stared wide-eyed, caught off guard by the unexpected scent. Was there another dessert waiting for them somewhere? Something pink, like cherry blossoms? Where was that smell coming from all of a sudden?

"Do you smell that—?"

"I don't think you should eat that, Kaguya."

"?!"

It was Sakura Arakawa. She was suddenly sitting at the end of the table from out of the blue. When had she gotten here?

"S-Sakura, you surprised me. What are you doing here? Actually..." Kaguya cocked her head at Sakura's appearance. "Why are you in uniform? Weren't you supposed to be off today, too...?"

"Kaguya," Sakura said, ignoring her question. She glanced disdainfully at the empty plates and ice cream on the table. **"Are you happy right now?"**

"What?" Kaguya furrowed her eyebrows. Why would Sakura ask

something like that? "Where did that come from? Where did *you* come from, for that matter…?"

"Just a minute, Arakawa," Kaguya's brother said, speaking up in Kaguya's place. "How disrespectful can you be, bursting in here without even announcing yourself first?"

"You're the last person I'm interested in hearing about disrespect from."

"Sakura, please…!" Kaguya said, rebuking Sakura. Why was she being so hostile all of a sudden? "I'm sorry. I don't mean to scold you, but Ren is right… You should at least say something before coming in uninvited. Technically, this is trespassing. You don't belong here."

"No, Kaguya. The one who doesn't belong here right now is you."

Kaguya was visibly confused. This conversation wasn't making any sense.

First of all, Sakura wasn't acting anything like herself. She wasn't the kind of person to do something so rude as to enter a person's house uninvited and interrupt their meal.

There was the sound of a chair sliding across the floor. Kaguya's brother had stood up. He stepped toward Sakura and grabbed her by the arm.

"W-wait, Ren…! Please calm down!"

Kaguya leaped to her feet to stop her brother. He did have a bit of a violent side sometimes, after all. Sakura, however, ignored Ren completely and continued to speak to Kaguya alone.

"There is an underground lab at Technical… You know it well, don't you, Kaguya?" For some reason, Sakura's smile looked pained. **"A place, like an operating room. It was dark. But sometimes the Director would come. She must have thought I was someone she could talk to, seeing as I couldn't speak. She told me a lot of things."**

A vision of the place floated into Kaguya's head. Yes, there was an operating room down there. She had been to it several times. But she was pretty sure Sakura had never visited.

"Sakura, how do you know about—?"

"That's my little secret," Sakura said, placing a finger to her lips with a chuckle. **"In any case, the Director spoke about you a lot. About how hard you were working. Too hard, sometimes."**

The Director and Sakura? Surely, they had never even met.

"Even the Director was worried about you. She had a lot of worries on her mind, which is why it was so sad, one of the saddest things I had ever seen when she died like that in front of me. She was a good person."

"Wait. What do you mean? Who died?" The way she was speaking, she almost made it sound as if the Director was dead. "Sakura, that's nothing to joke about. And when did you ever meet the Director? You're acting very strange! I never would have expected this kind of behavior from you!"

"Are you sure about that?" Sakura was not letting her off the hook. **"Kaguya, try to remember. Really remember. Just like you always ask others to do."**

Sakura's tone was gentle, but the words sounded accusatory to Kaguya's ear. As if, whatever it was Sakura was saying, Kaguya didn't want to hear what came next.

She didn't want to remember. She didn't know what it was, but she knew she didn't want to remember it. She felt a vague sense of terror. It felt like if she remembered whatever it was she was supposed to remember, she would no longer be able to stay here. As if all this happiness would just slip away.

"What do you mean, like I ask others to do? What do I ask them to do?"

"Don't you remember? You find people lost in their own chimerical dreams and make them confront reality."

Sakura's words shook Kaguya. She bit her lower lip hard. Sakura was just talking about what they all did, entering the heroes in order to wake them up. Wasn't she?

"B-but...that's something we all do. Everyone can do it, even you, Sakura..."

"I wish I had been able to do it..." There was a hint of regret in Sakura's smile. The sight made Kaguya feel uneasy. **"I know how hard this is, but let's go home, Kaguya."**

"G-go home...? To the barracks?"

"Yes and no."

There was a flash of glittering light.

The space around Sakura suddenly seemed like a different world, far away from this house. As if Sakura was repelling the space around her. The table, the food, the ice cream, the furniture, all of it.

"I'm not going to insist. I'm in no place to stop you. I'm the last person who would have that right. Not after having turned into a hero myself."

"A hero..."

This statement filled Kaguya with a sense of dread beyond anything else Sakura had said thus far. Did Sakura just say that she had become a hero? That wasn't possible. If Sakura had turned into a hero, then who was this person facing Kaguya?

"Well...i-if you're a hero, who's talking to me right now? Everyone knows that heroes can't speak!"

"You know better than anyone how untrue that is, Kaguya. You've talked with the heroes many times—so many times—before."

"Wh-why would you...?"

Why would Sakura say something like that? That was what Kaguya had begun to ask. If it could even be called a question. There were so many emotions behind that word *why* for Kaguya right now.

Why was Sakura here? And why would she say something so awful?

"Something very important is missing from this world."

Sakura glanced toward the sky-blue ice cream, which was already beginning to melt. Sprinkled with silver dragées. Those colors were giving Kaguya such a powerful sense of déjà vu.

"Kaguya, I know you can remember. Because once you take something into your heart, you never forget."

• • •

Azuma had thrust his katana into the hero, but in the end, it was pointless. The hero's powers of regeneration repaired the wound almost immediately.

The hero was still not showing any clear signs of hostility. But the rose petals continued to proliferate. They seemed to be doubling exponentially every five minutes. Each petal was as large as a human head.

Considering the size of Tokyo and Chiba, it wouldn't be long before the entire metropolis—if not the entire world—was buried in monstrous petals.

The scale of this attack could easily dwarf that of the hero from six years ago. In just thirty minutes, the petals would have increased sixtyfold. After an hour, this whole region would be covered.

Azuma sliced off one of the petals, trying to at least do something, but it was a fool's gesture.

If only he knew where the egg was. Now, when it mattered most. When they needed to find it more quickly than ever. He spoke loudly so that everyone could hear.

"Pull out all the stops! Whatever you can. We have to kill this thing!"

They all responded without hesitation. That was at least one saving grace. They were all in agreement when it came to saving Kaguya.

• • •

"What do you mean, you know that I can remember? What are you—?"

"Hey, Kaguya!" Kaguya's question was interrupted by her brother's voice. "Your ice cream is going to melt."

"Oh…!"

Right—they were eating ice cream. She extended her hand. She had to eat the ice cream before it melted. Just before her hand reached the bowl, however, Sakura suddenly snatched the ice cream away.

"Ah! Sakura! You give that back!"

"Absolutely not."

Sakura dumped the ice cream on the floor. How dare she! This wasn't like her at all! Kaguya's eyes went wide as she yelled at Sakura.

"Sakura! Why would you do something so—?"

"Seriously, Arakawa. What the hell?" Kaguya's brother said, standing up from his chair with a clatter and yelling at Sakura in Kaguya's place. "Why would you ruin food like that? What a waste."

Sakura paid him no mind. Kaguya hesitated. It wasn't like Sakura to do something so low as just to ignore a person.

"Wh-what's gotten into you, Sakura? You really are acting strange."

"No, Kaguya, you're the one who's acting strange right now."

Kaguya was taken aback by the expression on Sakura's face. A kind of desperation. Kaguya did not really know Sakura all that well, but she knew this wasn't the kind of face that Sakura usually made.

"S-Sakura…?"

"Here, Kaguya. You can have mine instead."

Kaguya's brother held out more of that same sky-blue ice cream. Sakura immediately tried to snatch it from his grip, but this time Kaguya's brother was too fast for her.

He was taller than Sakura, so he held the ice cream high over his head, which Sakura couldn't reach. Sakura began to climb up onto a chair, of all things, to try to get at the bowl.

"Sakura?! H-have you lost your mind?!" Kaguya cried.

Sakura would never stoop to being so disrespectful. Kaguya was beginning to wonder if this was really even Sakura.

No, I don't think it is.

Sakura would never behave in such a rowdy manner, not the Sakura that Kaguya knew. Kaguya began to feel a twinge of fear. The anger in Sakura's eyes was verging on hatred.

All this over some ice cream? But why would Sakura want to keep a little bit of ice cream away from Kaguya so badly? Didn't Sakura want her to eat it?

Kaguya's curiosity suddenly took over. That ice cream was the only colorful, shining thing in this entire sepia household.

As soon as her brother handed the bowl to her, Kaguya seized it from his hands. Sakura breathed in sharply.

"Don't—!!"

"No, do it." Kaguya's brother's voice changed completely. He could barely contain himself. It sounded like he was about to explode with joy. "Kaguya, this is what you've always wanted, isn't it? To sit around the dinner table, like a family, with me?"

Kaguya grew intoxicated with his words. They felt so buoyant and light. She started to forget what she had been doing. She had felt something like this before, hadn't she? But this time, it was different. This time, there was only one brother.

"Go ahead and eat up. It's always been your dream, after all."

Sakura was screaming at her, but Kaguya could barely hear. It didn't matter. The ice cream. Kaguya opened her mouth slightly and moved her hand. The sky-blue and silver dessert, which was already dripping off the spoon, entered her mouth without further resistance.

"...? Huh?"

Something seemed to shift, rewriting itself with a click.

What had Sakura been so upset about? This flavor was almost bafflingly delicious. It danced on her tongue. And yet there was something poignant about the taste, some indefinable sense of sadness or loss. Sweet? Bitter? It was impossible to describe the ice cream's flavor in a single word.

But what is this feeling?

It felt...as if she had just lost something very important. As if she had stumbled past some point of no return.

Sakura suddenly flew into a rage. Kaguya stared at her in a daze. Sakura's expression, as she rounded about on Kaguya's brother, verged on being demonic.

"Sakura... Did you really want to eat the ice cream for yourself so badly? Don't be mad. We can always just buy more," Kaguya said.

She had a feeling that wasn't the issue, though. Sakura looked completely shocked at what Kaguya had done.

"I already went down that path myself, Kaguya..."

Sakura was crying. Kaguya was starting to realize that she might have just done something that couldn't be taken back.

"...but I didn't want it to happen to you!"

A wind rose up—a breeze from outside the house that soon grew into a storm and then a tornado, rattling the house on its foundations. Yet Kaguya did not feel so much as a quiver. Like in *The Wonderful Wizard of Oz*, it seemed as if the entire house might go shooting off into the sky.

CHAPTER SIXTEEN
Awakening

The hero began to move.

The rose petals already covered the school grounds completely. In a few more minutes, the amount would double. It was easy to see how much damage would ensue.

The petals writhed as if they were alive. Through the air, on the ground, before their eyes, like they were searching. There were more and more of them with each passing moment as if whatever they were hungry for, it was never enough.

There would likely be deaths. The petals were fairly large, meaning a mass of them would easily crush people.

There was no way Azuma was going to let that happen. He sliced through several of the petals with a broad swipe, trying to work his way deeper toward the center.

Just as he was about to take another swipe, a vine coiled around his arm. Several more attacked simultaneously as if trying to drag him away. He shredded through all of them with a single effortless slice. He was certain now. The egg had to be this way.

It was heavily guarded, just as expected.

More specifically, the hero had formed with the egg at its center, leaving it inundated by stems, leaves, and petals. It was unlikely that anyone other than Azuma would have even been able to find its location in the first place.

"Erk...!"

Every time he took another step, the vines tried to stop him. Using brute strength, he tore free of the vines that coiled around his legs, leaving them in tatters as he made his way closer to Kaguya, step by steady step.

"Hang in there. I swear I'll make it before you turn into a real monster."

He just had to.

Azuma's body was almost completely covered in vines at this point. Every tendril in the vicinity was directed his way. Angry. Harrowing.

Entangled as he was, he could barely swing his katana properly. Nonetheless, he pointed the tip forward. The blade was so entangled in vines now that he could no longer see it.

"Someone clearly doesn't want me here..."

It was trying to reject him, an interloper interfering with their perfect world.

First things first, he needed to get rid of the vines. By changing the angle of his blade, he managed to make a significant notch in the vines entangling him. Once he had that gap, he was able to leverage it to cut the vines to ribbons with a single explosive slash. New vines coiled forward from the tatters of their remains, but Azuma quickly carved a path forward before the vines could ensnare him again. Doing this repeatedly, he slowly made his way toward the egg.

Once he was close enough to get eyes on the spot, he began to hear a faint pulse.

"..."

This egg's sound was very familiar to his ears.

He had once used it as a landmark before to search for Kaguya. The sound he had listened to the closest. At first, he had found it aggravating, but eventually, he had come to think of it as her second heart. He had been listening to it for so long that he now knew the rhythm by heart.

Azuma walked forward. That sound. That beating he needed to end.

"The truth is there was something I wanted to say to you."

No one else was around now.

"I'm not stupid. I knew. I knew what it was I was feeling."

It was his last chance to say what he needed to say to her. He could feel himself bleeding. He held his sword level, careful of the tight angles, as he closed in on the beating egg.

"—!!"

One of the large blossoming vines had Azuma in its sights. Kaguya was a hero now—it was one of her arms. It came for him. For Azuma.

Unable to disobey her instincts as a hero, Kaguya thrust a tentacle straight at Azuma's stomach.

"Erk—!"

Azuma had already been given the hero factor, however, during the attack six years ago. Targeting him now was pointless—it would only kill him.

Azuma's stomach split open. A wound so large that the one given to him by the dog hero, once upon a time, did not even compare.

The air froze. Koyuki, Rindou, and Haru all stared at the gaping hole in Azuma's stomach.

He wheezed, sucking in and exhaling something that did not constitute a breath. His blood spilled in shuddering torrents, drenching the hero, by way of its tentacle, in Azuma's fresh, hot blood.

It was obvious at a glance, even to Azuma himself. His fate was sealed.

His vision distorted and grew hazy. He was having trouble making out the hero.

The katana slipped from his grasp. Too weak to draw another weapon, Azuma placed his left hand on his left ear.

His cross. A keepsake from his younger sister and what Kaguya had once used to help save Azuma. His cross-shaped earring.

He tore it from his ear, causing a small trickle of blood to flow from the lobe. The earring, made of pure silver, glimmered brightly with his blood, more beautiful than anything else nearby.

He held the earring out toward the tentacle, which still pierced his stomach.

"Kaguya."

There was still something he had to tell her. A feeling he needed to share. The only last words he had now that he knew that this was his final chance.

"…I love—"

The words spilled from his mouth along with his life. He never managed to finish.

His confession, cut short in the end, was one he had only been able to bring himself to say because he knew she could no longer understand him. Slowly, almost comically slowly, he thrust the earring in her direction.

As it connected, all of his strength, all of his awareness, fled from his body.

• • •

"…!!"

It happened almost as soon as Sakura began to cry.

There was a heavy *thud*, and the world shuddered. Everything grew distorted, like when a movie screen warped. In the same instant, a powerful heat flared in Kaguya's throat.

Sakura noticed the change as well. Her face registered surprise. Kaguya saw it, a glint of light in Sakura's eyes—and there was more.

"Did I just hear…a voice…?"

She could have sworn she did. Although she had no idea what that voice was saying.

"Kaguya!!" Sakura took a step toward Kaguya, grabbing her firmly by both shoulders. **"There's still hope. You have to remember! Remember now!!"**

"R-remember what…?"

"Everything, Kaguya! Everything you've ever experienced, all the conversations you've had up until now!"

That was when Kaguya's brother intervened.

"It looks like there's a pretty nasty storm brewing out there, Arakawa," he said. "Don't you think it's about time you left?"

Sakura ignored him. She was only focused on Kaguya now, no one else. An image of those same jade-green eyes, sad, seemed to superimpose themselves in Kaguya's mind. She had a feeling, almost a certainty, that she had seen eyes like that staring at her once long ago.

The voice—

"—"

It sounded like it was coming from somewhere far away and yet also from inside herself.

But wait, she thought, *don't I know that voice?*

The heat, which felt like it was going to burn her throat, began to spread throughout her entire body. Meanwhile, the image of a young man began to rise up from the depths of Kaguya's mind.

At some point, the scenery had changed. The air smelled different—the colors she could see out of the corners of her eyes had changed. A dreary cafeteria. It was almost deserted. The smell of Lunch Set A wafted through the air.

"Huh...?"

She had been at home, hadn't she? Why was she in Technical's cafeteria now with Sakura?

Kaguya realized this was a reenactment of the day when she had been ordered to transfer to Charon. The captain of the squad, Sakura, had come to speak to her.

Her mind raced to thoughts of that first meeting. She was pretty sure they had argued. Neither was very receptive to the other at first. It had taken some time before they had learned to respect each other's guiding principles.

Wait, an argument...? With Sakura?

Something felt off with the way she was remembering things. When had she ever fought with Sakura? She couldn't even think of a reason why she might.

Her chest started to throb with heat. As if she was burning up. The heat had spread to her chest. She felt sick and dizzy like she had a fever.

Kaguya dove deeper into her memories. Right, they *had* argued. Neither of them had been able to see from the other person's point of view. But at some point along the way, as they continued to butt heads, they had learned to respect one another's perspectives.

But what changed? Yes, right, someone important had turned into a hero. And then Kaguya dove into that hero's psyche and learned that heroes possessed their own mental worlds.

A field of flowers. The gentle face of a mother, a little girl clinging to her side. That girl's name...

It was...

"...Sakura," said Kaguya. "It was you."

Sakura smiled, an embarrassed, almost resigned look in her eyes. Her pink hair swayed gently to the side.

Sakura had turned into a hero. And she hadn't been able to come back.

It was fascinating. All the pieces were beginning to click into place. But who was this captain she had fought with? What kind of conversations had she had after Sakura became a hero, and with who? Whose heart had she taken a peek into? Whose life she had saved, and who had she been saved by and made a promise to? Who had she let see her cry? Who was she planning to eat that ice cream parfait with?

"He's here," Sakura said gently. Kaguya raised her head. As she did so, the cafeteria suddenly filled with more people. **"It's just like it was on that day. I came first, and then he showed up later."**

A young man with icy silver hair was walking their way.

Even Kaguya, who barely took an interest in people's faces, noticed how handsome he was. There was a silver cross in his left ear. His sky-blue eyes bore a hole through Kaguya.

"Ah..."

She remembered him. She definitely remembered him. This wasn't their first time meeting. They had found themselves in this exact same situation a long time ago.

The young man stood before Kaguya without saying anything.

The heat was now circulating throughout her entire body. Hot and clammy, from the top of her head all the way down to the tip of her toes.

"Um…" Kaguya desperately tried to come up with something to say. The headache and dizziness were so overpowering that her voice sounded close to tears. "Can I ask your name?"

The young man stared back at her with the same sharp glare as before.

"—ri."

She could not hear him the first time. She was having trouble staying on her feet, and Sakura was no help. The young man repeated himself while Kaguya continued to stand there dumbly.

His name.

"Yuuri Azuma."

The wind rose up, enveloping everything. Rewriting this entire world. Returning it. Kaguya felt like she might pass out at any second as the scenery around her *flew away into the sky*. No, it was Kaguya who was falling. Falling away from the cafeteria, just as if she had fallen out of a plane. Falling down into the darkness.

• • •

Azuma was conscious again, brought to his senses by shouts from Rindou, Koyuki, and Haru.

There was the sound of a gunshot. Immediately, the tentacle piercing him exploded into fiery scraps, and Azuma fell toward the ground, into the waiting arms of Rindou.

But it was surely too late for Azuma by this point.

It's up to them now.

It was going to be difficult, however, for Rindou, Koyuki, and Haru to end this fight quickly on their own. There was a good chance Tokyo would be lost.

But that was no reason to give up. Kaguya had taught them that.

"Koyu—"

Instead of finishing a word, a spurt of blood escaped his lips. His lungs must have been hit. He was finding it difficult to breathe.

"Azuma!!"

Koyuki flew toward his side. But Azuma waved her off harshly.

"Enough… It's too late…to save…"

Any other person might hear that and assume he meant that it was too late to save the hero that had once been Kaguya and that Koyuki shouldn't hold back. But Koyuki understood what he really meant. That it was too late to save *him*. She needed to leave him and focus on killing Kaguya first.

"…!"

Koyuki couldn't argue—Azuma was obviously already beyond saving. She turned abruptly, a look of regret on her face.

Azuma, for his own part, was going to continue fighting for as long as he could. Even if he knew his death was already certain.

Picking up his katana, he began walking forward at a comically slow pace, deeper into the petals, coughing up blood as he went. Right foot first, he trudged forward doggedly, cutting wild swaths through the flourishing petals and hacking away at this infinite blossom at the center while his life steadily dwindled away. Despite his massive injuries, he was able to cut down five or so petals with every slash, moving forward another step each time before they could regenerate.

Finally, he arrived. Now that he was close, his ears picked up the sound again.

The egg belonging to Kaguya Shinohara's hero was right there in front of him.

• • •

The place Kaguya fell into was unfamiliar—no, that wasn't true. She knew this place.

It felt nostalgic for some reason. She remembered the sound and the smell. She watched the scene from a slight distance.

Someone was arguing far away.

A red rain was falling. A rain that smelled like rust.

Kaguya listened to their voices as the rain beat down on her. She heard them arguing.

"You son of a bitch, you wait! Kaguya still hasn't woken up yet!" someone shouted.

Another voice said, "Don't be ridiculous. She's already—"

"There's still time for her. She can still make it! I said stop!" the first voice shouted back.

She was on the ground, and the person's large, dark back was protecting her. As he glanced over his shoulder, she caught sight of a young man with chestnut-brown hair and pale violet eyes.

Several other people were standing around him.

"Ren…"

The voices continued. A memory dredged up from deep within her mind.

"But why Kaguya?" her brother demanded, his voice barbed. "It was me originally. I'm the only one able to dive into the heroes. If you wanted to go after someone, it should have been me."

The other person said something in response. But whatever they said was unclear. Either it was no longer in Kaguya's memory, or she simply hadn't been able to hear. But she heard what her brother said in response clearly.

"Fine. Then I'll go instead."

Instead…

The memories rustled in Kaguya's memories. He had said the word *instead*.

"I'll become your guinea pig in her place. Just leave Kaguya alone."

What was he saying? What did he mean? She understood intuitively. The memory was too insistent.

"So because you don't know what's going on and because the process failed…" Her brother's voice was incredibly low, like he was furious but also afraid. "…you want to make a new hero? Have you lost your fucking minds?"

Kaguya seemed to be watching that memory from someplace far away. Watching what really happened that day. The truth.

Her brother had gone to Technical No. 1 in her place.

The pain in Kaguya's head felt intense, threatening to make her hate this world and everything in it. It felt like her head was going to implode. A flood of memories came rushing back, along with the pain.

It was impossible to keep up the deception any longer.

"A hero…"

She was beginning to hyperventilate.

"I've become a hero."

She took a deep breath, trying to steady herself and get her pulse under control. Even if it was difficult, maybe even impossible, she had to try to make herself calm.

A voice spoke suddenly as if responding to Kaguya's efforts. A man's voice.

"I see. You're here now, too," the voice said.

There would be no calming down now. Kaguya spun around at the sound. She recognized the speaker.

Her brother was now standing before her.

Two brothers before her eyes. She remembered seeing something like this once before.

But this time, there was no need to decide which of the two brothers was the Goddess. It was obviously the one standing before her now, smiling. He was the Goddess.

Kaguya had a feeling she needed to settle this. To meet this brother face-to-face.

"Ren…"

Her brother grinned. **"Welcome, Kaguya. You're okay now. There's no more sadness or fear. You can stay in here with me forever."**

That smile, completely at odds with her real brother's, was almost dazzling enough to make Kaguya feel complacent. Although the smile was blatantly unnatural, the Goddess did not seem to care. He must have believed he already had Kaguya in his clutches.

The brother must not have cared for Kaguya's reaction. She saw a hint of brutality surface in his eyes.

"What's wrong? You don't seem very happy."

"Well…"

It was difficult for Kaguya to express what she was feeling with a single word. True, she wasn't very happy to be turning into a hero. But that didn't mean there wasn't some sensation of happiness involved. She couldn't deny that.

"I think it's a little more complicated than being happy or not."

Clinging to the happy dream that was playing out before her eyes was not an option. She may have already fallen into the fantasy, but that did not make it okay. On the other hand, she could not refute what this dream meant to her, either.

"I guess I could say…I feel *wistful*, perhaps."

She couldn't stay here. This was an image that the Goddess had created from her past self. But she did not hate it, either.

"Thank you for the ice cream. It made me happy, even if it wasn't real."

"I see…" The brother smiled as if he had been half expecting her answer. "**Are you sure, though, Kaguya? That you really want to return to reality? Aren't you sick of all that by now? Being forced to cope with everything all on your own? If you wake up again, they're all going to start depending on you for things again. It doesn't matter how worn out you get, they won't care. Haven't you had enough of that?**"

"You're wrong…" Kaguya shook her head gently. "They wouldn't do something like that. And even if they did, I'm not as shortsighted or as self-destructive as I once was. There's always a way out when things get too tough. I'm done choosing this suicide pact with the heroes."

There was more.

"I don't think Azuma and the others want me to keep doing this anymore, either. I'm pretty sure everything is going to be okay."

"**Are you really?**" The brother's expression changed into a sinister, inviting smile. That face didn't suit her brother very well, but it did suit the Goddess. "**How much do you really know about them,** though? You've only just met them, after all. They come from very different backgrounds from what you're used to."

Having peeked into Kaguya's dreams, the Goddess was able to verbalize ideas that Kaguya had only formed subconsciously.

"Their first priority is always going to be on fighting heroes, you know. If you stay with them, you'll be ground down to a pulp. Just like when you fell into that coma. If it happened once, it will happen again and again and again."

Kaguya had fallen apart once. But not everything the brother was saying was true. He did not really know anything about Azuma and the others.

"You don't know them at all, do you? You don't know anything about Captain Azuma and the others."

Kaguya pieced her words together with tender care.

"Azuma—Captain Yuuri Azuma—can be a little irritating at times, but the truth is he's incredibly kind and gentle. Koyuki is my friend, and she's probably more passionate and heartfelt than anyone I know. Rindou might be a little rough around the edges, but he always thinks of his friends first. And Second Lieutenant Takanashi is strong. Strong enough to stand up and fight for her principles and the things she believes in."

Kaguya had only been with them for a few short months so far. Maybe she didn't know everything about them, but there was one thing she could say for certain. Her time with them had been happy.

"They're why I still want to go back."

"I see..." The brother smiled gently for a moment. **"You're a real bitch."**

His tone of voice changed suddenly. Kaguya froze when she saw the look on his face. It was pure, unbridled hatred. He glared at with rancorous resentment, speaking in a low—such a low—voice.

"It's your fucking fault I became a hero! You're the one who did this to me."

It was like he couldn't stop himself.

"I'm your *real brother*, your *actual brother*. Do you understand what I'm saying? I've been wandering, untethered, ever

since that day and it's all your fault. You fucking did this to me, Kaguya."

The way he was speaking.

"If you hadn't become a goddamn hero, I would have never wound up like this. Do you even care? The least you could do to make up for what you've done to me is join me in here!"

"R...R-Ren..."

Kaguya had been wrong about one thing.

This brother before her eyes had been *her real brother* after all—his own memories, his self, and his consciousness were long since gone. Transformed into a Goddess, he was now just acting the part of who he had once been from those former memories. But it still came as a punch to the gut for Kaguya. This was her real brother. The one she had been searching for all this time. Right in front of her.

"It happened six years ago. I was turned into a hero by those jackals at Technical No. 1."

"It's you...! You were the hero six years ago...?!"

"I took your place. When they tried to take you away, I went instead—"

The hero from six years ago had been her brother all along. Kaguya stepped back, overwhelmed by the truth.

"Aren't you disgusted with yourself? You made me like this, and now you think you deserve to be saved without me? Do you really hate me that much? Even after, for your sake, I—"

"Stop," came a voice, slightly deep for a woman.

The word carried power, like a curse. Kaguya spotted a splash of pink out of the corner of her eye. A young woman was suddenly standing next to her.

It was Sakura. But she wasn't in her uniform anymore. She was wearing a dress. Just as she had appeared after she had died when Kaguya had seen her off.

This Sakura, however, was no longer wearing the sad smile she had worn that day, as if she had given up on everything. Instead, she wore the old smile that Kaguya remembered best. It was trustworthy, animated, and even a little combative.

"You aren't Kaguya's brother anymore. You're just pretending to be him. How long are you going to keep up this sloppy charade?"

She's right, thought Kaguya. This wasn't really her brother. It was just some *thing* masquerading as him, using Kaguya's memories—and her brother's—in an attempt to lure Kaguya to her downfall. Her brother's consciousness was already lost to this world, and this creature was debasing his dignity and his memory by pretending otherwise.

"She's right! My brother would never say anything like that!" Kaguya shouted, carried away in a sudden flurry of rage. "What would you know about him? Or about Azuma and the others? Don't act like you know a damned thing!"

The scenery around them suddenly disappeared. It was dark. Just pure darkness, with no left nor right, no up nor down. And in the darkness, Kaguya, Sakura, and Kaguya's brother. Just the three of them floating, with nothing visible beyond each other.

Kaguya spoke sharply, almost as if she was speaking for her own benefit.

"I'll decide how I end. I'm not going to become someone's hero. I *will* become human again. And also…"

As she spoke, she remembered her reasons for originally wanting to become a scientist. That same passion now sparked to fiery life inside her chest. She had come this far and had fought for so long, all in order to turn heroes back into humans.

In the end, she had been wrong about her brother turning, but she still remembered how she had felt at that time. That feeling had only been strengthened and solidified when Sakura had turned.

There had been enough grief already.

"And also, Azuma and the others are still out there, fighting. I can't take hope away from them."

Somewhere the darkness cracked. A decisive fissure opened up in the blackness between Kaguya and her brother.

"But what about me?" Kaguya's brother's face contorted. "What about the people who died? Do you even care about them? Don't you remember, Kaguya? We got along pretty well back in the day. Didn't we?"

"We did. But that was the brother in my memory."

Kaguya's brother glared at her hard from across the fissure. She felt a little sad, but she was okay with that.

Her brother was already dead. She had to focus on the living now.

She was pretty sure that Azuma would tell her the same.

"I'm sorry, Ren," Kaguya said, rejecting this ideal world, "but I'm going back. To where everyone is waiting. To Captain Azuma and the others. Before I become a monster. Back into the light."

Just then—

The world shuddered, gently collapsing around the edges. She could catch glimpses of something through the gaps. The light from beyond grew brighter. Something was beginning to break.

A shard of darkness tumbled away, blotting out the sight of her brother, who had been standing directly beneath it. She could only hear its voice now, an insectile screech, bitter and tremendous.

In contrast, Sakura sounded overjoyed. She glanced up, a smile peeking out from the corners of her mouth.

"The captain is so impatient. He's never going to get a girlfriend if he can't learn to give us ladies our time."

"Sakura, does this mean...?"

"Don't worry, Kaguya. We won't be late. There's only a moment, but time flows differently here than it does in that world."

Azuma must have been trying to break the egg. She could feel it.

Earlier, Kaguya said that she was going to return to reality. But that wasn't actually possible anymore—she had already fully turned. All she could do now was wait for Azuma to deliver final mercy.

But her mind continued to race. There had to be some other way. Even if coming back now would be like the equivalent of unboiling an egg, that was still no reason to give up.

Why did humans become heroes?

What was the catalyst? What actually happened when a person died?

There were three types of death—physical death, the second death that came from being forgotten, and spiritual or psychic death. This had to be a matter of either physical or psychic death.

But everyone who has come back just before turning into a hero, so far, has had their physical body restored.

People became heroes after being lured away by the Goddess while on the verge of death. That meant the young men and women were already mortally wounded by the time they began to turn. Even after becoming human again, they should have died in a matter of seconds.

But they didn't. Meaning the trigger must not have been physical death.

Spiritual death, then. Humans become heroes when their psyches die.

So perhaps, by dying a psychic death, humans attain the right to become a hero. Taking the Goddess's hand allows their spirits to reach true death in the end, and thus they are no longer able to come back.

Meaning I'm already immersed. My soul has fully crossed over to the other side.

Kaguya was no different from one of the dead now. Bringing back the dead was impossible, but what if that death was spiritual rather than physical? What about the soul?

"It's...worth a shot."

She could think of just one possible way.

The transformation from human into hero was caused by psychic death. In this case, all that needed to be done was to revive the deceased spirit. And if something that had died could not be brought back...

...then why not just reconstruct it?

Reconstruct the psyche. If her old psyche was dead, why not just remake it?

"Sakura, can I borrow your katana?"

Sakura wasn't supposed to be wielding a sword, of course.

"My katana? For what...?"

"I'm going to try rebuilding myself. But in order to do that, some destruction will have to occur. That means I'll destroy myself by my own hands."

"...?! But Kaguya, that's..."

The method, which Kaguya had come up with on the fly, was to die within her mental world—in other words, mental suicide.

It was a shocking idea, but Sakura said no more. She simply handed over the katana that she was in fact carrying.

It was very heavy. Far too heavy for Kaguya to swing.

With a fair amount of difficulty, Kaguya managed to draw the sword and place it against her throat. Even now, her throat burned with fiery heat.

"I can't believe it. Aren't you scared?"

"I'm very scared."

Seeing how difficult it was to pierce her own throat made Kaguya realize once again that the Director definitely had not committed suicide.

"I could be wrong. The very thought makes my skin crawl. And even if my hypothesis is correct, I will still be dying in here along the way. The next time I open my eyes, I might not even be me anymore. If I choose to erase my internal self, the next time I wake up, I might be a completely different entity that looks exactly like me. But I have to do this, all the same."

She was the one who had created this world. She was the only one who could end it.

And so...

Kaguya could not reach the hilt with her hand, so she gripped the blade directly. She felt sharp pain as the blood began to flow. A drop of it reached her neck after trickling down along the blade.

"Thank you, Sakura." Before she pushed in the blade, Kaguya glanced toward Sakura and smiled at her. "You were able to come here because Captain Azuma used his Chronos, weren't you? That's the only reason I'm able to leave."

"**That's the Kaguya I remember. Smart as a whip.**"

Sakura flashed a bright, sisterly smile. Kaguya moved a little closer to her.

"I'm sorry...that I didn't notice sooner."

"**That's okay. I'm the one who should be apologizing to you. It seems I left a lot of responsibility on your shoulders.**"

"No. If it hadn't been for you, I don't know if I would have been able to keep going all this time. I'm glad I got to see you again. Thank you, Sakura."

"**I'm glad I got to see you again, too, Kaguya. Don't worry. I'm sure you'll be able to become human again. As long as you want to go back, you can.**"

"Hngh..."

"**Don't cry. You're going home!**"

Kaguya could only smile in response.

"**Go be happy enough for the both of us out there, Kaguya.**"

"You've been so kind, Sakura, right up to the end..."

"**Why wouldn't I be kind when we're such good friends and comrades? And besides, I was watching you all this time while you worked so hard. So—**"

Farewell, this time forever.

"**—go be happy, Kaguya. Farewell.**"

"Farewell," Kaguya whispered back.

What followed was a sickening *crunch* as Kaguya thrust the blade into her own pale throat.

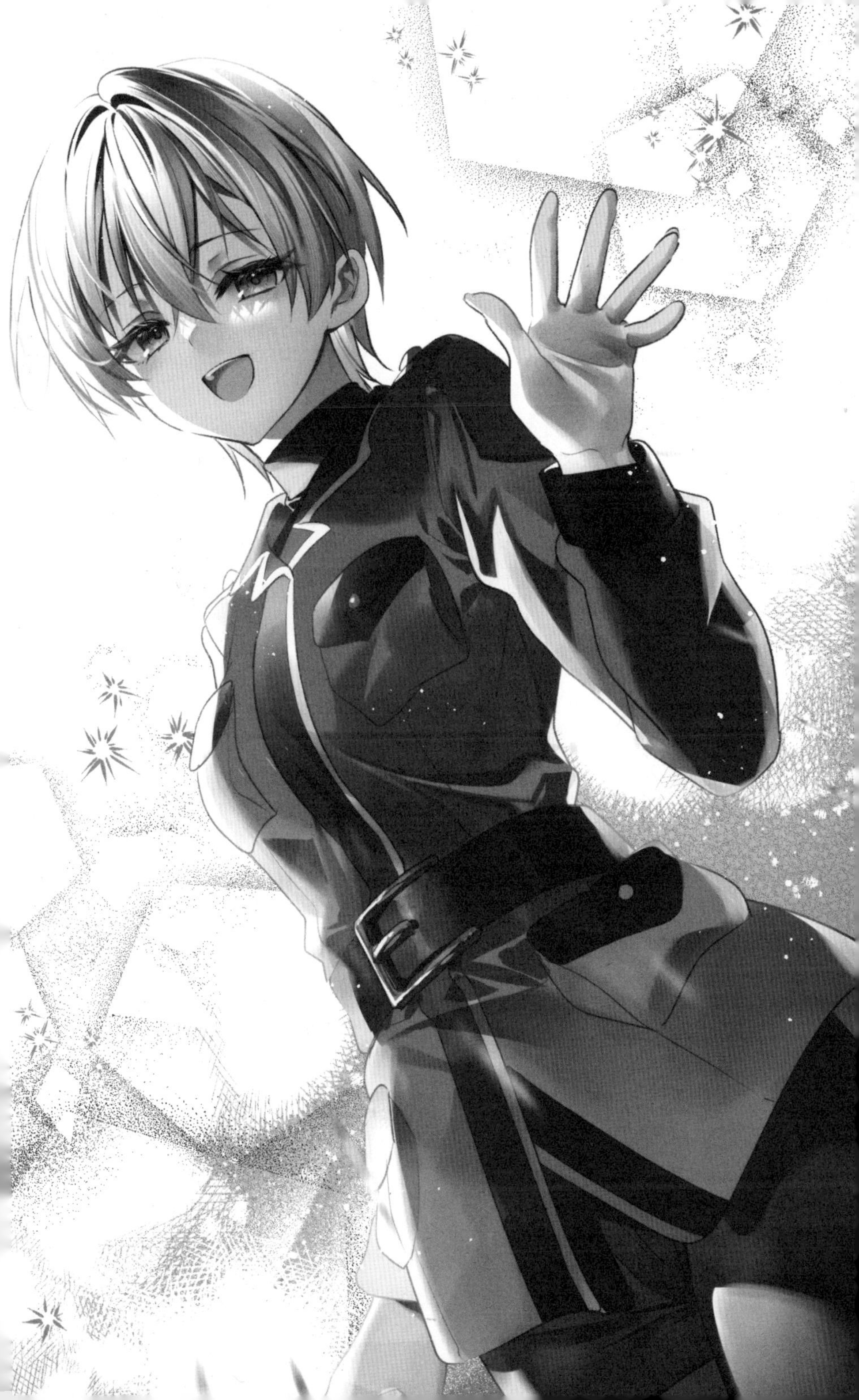

・・・

"—!!"

There was a pulse.

"Ah…!!"

Despite being on the verge of death, Azuma could not resist leaping to his feet.

The sound of the egg clearly changed just as he was about to stab it.

And then the hero began to retract. Its body began to grow smaller, like a video played in reverse. The petals withered and fell. The propagation stopped.

Using the last of his strength, Azuma chopped off the tentacle piercing his stomach in a panic. It was the only thing that was just barely stopping him from bleeding out immediately. He couldn't allow it to retract along with the rest of the hero.

The blossoming petals gradually converged together. At first, Azuma worried it might be another attack, but he stared in disbelief when he realized the hero was contracting into the shape of a certain silhouette.

That of a woman lying on the ground—it was Kaguya.

The petals were being sucked backward into her throat. It took less than a few seconds for them to all disappear. The other changes vanished as well. For all appearances' sake, she was back to her original human self once again. Azuma struggled to his feet.

"Did the hero just…?!"

It almost looked like…it had just turned back into a human.

"But it's already too late, isn't it?! What just happened here?"

The hero had already turned hostile. Without Kaguya's help, there should have been no way to pacify it. They were all thinking the same thing. This had to be some new form of attack. Just then, however…

She opened her eyes.

"Kaguya…," Azuma said, still struggling to stay upright.

He was losing more blood, but he had other things to worry about right now. They had no proof she was human again. This could all be part of one of the hero's attacks.

Now that she was awake, she stared blankly at them. They were all headed straight toward her, preparing to attack. She didn't blink an eye. Azuma clucked his tongue.

No normal human being would wake up to a sight like that without at least flinching.

"I guess it was too much to hope for…"

That settled it. She was still a hero. Just as he began to point his katana in Kaguya's direction once again…

"My name…," she managed to croak out. "My name is Kaguya Shinohara."

Still oblivious to the aggression that had been pointed her way just moments ago, Kaguya began to rise to her feet. She was no longer bleeding. There was still a trickle of blood coming from the remnant of her wound, but it had healed almost entirely. It was just a minor cut now.

Azuma wasn't sure what was going on. For a person to turn completely but then become human once more—it was impossible.

Her scarlet hair clung lightly to her cheek. He still couldn't see her face. His eyes suddenly went wide as he realized something.

I can't hear it.

The sound of the egg, which should have been coming from inside her body, was gone now.

"Kaguya…?"

As Azuma called her name, she glanced his way. A chill ran down his back as he saw himself reflected in her blank eyes. It was like she was staring at something else. Somewhere else.

The next thing she said…

"…Ren."

She turned her eyes toward the sky as she spoke.

There was a Goddess there, right in the path of her gaze. It looked almost like a bee but was clearly something else entirely.

"Ah…!"

This Goddess was far more dreadful than any others they had seen thus far. It was massive.

It changed into Azuma's younger sister. It was trying to lure him instead. But those tricks weren't going to fool Azuma anymore.

Azuma stared at the illusions it presented. First, his sister. Then Kaguya. Then Sakura. Visions of everyone he had watched leave until now. For a brief moment, he felt like he wanted to go to them.

He sensed instinctively that he was close to becoming a hero. He wasn't just going to let that happen, however. Not at this point. He took a step back as if to refuse the creature.

Kaguya suddenly spoke to him softly.

"Captain Azuma, I'm not giving up on you yet. I promise I will save you."

He tried to ask her what she was talking about, but all that came out of his mouth was another spurt of blood.

Azuma was moments from bleeding to death. He was as shocked as anyone that he was still conscious at this point. He had already lost around a tenth of the blood from his body. His death was sealed. All that was left now was to decide *how* he died.

It took genuine effort for him to raise his head, look Kaguya in the face, and shake his head from side to side.

"It's...too late."

It took monumental effort to get even those few words out.

"I..."

I'm already past saving.

But there was something more important he needed to tell her— that it wasn't her fault. She wasn't responsible for his death. If there was anything he needed to tell her now, it was that. His death was sure to weigh on her. Even if she understood it wasn't really her fault. That was just her personality.

"Y-you're not...to blame—"

Kaguya, however, was not interested in his last words right now.

"Yes, obviously I know that."

Kaguya had not even entertained the thought. She brushed a hand over his eyelids softly, closing his eyes. He was submerged in a pool of stagnant blood, and darkness consumed his already cloudy vision. Eyes closed, he felt pressure against his solar plexus. She was trying to stop the bleeding.

"Major Mirai has probably already called for an ambulance. Before it gets here, there's something I need to tell you."

What was she going to tell him? He had a bad feeling about this.

"Captain Azuma, I've found a way to turn heroes back into humans and—ah!!"

Just then, Kaguya suddenly flew away into the sky. No, she was snatched. By the Goddess.

Azuma tried to clamber to his feet. However, he no longer had the strength. Even his toes had stopped working. All he could manage to do was to drag himself through the dirt like a worm, his arms screaming out in pain.

Kaguya didn't even make a sound, she just glared at the Goddess as it snatched her into the air.

"Ren."

She spoke her brother's name. The Goddess didn't respond, simply flying higher and higher. As if it was trying to take Kaguya away with it somewhere.

She was too far away for Azuma to hear her directly by this point. In a panic, he turned on his comms receiver.

"I'm sorry, Ren. But I can't save you."

There was no deep sorrow in the voice that he heard on the other end of the line. Only firmness, determination, and resolve.

"All I can do for you now—"

He heard a sound on the line. Like the cocking of a pistol. Azuma went pale as he realized what she was about to do.

His veins ran cold. She was being carried up into the sky and was about to kill the very thing carrying her. If she did that, she was going to fall from an incredible height.

"Hngh, urgh—"

He tried to lift himself with a grunt, but his arms failed him. His mind was growing dim.

Death was close now. It would have been easier just to give in and pass away peacefully instead of trying to grit his teeth and withstand the pain for a little while longer. All he had to do was relax, just for a moment, and he would be able to slip over to the other side.

But he continued to try to rise to his feet.

He'd lost a tremendous amount of blood. His body was immersed in a pool of it. It was unlikely he would be able to defeat the Goddess in this state.

There was only one reason for him to continue now.

If he was going to die anyway. If it was too late to be saved. Then he wanted to at least save Kaguya before he went. If she fell from that height, she was going to be seriously hurt. There was no getting around that, but if he could get there first to cushion her fall, she might at least still live.

Where? Where are you going to fall, Kaguya?

She suddenly began speaking into the comms, oblivious to what was going on in Azuma's head.

"Captain Azuma. Listen. I've found a way to turn heroes back into humans."

The wind was whipping loudly over the line. For some reason, though, he could hear her voice clearly.

"It's silver. For some reason, when you turned into a hero, your earring was the only thing that was left untouched, Captain Azuma. You stabbed me with it earlier, too, didn't you? With your silver cross earring."

Glancing up, Azuma spotted a twinkling flash of silver. He frowned, realizing it was his earring, which he had been clutching in his hand up until a moment ago. When had she taken it from him?

"The inner world a person sees when they're pierced with silver. It's dark and bright. It's hot and cold. The kind of world you understand you need to leave."

"What are you—?" Azuma had to strain to make his vocal cords work. "What are you…trying to say?"

"Thank you for everything. The time I spent with everyone at Charon was truly fun."

Azuma saw where this was going. Kaguya…was planning to take herself out along with the Goddess.

Why? Azuma didn't understand. But it sounded like she had already given up on life. That was why she was trying to tell him what she knew before she went.

But Azuma wasn't going to allow that.

"Wait... Kagu—"

"Captain Azuma. Sakura is the one inside that sword you're wielding."

And with that, he heard the soft bang of a gun. The Goddess issued a scream, and the static on the line grew more frenetic. He heard a faint scream from Kaguya as well. The Goddess contorted in the air above, dancing in pain.

She had shot it, but the shot had not been fatal. However, the Goddess had slowed down now. Its altitude was dropping.

"Kaguya, wait!!"

"Make sure that you save her. I'm pretty sure..."

Kaguya paused for a breath. For some reason, Azuma could hear her clearly despite the howling wind.

"I'm pretty sure we aren't going to need them anymore. This entire Bureau should be gone soon enough."

Azuma heard another noise over the line. Like something whistling through the air. Kaguya's voice grew smaller and farther away. The thing must have flown even higher.

"Captain Azuma, you and the others will—so you—"

Kaguya's voice was breaking up because there was too much noise. She must have left the transmission range. The line suddenly cut out.

The giant bee continued to dance in pain in the sky above, leaving the trailing scent of osmanthus in its wake. Kaguya, meanwhile, was clinging to the anthropoid creature. She was trying to climb onto the Goddess's back.

Half of Azuma's vision was stained red with blood, but he could still see clearly that Kaguya was trying to bring the Goddess down.

There was the sound of another gunshot—the second one. The Goddess dropped lower, and communications came back online. But when he called out Kaguya's name, there was no answer. He wasn't even sure if his voice was being transmitted to her.

She had woken up. She had become human again. But if they didn't do something, Kaguya was going to die now.

He felt helpless. He couldn't even offer himself as a crash pad for her anymore. All he could do was watch silently as she fell from the sky. All alone, he watched her—

"What did I tell you about hogging the spotlight?!"

A young woman's shout changed everything.

Koyuki was back in the fray, and she had the Goddess in her sight. "Takanashi! Tell me when to go!"

"Not yet. Just a little more. Three meters!"

"Kaguya, did you hear that?!" Koyuki yelled into the comms. "Let's see... That's it. The wings!! Shoot the wings!! Drop it down by three meters!"

There was no answer from Kaguya. It seemed like she was too shaken up.

"If we drop it down by three meters, Second Lieutenant Asaharu, that will be low enough for Lieutenant Shinohara to jump, right? But then what?! If she just falls—"

"Don't worry. You've got it covered, right, Rindou?"

"Who do you think you're talking to here?"

They all knew exactly what they were doing.

Azuma tried to shake off his stupor and think. Was there anything he could do right now to help? He was nearly dead, so there was no way he was going to catch Kaguya. Besides, while it wouldn't really matter if he were to die in the process of breaking her fall, he doubted Kaguya would be too happy about that fact.

"Everyone..."

Azuma could hear the tears in Kaguya's voice.

"Don't. Don't you get it? I...I..."

He had never heard her sound like that before. Her voice was plaintive, as if she had lost all control.

"My brother became a Goddess in my place."

The static was terrible. Azuma could barely hear her, but he understood what she was trying to say.

"Kaguya."

Azuma's breath was ragged, his voice no more than a whisper, but for some reason, they all grew quiet and listened. The only other sound was the screaming of the Goddess.

"Did you forget...?"

He could only get out a few words at a time. His lungs were filling with blood.

"Or can you just not see?"

He could feel the life draining from his body with every word he spoke.

"You are human. A human, living in this world."

Azuma wanted her to remember. What he had said to her that day in that hospital room. The dead could be left to their own devices. It is the living who we should prioritize.

"Don't give up over something like this. Don't give up on yourself."

Azuma, at least, was not going to give up.

"Hold on. The Goddess's trajectory just changed!!" Koyuki shouted in distress.

Looking up, Azuma saw the Goddess swerving erratically as it hurtled swiftly toward the ground. But the trajectory was all wrong. It was branching far off from where Koyuki and Rindou were waiting. Kaguya crouched down on the Goddess's back, hanging onto it tightly, but if they crashed together, it would almost certainly mean her death.

They were headed far off course. Rindou would never make it in time, not even if he ran. But Azuma wasn't giving up hope yet. There was still a way to save her. The only way left was for someone like him, someone who could no longer move, let alone run.

"My brother."

He felt the presence standing beside him. A possibility. He turned his eyes toward it now.

It was his sister. She extended a hand toward him gently. All he had to do was take it, and he would become a hero. And when he did, the wind would blow. It always did when a person became a hero, without exception.

Azuma made a calculated decision in the back of his head. Even if the wind didn't get Kaguya and the Goddess back onto their original course, it would likely still be enough for Rindou to make it in time.

"Fine, then..."

Azuma extended his hand without hesitation. But he obviously had no plans of making things easy.

"You can use me this time instead."

As soon as he took its hand—the wind began to rage. Azuma turned his eyes toward Kaguya as she hurled toward the ground. The trajectory of their fall had changed. He spotted Rindou leaping into the air from the side. Azuma started to speak, as if offering up a prayer to Kaguya, who was prepared to give up on life.

"Kaguya. I believe in you. I believe in you, so come save me. You're the only one who can bring me back, right?" Just like he was the only one who could save Kaguya. "In that case, don't you die on us, okay?"

He had to tell her how he really felt.

"But even if *it's too late for me*, pass it on to the next person. But in order to do that, you can't give up on yourself first."

Because no one else could do what she could do.

Having said everything he needed to say, Azuma allowed himself to be lured of his own volition into his ideal world.

• • •

After her trajectory changed and she fell, Kaguya was safely caught in Rindou's arms. She was now back on solid ground. She had seen Azuma change with her own two eyes—she wanted to run to him immediately, but she suddenly realized that the silver cross, which should have still been in her hand, had been knocked from her grasp at some point.

She went pale and glanced around, eventually spotting it at quite a distance from where she now stood. Its current location, unfortunately, was far from ideal.

Due to the wind that had surfaced after Azuma turned into a hero, Kaguya was now positioned second closest to Azuma, along with Rindou. Koyuki was the closest.

The cross was much farther away. Even worse…

"Oh no… It's in there!"

Nestled in the rubble of the decimated school building. It was not completely buried—she could still make out a glint of silver—but there was no telling how long the remains would continue to stand. If the rubble collapsed completely, they would all be out of luck.

Kaguya only realized as she tried to run toward the earring that her ankle was broken.

"Why…?!"

She must have hit it when she fell. Either that or she had somehow hurt herself without noticing while wrestling with the Goddess in midair. Either way, she could no longer run.

The hero suddenly roared. Maybe it was because he had taken the Goddess's hand of his own accord, but Azuma was transforming into a much more fearsome shape than the katana hero he had once transformed into before.

"Ah…"

Kaguya stared at him as she tried to think.

If she tried to crawl all the way to the earring, she would never make it on time. Azuma would attack them first, resulting in an irrevocable outcome.

How was she supposed to save him? How was she supposed to get the one key that worked into his hands? She needed to get to that rubble and dig the cross free. She could always try diving in and saving him again herself, like last time. But who knew if she would be able to come back this time?

"Kaguya!"

Just then, a rough, boorish voice yanked Kaguya back to reality. She caught sight of him out of the corner of her eye, the same person who had just caught her when she fell from the sky. It was Rindou.

"What do we do next? Tell me what you need!"

He was out of breath, but he was staring at Azuma, just like she was.

Kaguya suddenly remembered something that Azuma had told her before. That she needed to rely on everyone more. To trust them a little and not try to handle everything all by herself.

She made up her mind immediately. Charon trusted her. There was no reason not to trust them in return.

"Rindou!! Can you do something about that?!"

She pointed toward the cross buried in the rubble. Rindou was speechless. Doing "something" about it was clearly going to be difficult. But *difficult* wasn't the same as *impossible*. Kaguya knew he could do it. She shouted once more.

"Please!!"

Clicking his tongue softly, Rindou began running toward the rubble without another word. Even Rindou looked ready to drop from exhaustion at this point. After all, he had just fought two heroes in a row. Kaguya knew he was barely standing now.

The rubble looked like it was ready to collapse. They could still see the silver cross but just barely. Once the rubble came falling down, it would be lost entirely. He made it—mere moments before a large chunk of debris that sloughed off from the building would have crushed the cross. However, Rindou took the brunt of the falling rubble in the cross's place. The debris fell on top of him. Despite this, he grasped the cross firmly in his hand.

He threw his arm backward, tossing it away from the collapsing wreckage. He couldn't even see where he was throwing.

A pond—the cross was headed straight for water! Just as it was about to hit the surface…

Someone else snatched it out of midair.

A young woman with teal hair and jade-green eyes—it was Haru! She caught the cross and just kept running as fast as she could. She wasn't as spent from battle as Rindou was and still had plenty of stamina left over. She bought even more distance, but there was a problem.

"Th-the wind...!"

The wind was cloaking Azuma, keeping her from getting any closer. Haru was hardly a flimsy girl, but she wasn't nearly as strong as the other members of Charon. All she could do was try to dig her heels in so that she wouldn't be blown away. She reached out, trying to deliver the cross into Kaguya's hands, but it was blown from her own hand instead!

"Ah!!"

Fortunately, there was someone there to catch it before it could fly away.

"Koyuki...!"

Koyuki tossed her gun aside and held onto the cross as tightly as she could instead. She passed it to Kaguya as Kaguya shouted her name before grabbing Kaguya's arm tightly with one hand.

"Go get him for us...Kaguya!!"

And then she tossed Kaguya bodily through the air, straight toward Azuma. The counterforce caused Koyuki to lose her footing and be tossed backward into the wind, disappearing from sight.

The wind was even stronger than her. Stronger, colder, and so much fiercer than any wind Kaguya had ever felt before. An implacable barrier. But strangely, the storm seemed to be pointed inward. The wind coming off Azuma's hero was actually sucking Kaguya in.

Kaguya held the silver cross in her hand. This was it. There was no hesitation, no second thoughts, no fear, and no despair.

"We're waiting for you." Kaguya's long hair whipped against her cheek. "Everyone is waiting for you, Captain."

The cross—which Rindou had dug free, Haru had delivered, and Koyuki had passed into her hands.

"So hurry up and come back to us. Come back to us, Yuuri Azuma!!"

As the inward-facing storm drew her in, Kaguya extended a hand toward Azuma's right eye and stabbed it with the silver earring. There was no scream. Blood spurted forth, staining Kaguya's scarlet hair an even deeper red. Despite the intensity raging around her, Kaguya's worry was no more than fleeting.

The moment she struck, as the wind threatened to tear her away, Kaguya had a thought.

This isn't like last time. I'm not alone. There's hope. A hope that we came together to create. A hope that I know will save you.

• • •

The moment Kaguya stabbed him with the earring, the wind ceased.

Kaguya lost her balance and clutched frantically at the dirt, fearing the wind would soon return.

However, all was quiet.

Without warning, the hero began to move. Kaguya braced herself, but the hero had simply started to fall backward. She stared at the creature intently as it crashed down to the earth. It soon took on the silhouette of a young man sprawled in the dirt.

"Captain…Azuma?" she called softly, moving closer.

Azuma's bleeding had subsided.

If Kaguya's hypothesis had been correct, Azuma was human once more. But what if he was still a hero? What would they do then? She hadn't thought that far ahead. It was all a gamble—one last bid based on a private theory drawn from subjective experience.

"Ugh…"

Azuma opened his eyes. The others held their breaths. While they watched, Azuma casually sat up—and then realized several things all at once. His wound had closed. He was no longer on the verge of death. And the Goddess was still there.

"The egg…"

Azuma touched his right eye.

Having awoken from her own hero's dream, Kaguya understood what he was thinking. His egg was probably gone. A look of stunned surprise, like Kaguya had never seen before, solidified on his face. He stood up with a gasp.

Azuma's katana was currently thrust into the ground just next to him. He grabbed the hilt and pulled it free, flicking off the blood lightly.

Kaguya stood next to him, Koyuki and Rindou behind them. Haru was located a little farther away, but her eyes were fixated on the same point as theirs were.

The Goddess.

It was gigantic.

But they did not despair. Not one of them. A myriad of possible outcomes flashed through Kaguya's head, but not a single one of these options included the word *defeat*. It was time to end this for good.

The clacking of metal filled the air. Rindou had struck the brass knuckles on each of his hands together in anticipation.

"The hell are you doing still alive?!" Koyuki said in surprise.

"Sorry to disappoint you," Rindou answered, not looking her way. "Anyway…I think these Chronoses have a bone to pick with that thing."

"I bet they do…"

Koyuki readied her rifle.

The Goddess appeared in the shape of a bee again and was still flying in the air, but it was already on the verge of death. Azuma headed toward it first. The Goddess did not try to run—it simply continued to face them, hovering imperiously. As Azuma brandished his sword once more, Kaguya whispered to him softly.

"I…met Sakura earlier," she said.

To which Azuma replied, "So did I."

Kaguya glanced at Azuma's sword. The image of Sakura, likely suffering inside that blade, floated into her mind.

"Don't worry, Sakura. It will be my turn to help you next."

The Goddess was already severely damaged. Kaguya had shot it several times and brought it crashing into the ground. It was still attempting to lift into the air, like the insect that it appeared to be, but its altitude was piddling at best.

The Goddess teetered sideways.

Koyuki took a shot at its flank to knock it off balance even further. The powerful anti-materiel-class rifle shaved off a chunk of the creature's body, causing the Goddess to crash into the dirt with a screech.

Goddesses lacked offensive power but were highly durable. Rindou moved in close and grabbed the downed creature's wings in a joint lock to prevent it from flying back into the air. Azuma seized the opening, pointing the tip of his sword toward the creature—

"Azuma!!"

Just as the blade was about to hit, the Goddess began to flap its wings. Azuma checked that movement with a single kick and then pressed the blade—Sakura—to the creature's neck.

"Agh…! It's too tough…!"

Either he had chosen a bad spot, or he wasn't fully recovered yet. Either way, the toughness of the creature's skin won out against Azuma's attempts to chop off its head. The katana slipped from his grasp mid-strike. Ignoring the blade, Azuma kicked the Goddess as hard as he could instead. That force was enough to leave the Goddess's head half-crushed, causing it to collapse fully into the dirt.

And yet somehow—it was still alive.

Its head was only connected by a thin scrap of flesh. It was bleeding intensely and did not look long for this world. After slipping from Azuma's grasp, the katana had once again embedded itself in the earth. But the Goddess's breathing was shallow. It would likely die soon, even without a finishing blow.

Hence why no one made a move.

No one, however, except for her.

Kaguya was standing closest to Azuma's waylaid sword. She retrieved it, this sword that still held Sakura's soul, and used it like a crutch as she approached the Goddess.

"Kaguya."

Somebody called her name, but Kaguya ignored them. She had to be the one to finish this. She had already made up her mind on that point.

"I'm sorry, Ren. I wasn't able to save you in the end," Kaguya whispered as the insectile Goddess continued to hover on the verge of death.

The older brother she had been searching for all this time—his transformation into a hero had been the catalyst for all of this.

"I'm going to go on living. For both our sakes…forgive me."

Kaguya thought she heard a voice, like some sort of hallucination. *No, forgive me.* It seemed to be coming from the Goddess, but Kaguya knew that Goddesses couldn't speak.

I couldn't say it until now.

But the voice was speaking to her.

No, the truth is I hadn't even noticed. But I finally understand.

She knew this voice. It was real this time. *Please*, thought Kaguya. *Please don't say the rest.*

Thank you, Kaguya.

How was she going to stop herself from crying once he said it? How would she keep from drowning in all the sorrow and pain? If he said it, she would have to face the fact that she was really losing him.

I love you, Kaguya.

"I love you, too, Ren…"

It was time for their last farewell. At the end of a blade. She didn't care if the rebound sent her flying. Even that pain would be transformed into love and commitment.

"Thank you."

And with that, she cut off the Goddess's head.

Kaguya then collapsed.

Departing upon another comatose journey—into a sleep from which no one could shake her.

CHAPTER SEVENTEEN
Normalization

Another week passed before Kaguya opened her eyes.

Many things happened during that week. First and foremost, the Extermination Bureau's deception was exposed.

The Extermination Bureau was no more than an experimental setting for the development of new weapons—that truth was revealed to the rest of the organization, which quickly threw the Bureau into chaos.

After being confronted by the fact that their whole lives had been nothing but pretend, many of the Bureau's soldiers lost control and resorted to rioting and violence. The others, particularly Azuma and Charon, managed to quell the unrest, but Bureau morale suffered greatly. For all intents and purposes, the Extermination Bureau had been effectively dissolved.

Meanwhile, a change occurred in the way they fought the heroes. They now knew that what Azuma had done was effective—how he had pierced Kaguya with his cross.

Silver was what worked against the heroes. There was obviously no silver in the Chronoses. Standard weapons, meanwhile, were generally made primarily out of materials such as iron and lead. More importantly, silver did not cause rebounds.

There was no more need for Chronoses.

Once the mistaken assumption that only Chronoses could work against heroes had been undermined, their value drastically plummeted. The people inside those weapons could finally be laid to rest.

The few dozen Chronoses currently in existence—with the exceptions of Rindou's brass knuckles, Koyuki's anti-materiel-class rifle and handgun, and Azuma's katana—were destroyed. They had used their own Chronoses to destroy them.

That included the ax the Director had occasionally used, finally freeing the young girl who was apparently trapped within.

The Extermination Bureau managed to find equilibrium by changing its name and structure. The ostensible military system was abolished, and participation was made voluntary. Its ranks, which originally numbered quite high, dropped by half, and even the members of Charon began to leave, one after the other. Before long, everyone besides Azuma, Koyuki, Haru, and Rindou had moved on.

After picking through Inspection's databanks, Haru had expected something like this. While she saw no reason to announce her suspicions, she had seen the Extermination Bureau's end on the horizon.

"It will all be clear soon," she had said. Although Azuma only heard this from Koyuki after the fact.

All this happened in a week's time.

"You found out who killed the Director?" Sitting in his own room, Azuma furrowed his eyebrows at the report he had just received. He was in the middle of a call. "You found them…? Who was it, in the end?"

"Oh, I forgot you hadn't been informed yet," the person on the other end of the line said. It was Mari. *"It was someone from Inspection, just as expected. The very same person who sent Haru Takanashi into Charon. They were likely worried about someone finding out the truth, that Chronoses were sentient. The person's name was—"*

Azuma exhaled deeply and sank further into his chair. It was the same person who had once urged him to transfer Kaguya.

"That was impressive work, uncovering all of that. How did you manage to do so in such a short period of time…?"

"*It was Major Mirai's doing…*" Mari's voice grew just a little softer. "*She was like a dog with a bone when it came to this…*"

Mirai's tenacity in avenging her old friend had surprised even Haru. In the end, everything came out, even the details of that photograph.

The photograph in question, discovered by Kaguya and Mari, had been taken by an ordinary layperson but had later been found by someone at Technical No. 1. The reason that it remained after every other document and record had been destroyed was likely just an oversight, due to the loss of Technical No. 1 amid all the chaos.

"I guess things will also be wrapping up for us soon, then…"

"*There are still Goddesses and heroes remaining out there, so it won't happen immediately… But it shouldn't be long now. I heard talk, actually, that Charon is going to be dissolved in the near future.*"

"*Dissolved* is probably too strong of a word. But there isn't much of a need for us anymore, is there?"

An awkward silence from Mari ensued.

What Azuma said was true. Now that they had identified a clear weakness in the heroes, there was no need to rely on just Charon any longer. As for what that meant for Charon—well, Azuma was under no obligation to explain that to Mari.

"Putting all that aside, I assume you actually have a different reason for calling, Ezakura?"

"*Oh, y-yes. You remember that Kaguya finally woke up a little while ago, correct?*"

Of course he remembered. He had never felt so relieved in his life as when Mari had told him the news.

"*Well, as it turns out…she's lost her memories. Completely.*"

"Her memories…?!"

"*All of them. She has zero episodic memory from before she fell into the coma. At first, she didn't even know her own name…*"

"I...see. Even though I came out fine..."

"*I think it must be some kind of defense mechanism. Kaguya went through a lot of painful experiences. Honestly, I was worried something like this might happen someday.*"

Mari's voice, over the line, sounded so sad that even Azuma could sympathize.

However...

"*On that note, there's something I wish to discuss.*" Mari's tone suddenly undertook a drastic shift. "*Since she was lucky enough to forget things—I'm sorry. I shouldn't have said it like that. But since she's lost her memory anyway...could we just pretend like the last few months at Charon never happened?*"

They could concoct false memories for her—for just that period.

"I understand. We'll do as you say... Believe it or not, Warrant Officer Ezakura, you and I agree on that point. I was thinking the exact same thing."

There was no need for Azuma and the others to drag Kaguya back into their ranks. No one wanted to get her any more wrapped up in things than she had already been.

"We'll pretend she's just a stranger, someone we would have never met, let alone exchanged two words with. I was thinking of proposing the same thing. Let's just leave it at that."

"*That makes things easier, then...*"

Mari's request for Azuma and the others was as follows: They were to act as if Kaguya's experiences up until now did not include the several months she had spent at Charon. Instead, they would pretend that she had been in a coma that entire time.

"*I want you to promise,*" Mari said. "*Promise you will never see Kaguya again. That you will pretend like none of this ever happened. I know what I'm asking is terrible, but—*"

Mari's voice grew even more serious than before.

"*—I just can't watch her do this to herself anymore. I know you all know what I mean.*"

He did. Azuma knew very well.

"That means…this will be our last time speaking together as well. Technical and Charon were never supposed to be involved in the first place. So let's call it a day."

"Yes… Let's."

If they really had Kaguya's best interests at heart, this was the right choice to make.

Azuma had made a similar decision several months ago. But that time, Kaguya had returned to Charon on her own. This time, however, her memories were gone. There was no way the same thing could occur.

It truly was farewell this time.

"I'm sorry for all the trouble we've caused up until now. For you, for Kaguya, and for the Director."

"No, Kaguya's presence at Charon was necessary. I understand that now." Despite her previous sharp tone, Mari's voice grew soft. "Is there anything you want to say to her by way of good-bye…?"

"That's not like you. What's wrong? You're not feeling sorry for us, are you?"

"Of course not. But I understand now how much Kaguya needed you all. I just thought there might be something you wanted to say."

"But if you gave her a message from us, it might cause her to remember things… It's better if we just keep our good-byes to ourselves."

"Well," said Mari, sounding a little regretful. "If you say so. I plan on disposing of any possible links on this end anyway."

"Yes, as do we. I've already gotten everything in order."

"That's good to hear. I know I can trust you to keep your word. Farewell, then."

And then she hung up the phone.

Azuma deleted all their relevant contact information, just as Mari had requested. Kaguya's. The Director's. The documents and terminals in the room had also been scrubbed in advance.

"Wait. There was one more piece…," Azuma muttered, remembering.

After dealing with the other documents, Koyuki had mentioned one last piece of paperwork she had apparently found in a desk drawer in Kaguya's room. But it was just a single sheet of fairly low importance. Azuma planned just to tear it up and place it in the repository's shredder box.

They decided to pretend the bottom bunk had always been Haru's, thus eliminating any evidence that Kaguya had been there at all.

For his own part, Azuma made up his mind to forget all about Kaguya.

Made up my mind…? Who am I kidding…?

No, he realized. He *needed* to forget her.

He set his terminal down on the table, letting go of any last faint connections.

CHAPTER EIGHTEEN
Separation

Approximately two months had passed since Charon had severed connections with Kaguya Shinohara.

The number of heroes was steadily decreasing. Naturally, as the larval hero forms diminished in numbers, so too did the adult Goddesses. At this point, they were only encountering about one hero per month. The frequency continued to drop, and the prospect of total extermination was now in sight.

The members of Charon had started to think differently, their minds naturally turning to what might come *next*—after the Extermination Bureau was totally gone.

"..."

That included Koyuki.

She was still lying in her bunk bed in the new barracks, in the room she shared with Haru. Koyuki was on the bottom bunk this time around.

On that particular morning, after waking up, Koyuki just didn't feel like moving. As she lay in bed, a voice called out to her from above.

"Koyuki, what are you doing?"

"Oh… Haru."

At some point, Koyuki had just started calling Haru by her first name instead of her title. She slowly got out of bed. After getting herself ready, she left the room, somehow managing to drag her feet to the meeting hall, where everyone was gathering today.

They were all present—their Chronoses already placed on the table.

That's right. Today was the day they were going to destroy the remaining Chronoses.

Charon's numbers had dwindled, and there were plans to dissolve the unit entirely in the near future. The formalities were still a month away, but the Chronoses were no longer being used.

The looks on everyone's faces were complicated.

The pair of brass knuckles. The anti-materiel-class rifle, which had been propped up against the table, was too large to fit on top. Two handguns. And Azuma's katana.

Koyuki had spent a little time investigating the weapons. She hadn't been able to find out their names, but she had learned their ages and sexes. The brass knuckles used by Rindou had once been a twelve-year-old boy. The anti-materiel-class rifle used by Koyuki had been an eighteen-year-old girl. And the handgun she used had been a seventeen-year-old boy.

Of course, they knew who was in Azuma's weapon. The gun that Kaguya had used once upon a time, meanwhile, had been a sixteen-year-old boy.

"Let's get started. We'll use this gun to destroy them... I know watching this will be painful for some of you, so feel free to leave if you need to."

However, no one left. Even Haru, who had almost no involvement with the Chronoses, remained in the room.

Normal bullets worked fine. He loaded the Chronos gun, cocked the hammer, and lined up the sights. He placed his finger on the trigger.

Just as he was about to fire the gun and destroy the first Chronos—

"Wait," Koyuki said, stopping him. A thought had just occurred to her. "What...will we do for this one?" She meant the gun in Azuma's hand. "Chronoses can only be destroyed by other Chronoses, right? Then how will we free the person trapped inside the last Chronos?"

"I figured we could induce a hero to destroy it," Azuma said offhandedly. He had already given the matter some thought.

He had never even considered leaving either Koyuki's or Rindou's weapons for last. It felt right that they should destroy them themselves. He had chosen the gun instead out of purely personal feelings—favoritism, essentially. He didn't want to make Sakura suffer any longer than she had to.

"Once this is done, everything will be over. All of it..."

And then he pulled the trigger.

It took two shots to reduce Rindou's brass knuckles to smithereens.

The anti-materiel-class rifle took a little more work, requiring three shots to get it into a state that could finally qualify as being destroyed.

The other handgun, the one that had been wielded by Koyuki, was soon shattered into pieces as well, leaving behind silence.

That left only one weapon to destroy.

"Sakura."

The katana-shaped Chronos that Azuma had been using, which even now supposedly contained Sakura's consciousness.

They were all there to see Sakura off in her final moments—Rindou, Koyuki, and even Haru, who had never even met Sakura. Koyuki realized that unbidden tears had risen to her eyes. Rindou turned his face away. Apparently, even he was crying... This farewell would be forever.

But it's better this way.

They couldn't leave Sakura in pain any longer.

There was a cocking sound as Azuma readied the pistol. His hand trembled ever so slightly, but he quickly got himself under control.

"Farewell, Sakura."

The sound of the gunshot was surprisingly soft as the katana split in two.

Sakura Arakawa was finally free of this world.

• • •

"Oh, look! They've changed the menu! When did that happen...?!" shouted a young woman with scarlet hair and pale violet eyes.

It was Lieutenant Kaguya Shinohara. Her eyes went wide with excitement.

They were in the cafeteria at Technical No. 3. She opened the menu, her attention fixated on one item in particular. And that item was…

"A limited-time, seasonal pasta set…?! And it says it's back by popular demand. I don't remember this being on the menu before…"

"They had it while you were asleep. They just brought it back last week, so I guess you're in luck."

Lieutenant Kaguya Shinohara was taking a late lunch together with her junior colleague, Warrant Officer Mari Ezakura.

About seventy days had passed since Kaguya had woken up. During that time, she learned that she had lost her memory, had once been in a place called Technical Research Lab No. 2—which had been abolished—and had learned Technical No. 3 was newly established to take its place. At first, Kaguya had been very confused, but Mari had been patiently teaching her everything she needed to know, so she now had a basic grip on things once again.

"So we were trying to turn heroes back into humans…"

She still found it hard to believe they had actually been carrying out that sort of research.

She had forgotten about the existence of heroes as well. When she saw videos of the creatures, they just seemed like monsters to her. She certainly couldn't see how they could possibly be turned back into humans again.

"But you already succeeded, right?"

"Yes, thanks to the Director's hard work."

According to Mari, a lot of things happened while Kaguya was in her coma.

First of all, there had been the death of this person known as the Director. She had supposedly died in an accident related to the weapons known as Chronoses.

Unfortunately, as Kaguya's knowledge of the Director was purely intellectual, she was unable to feel any acute sense of sadness over that person's death. She did feel oddly forlorn about it, however.

From what Mari told her, this Director had taken Kaguya under her wing. The Director had been carrying out research into the Chronoses but had died before she could finish.

"She could be all over the place at times…but she was a very good person. I suppose you don't remember her, though…"

"…"

"Oh! I shouldn't have said that. I can't imagine how it must make you feel."

"N-no… It's okay. Don't worry about it."

From what Kaguya had been told, there were only three people stationed at Technical No. 2 to begin with. After the Director's accidental death and with Kaguya in a coma, Mari must have been all alone over there.

"I'm impressed. It's amazing that you were able to accomplish all of this on your own."

"Well, actually… I mean, yes, I suppose."

It sounded like Mari had been about to say something but then thought better of it. After a moment, she thrust her chest out with pride.

"It was so hard! I had to struggle so much to get by, with nothing to go on but the little bit of information the Director had left behind. I really wish you had been there to see it."

"Ha-ha, I would have liked that." Kaguya meant it. She would have loved to have seen what Mari was capable of. "But…if what you said is true, we already know how to turn the heroes back into humans, right? So why does Technical even still exist?"

A frown, part distress and part sadness, appeared on Mari's face.

"I told you about the Goddesses, right?"

"The Goddesses? Oh, the creatures that turn humans into heroes, right…? They were originally humans, too, weren't they?"

"They were. I'm working on a different project now. I'm trying to figure out if there's a way to turn Goddesses back into humans."

Kaguya tried to look impressed. "Wow, Mari, that's incredible. If anyone can do it, I know it's you! Give it your best!"

"Ha-ha… I guess I should have expected that…" Mari smiled,

although, for some reason, she looked closer to tears. "Anyway, I'll try. But I still expect you to help, Kaguya."

"You can count on me. Not that I have any idea about what needs to be done!"

Kaguya laughed in what she meant to be a self-deprecating way. After all, she really couldn't remember a thing.

Well, not exactly. She still had her semantic memory—the kind of stuff required for daily living. That was why the information entered her head so easily when Mari started teaching her the basics. But even now, she didn't understand why any of it was supposed to be significant for her. She knew she had been working on something called the Revival Project—but none of that felt real to her. It just didn't seem very important.

She turned her eyes toward the cafeteria menu.

"All these options look so delicious. Which one was my favorite before?"

"Hmm? Well… I wouldn't really say you had a favorite. Or I guess I could say all of them."

"Of course," Kaguya muttered absently, not really meaning anything by it.

"There wasn't really any food you didn't like, to be honest. You even cooked for yourself sometimes."

"Really? I did?"

Kaguya was somewhat interested to hear that. She wondered what kind of food she used to make.

"You know, things like instant noodles or microwavable pasta."

"I'm not sure that really qualifies as cooking."

"And lots of soup in pouches. You know, the kind you heat up in the microwave."

"Ah…" Kaguya's thoughts began to wander. "Now that you mention it, I do remember something like that. In retort pouches, right? I remember I was heating it up like you're supposed to, but there was someone else who just threw the whole pouch into a fry pan."

Kaguya was piecing together her words as she spoke. Her attention, along with her eyes, was still pointed toward the menu in front of her, and she wasn't investing much significance in what she was saying.

"After that, they tried to stick some eggs straight into the microwave as well. Isn't that funny?"

Mari was sitting next to Kaguya. With her eyes still on the menu, Kaguya didn't notice the look on Mari's face. It was only after glancing up because Mari wasn't responding that she noticed the look of fear in Mari's eyes.

"That's... Who are you talking about...?"

"What?"

Kaguya was taken aback. Why was Mari reacting so strangely?

"It's just... Nothing like that ever happened at the dorms. We've only ever gone out to eat since you came to Technical, remember? Who are you thinking of?"

"Well..."

Kaguya wasn't sure how to answer. Now that she thought about it—she couldn't remember the person's face or their voice. Or anything about what had happened before or after that incident. It was all absent from her head.

But she did seem to have a vague memory of this incident she was describing—no, not a memory, exactly. Even when she tried to focus on it, the details remained unclear.

"Huh... Who could it have been...?"

There was only one possibility.

"Maybe it was just a dream..."

She must have experienced something like that in a dream. It was the only explanation she could think of.

"Kaguya, can't you even tell the difference between reality and a dream?"

"Honestly, lately, it seems like I can't. I keep convincing myself that things that happen in dreams actually happened in real life. Maybe I'm just tired."

The exact same thing happened the other day. She had remembered being in a physical fight with someone—something that obviously would never have happened to her. Specifically, she had been holding some kind of long stick, and her opponent—well, she couldn't really remember her opponent, but the person had been attacking her. Kaguya had been at Technical this whole time, however, so obviously she wasn't going around with a stick in her hands getting into fights.

There was more, too. She remembered being in a place that was all white in every direction like it was dipped in a white shadow, and she had been talking to somebody there. But she couldn't remember the person's voice or their face.

And she remembered an unbroken field of flowers for some reason. *Something* had happened there—she just couldn't remember what.

And also—

"Dreams are just dreams, Kaguya," Mari said, sounding concerned.

Kaguya lifted her head, snapping out of it.

"Anyway, I can't blame you for being tired. You were asleep for months, after all. Besides, this work isn't like with the heroes. Trying to turn Goddesses into humans is a whole different ball game."

"Y-yes, I suppose."

Mari's words did little to dispel Kaguya's unease, however. Besides, an image passed through Kaguya's head. The image of a silver—

"Huh?"

Kaguya suddenly felt someone's gaze on her.

Not even a gaze, exactly. Just a feeling that something was off. She glanced around restlessly before releasing a little exclamation of surprise.

A young man in a uniform whom she had never seen before was loitering in a corner of the deserted Technical cafeteria. She couldn't see his face, just a tiny bit of his hair, like silver ice.

"That guy over there… Who is he?" Kaguya muttered.

Mari looked at the young man.

"Ah…?!"

Visibly shocked, she stood up, her chair falling over with a clatter. There was both surprise and anger in her eyes. Enough to make Kaguya feel a little afraid.

"M-Mari?"

"I'm sorry, Kaguya… Wait right here for a moment. Don't move. I'm going to go talk to that person."

"What? Well, okay."

He must have been an acquaintance of Mari's. She stomped toward the person with long strides, a look of incomprehensible annoyance on her face.

"Well, now I need to know what this is about…"

Quietly and casually, Kaguya inched her way closer to Mari and this unknown person, trying not to be noticed. Mari seemed to be accosting the person for some reason. She was acting menacingly, in a way that Kaguya had never seen her behave before.

"This isn't what you promised…! What do you think you're doing, lurking here?!" Mari was keeping her voice low, but even from this distance, Kaguya could tell she was getting worked up. "Wait. You're not trying to see her, are you?!"

The young man shook his head back and forth wordlessly as if to say that was obviously not the case.

"I didn't come here to see her," Kaguya heard him say.

Kaguya leaned forward eagerly. *"Her"?* Who did he mean by *her*?

"I came to give you this," the young man said, handing something to Mari. "It was the only thing of hers still left at Charon. It didn't feel right just to get rid of it."

A white earpiece. Possibly a recorder in the shape of an earpiece. Maybe there was something important on it. Mari took it, looking displeased.

Kaguya, however, had picked up one important piece of information from this conversation.

Charon? That's one of Tactical Infantry's squads, isn't it?

Mari hadn't shared many details, but Kaguya had heard of this group. Shouldn't Mari have been more surprised to see someone from Tactical show up around here? How did she possibly know him? Kaguya tried to move a little closer, her interest now piqued, when she suddenly caught a glimpse of his face.

He had light silver hair and blue eyes. Even to Kaguya, who didn't take much of an interest in people's faces, his features seemed handsome and well-formed. His expression betrayed a blatant lack of interest in his surroundings.

"Ah!"

As soon as she saw his face, Kaguya's heart seemed to beat faster.

But the feeling soon subsided. Kaguya wasn't sure what to make of it. It almost felt like a palpitation. But why? Nothing Mari had told her so far had had much of an effect on her, but for some reason, the mere sight of this young man had managed to capture Kaguya's attention completely.

"Later," the young man said, waving his hand lightly as he began to leave.

Apparently, he had accomplished whatever he came for. Just as he was about to turn around, for the briefest moment, his eyes moved her way. They were sharp and blue as if they could penetrate through anything.

At that moment, she saw it. There, dangling from his left ear. An earring in the shape of a cross.

"E-excuse me…!"

Kaguya called out to the young man without thinking, abandoning her efforts to hide.

"Kaguya," Mari said, in shock. But Kaguya wasn't looking Mari's way.

That cross…

That cross. She had been seeing it so often lately. But it surely couldn't be the same one that was showing up in her dreams.

"…"

Upon being spoken to, the young man pointed his sharp gaze wearily in Kaguya's direction. A moment later, without a word, he turned his back to her once more as if rebuffing her attempt to speak with me.

The idea of speaking up again was daunting. This was her first time meeting this person. But if she let him get away now, she would probably never see him again.

"Wait!"

As she called out for him to stop, the young man turned around. His blue eyes narrowed with displeasure, and Mari looked surprised. It didn't feel as if any of this was happening for the first time.

No, it wasn't—Kaguya was certain of it. She had seen all of this before. But for some reason, she couldn't remember.

"Umm…I'm sorry to bother you like this. But would it be all right if I asked your name?"

"…Why?"

His voice was sharp and curt. She had a strong feeling she had seen him before.

Why? Kaguya was at a loss for words. She couldn't think of a good answer. She had just asked him to wait. She could hardly say it was because she had "seen him in a dream."

She remained silent. The young man spoke again.

"You're…with Technical No. 3, right? What possible reason could you have for speaking to me?"

"W-well, you'll probably laugh at this, but I have this feeling like we've met before."

"…"

There was silence between them for a moment. She thought she saw the young man's eyes widen temporarily, but they soon narrowed once more.

"You must be mistaken. I've never met you before in my life. This is our first time speaking with each other."

"Yes, I suppose, but—"

"And I'm sorry, but I just don't feel like sharing my name. Telling you my name would be pointless."

With that, the young man turned around once more and began to walk away rapidly.

"Kaguya…," Mari said timidly as Kaguya watched the young man leave. "Did you rememb—? I mean, do you know him from somewhere? Why did you just speak to him like that?"

"Because… Well, I'm not really sure why. I'm sorry. It seems like I interfered in something important. I just had this feeling that it wasn't my first time seeing him."

"O-oh... Of course, didn't I mention before?" Mari said, her voice sounding a bit panicked as if she was trying to come up with an excuse. "It probably has to do with this."

Mari waved her personal Bureau terminal in front of Kaguya's face.

"Sometimes he shows up on the Bureau's video feed. You must have caught a glimpse of him on a terminal somewhere, and the image just stuck in your head."

"Oh... I guess that would explain it."

She must have seen him somewhere without remembering, and the image had gotten lodged in her memory. What with her amnesia and everything, she must have just gotten confused.

Unless... I wonder...

The explanation did make sense. But something wasn't sitting right. She wasn't sure what that *something* was exactly. But she did know one thing for sure.

That man...was so infuriating!

She instinctively suspected that the two of them would not get along.

"You see, that's all there is to it. Anyway, Kaguya, what did you decide? Should we get the seasonal plate, then?"

"Why not?"

Kaguya turned back around. It was better to not get involved with someone so disagreeable. She had probably just seen him somewhere else before. She would forget about him soon enough.

"While we're at it...I think I'll order Lunch Set A and Lunch Set B, too. I've got a feeling the special won't be enough."

"I guess that's one thing about you that will never change."

• • •

The recorder contained the last words of the departed Sakura Arakawa. He just couldn't bring himself to throw it away. Having something like that at Charon could raise questions, however, so that was why he had decided to return it to Mari.

"You never introduced yourself. What's your name?"

Azuma could hear her voice again in his head.

Why? That was what he had asked her at that time. What was she—someone who had an egg inside her—doing at the Extermination Bureau? That was what he had originally meant by his question back on that day.

But not now. What he wanted to know now was why she had spoken to him.

She didn't remember him, after all.

"It's better this way," he whispered.

This was sure to be his last time visiting Technical, and she would not be coming to Charon again.

"Farewell, Kaguya. This time, for good."

And then they each went their separate ways. Just as they had done before.

From then on out, they would have nothing to do with each other. Not until the day when heroes disappeared from this Earth.

EPILOGUE ONE
Memory

Several months had passed since Kaguya had encountered the young man.

She had forgotten him completely by this point, throwing herself into her new research. They had to tackle the question of whether or not Goddesses could be turned back into humans, after all.

Kaguya had come to Headquarters earlier in the day with Mari, but Mari had other matters to attend to at the moment, so she was spending her time in the archives while she waited.

"Hmm, this isn't quite right, either."

She had been gathering whatever documents she could find that were related to the question. She had already rifled through several books and papers that seemed to bear a connection but couldn't seem to find anything that looked like it might actually be useful.

Kaguya had figured out one thing at least: Turning a Goddess back into a human was impossible. It wasn't a problem with her own powers of intellect. It was just plain impossible, no matter how far they went. Turning a Goddess back into a human would be akin to bringing back the dead.

Although…they apparently managed to turn heroes back into humans.

That was supposed to be impossible as well, but the Director had apparently found a way. If they could do that, then it should be possible to return a reconstructed and changed soul back to its original form.

However…

After looking through nearly every related book and document she could find, Kaguya was at a dead end.

"Ah…"

Just then, she remembered that there was a box where documents and materials that were waiting for disposal were kept.

Usually, these documents were collected and disposed of once per day or at least once per week—in theory. Since few people still used these archives, there were naturally very few documents to dispose of nowadays, and the box tended to be forgotten.

"Not that I imagine I'll find anything worthwhile in there…"

Seeing it as her last hope, Kaguya decided to take a peek into the box anyway.

The box was less than half full. As she was skimming through the documents, expecting to come up empty, she noticed one item that was clearly different from the rest.

"Wh-what is this…?"

It didn't look as if it belonged there. It was a report. Paperwork of some sort.

The piece of paper had staple marks in its upper right-hand corner, which told her that it was one sheet torn from a larger bundle.

While she had no idea what something like that was doing here, it was the contents of the reporting and the handwriting that truly grabbed her attention.

The report detailed the results of a physical and mental exam of a certain person—a young man, apparently. It was mostly written in handwriting that Kaguya did not recognize, but the handwriting of the notes and addenda was clearly her own.

But the date was from five months ago. A period when she was supposed to have been in a coma.

"That doesn't make any sense…"

Supposedly, she had been asleep for eight months. That was what she had been told.

"Maybe the handwriting is just similar. This doesn't seem like something I would spend my time on..."

However, she couldn't stop herself from reading further.

"Elevated pulse, increased body temperature, sweating, redness in the face?"

Elevated pulse? Kaguya had felt those same symptoms before herself, hadn't she? Yes, she definitely had. That time with that young man. She had experienced the exact same thing after coming face-to-face with him. It had only happened that one time, but she remembered it clearly. It was obviously an abnormal reaction.

Was it just an isolated occurrence, or could it be reproduced under the same conditions? She had to confirm. Which meant—

"I need to find him again in order to—"

Kaguya broke off mid-sentence as she remembered the young man's attitude that day.

"I'd rather not, to be honest..."

He had behaved so arrogantly, despite it being their first meeting. Just remembering the incident left her feeling annoyed. Although she wasn't sure why she cared so much.

"Now that I think about it, I probably couldn't find him even if I tried..."

The special ops squad that the young man apparently belonged to was being disbanded this very day, or so she had heard, in order to be absorbed back into Headquarters. From what she had been told, there weren't many people left in the squad these days, and it didn't make sense to maintain their barracks anymore.

Putting that aside, why was only this one page in the box and not the rest? And what was it doing here, of all places?

She continued to read through the handwritten notes. As she looked more closely, ignoring the feeling that something wasn't right, she eventually landed on one note in particular. But this note was strange as well. It was just one word written on the back of the page—not in her handwriting and not in the other person's handwriting, either. It was in a third person's hand.

"Love...?"

Love—as in *love* love?

That feeling that one human being could have for another?

"...I don't understand..."

Why would somebody write something like that on a report and then scribble it out like they had? It wasn't making any sense to Kaguya.

"But...maybe it has something to do with me..."

Something about Kaguya's own self, right now, felt off to her. Even if this all turned out to be silly, she couldn't quell her desire to know more.

Since there was only one page, there was no need to take it back with her. While glancing through the contents quickly, she soon discovered a name.

"Yuuri Azuma..."

For some reason that name almost felt nostalgic to her. She stroked the spot where it was written on the page.

"Captain Azuma..."

She startled herself by saying the name out loud. For some reason, the sound felt familiar on her tongue. As if this was not her first time saying it.

"Do I...know this person?"

Since the page had already been placed in the box for disposal, there was no need to ask for permission to take it. Besides, these archives were already in the process of being shuttered. Kaguya carefully folded the page in two and tucked it away before heading toward the building for Technical.

The cafeteria at Headquarters was located along the way. As she passed it, several things caught her eye all at once.

"Parfaits..."

The menu out front proudly proclaimed that ice cream parfaits were on sale.

This cafeteria was also going to be closed down before long. As a result, they were trying to get rid of their inventory. For some reason, when Kaguya saw parfaits written on the menu, she felt a pain in her chest.

"Wait, didn't I tell someone…?"

It came suddenly, like a lump in her chest, this feeling that something was wrong. Kaguya searched her heart, trying to identify what was making her feel this way. She furrowed her brow as the answer finally came to her.

For some reason, she had the strong feeling that she absolutely needed to go eat ice cream parfaits with somebody.

However, Kaguya had lost all her memories from more than a few months ago. When she tried to recall who that person might be, the only person she could think of to whom she could have possibly made such a promise was Mari. But she hadn't made any promise of the sort to Mari—had she?

In which case, could this be a memory from the time she had forgotten?

Or maybe she had just gotten her wires crossed again. Maybe she was just in the mood for ice cream and had cooked up the idea of a promise in her head.

"No. I…definitely made a promise with someone. Somebody—"

But she couldn't remember who. They must have been fairly close if they were going out to eat together. Was it a man? A woman? She couldn't even remember that much.

But she had the strong feeling that she needed to remember this if nothing else.

"Who was it…?"

But no memories came to mind. The oldest incident she could recall was waking up in her hospital bed with Mari peering down at her.

"Who could it have been?"

Kaguya clutched the paper in her hand, feeling at a loss. She stood there, frozen and no longer looking at the crumpled piece of paper in her hand, as she desperately tried to drudge up anything at all from her memory. However, as soon as she dug back several months, she collided with a brick wall and could not dig any farther.

Who are you? What was your name? What did your face look like?

She took a step forward. As she did so, she felt a vague presence behind her. Turning around…

"Kaguya!"

"Ah…! Oh, Mari…it's you. Did you finish everything you needed to? I thought we might—"

"What is that in your hand?"

With a forcefulness that Kaguya would have never expected from her, Mari stepped closer and deftly extracted the page from Kaguya's hand.

Mari spread the paper open. After getting a better look, she held her breath and then exhaled heavily.

"I always wondered where that missing page went after they handed over the report. I knew I was right to worry."

"The report…? There's more? More pages like this…?"

"They're not necessary anymore. Forget about it."

"B-but that name written there, Captain Yuuri Azuma, I need to—"

"I said forget it!" Kaguya took a reflexive step backward. She had never heard Mari shout like that before. "I'm sorry. But I can't do it. I can't stand to see you wind up like that again."

"Wind up like what…? Mari, what are you saying? Wasn't I asleep all this time?"

Mari didn't answer.

"You're curious, aren't you? About Captain Azuma."

Not really, Kaguya tried to say, but she found herself nodding her head slowly. She took the spread-out report back from Mari gently and stroked the date in the upper left-hand corner with her finger.

"This is my handwriting…but the date doesn't make any sense. I just felt like there might be more to this."

Kaguya was realizing something about herself for the first time. Once she sank her teeth into something, she couldn't let go of it so easily.

"That's not all, either." There were other things that were bothering her. Things that had come back to her, one after the other. "Like that thing with the soup. I just feel like there are so many things that I *need* to remember. Also, I'm pretty sure that I made a promise to somebody."

"A promise…?"

"A promise to go eat ice cream parfaits."

Kaguya felt herself getting worked up. It was like the words were delivering a shock to her brain.

"But who? Who in the world could it have been?"

Mari was standing right in front of Kaguya, but Kaguya couldn't see her now. She was digging through her memory once more. But once she hit that brick wall, she couldn't dig any farther.

But if a wall was in her way, then all she had to do was destroy it. There were memories sleeping beneath the surface that were too important for Kaguya to give up. And one of them was this name.

"Who is he? Captain Yuuri Azuma…?"

At that moment, Kaguya's thoughts were interrupted by the sound of someone chuckling. Kaguya looked up in surprise. It was Mari, her laugh uncomfortable. Almost like someone would laugh at a precocious child who was being naughty.

"It's just like the Director said …"

"M-Mari…?"

"Once you decide how things are going to be, there's nothing we can do to stop you."

Judging from the expression on her face, Mari's words seemed to be directed elsewhere.

"Kaguya, I'm sorry for lying to you. The one who found a way to turn heroes back into humans was actually you, not me."

"What…?"

"I was also lying when I said that you had been asleep… You really were in a coma for a while, but that was over half a year ago."

These were shocking words, but for some reason, hearing what Mari said put Kaguya at ease. The report, at least, was starting to make more sense now.

"Th-then what in the world was I doing before…?"

There was a clear hint of desolation in Mari's eyes.

"You should go find that out for yourself," Mari said simply before moving back. That was when Kaguya thought she saw—yes—a look of resignation on Mari's face. "Technical No. 3 probably won't be around for much longer, either. There aren't that many Goddesses left, after all."

Meaning this place was no longer really needed. Goddesses were only showing up at a rate of about once per month. There was always the option of just giving up on them.

"You won't give up, will you, Kaguya? I probably couldn't make you if I tried. Only..." Mari hesitated. "Only...whatever else happens, you'll always be my mentor, Kaguya. And mine alone."

"Mari..."

"Now go. Before it's too late."

"What do you mean, too late...?"

"Don't you already know? Charon is being disbanded today. Who knows what will happen to Charon's members once the squad is gone? We don't have any contact details for them, either. If you want to see them, today is your last chance."

Kaguya wasn't entirely sure what Mari meant by "too late," but the heartbreak on Mari's face made Kaguya feel a pang in her chest. Though she still wasn't able to process half of what Mari was saying, Kaguya found herself hugging the girl tight.

"I'm sorry, Mari. And thank you."

Kaguya gave Mari's face one last look. Although still resigned, Mari appeared brighter now. It was an expression Kaguya had never seen on her face before. As if Mari had discovered some sort of peace.

Kaguya needed to find this Captain Yuuri Azuma and speak to him face-to-face. She was certain of it, even if she wasn't sure why.

But how was she going to find him?

"Call this number."

Mari had apparently anticipated Kaguya's question before she could ask it. She wrote down a number on a scrap of paper torn off from the report.

"Major Mirai will understand…but I think you probably know that."

Kaguya had a memory of being whipped around in a vehicle that raced like the wind. Of a woman, asking her if she was truly ready. Something she must have once experienced long ago.

She finally knew for sure—that none of it had been a dream. These were memories. Forgotten, but important.

EPILOGUE TWO
Reunion

By this point, barely any heroes were appearing. They had steadily picked off the few remaining Goddesses, and peace was returning to the world.

Koyuki could see the end coming. They weren't completely in the clear yet. For instance, there were still problems with what to do with the humans who had come back from turning—but the need for fighters was a thing of the past.

Just the other day, they had defeated what they believed to be the last Goddess, and nothing unfortunate had occurred since. It seemed as if the heroes and the Goddesses had been eradicated completely.

"What do you say, you three…? You don't have any regrets, do you?" Azuma asked.

"…No."

Koyuki forced herself to shake her head. Haru and Rindou did the same.

"What would there be to regret in the first place?" Rindou said, putting on a show of annoyance. "It's over now. We left everything out on the field."

"Exactly. I learned everything that I needed to know," Haru added, seemingly indifferent. But the truth was she was just doing her best to hide the emotion in her eyes.

"Yeah… Me too. I don't think there's anything left to regret."

Koyuki forced herself to smile along with them. Azuma could tell that Koyuki didn't really mean it, but he didn't say anything.

"…"

All was silent for a while.

They were all thinking the same thing. Koyuki was sure of it—that they were all thinking the same thing and that they all knew it.

"Well, I guess this is the end of the line."

Haru was the first to speak. Her jade-green eyes narrowed, her teal hair reflecting the light like a gem. Koyuki supposed this felt like a relief for her.

Only…

"This is a little disappointing, to be honest…," Haru said suddenly. "There's someone else who should be here."

"Takanashi… You know she's—"

"I know," Haru said, her face a peaceful mask of resignation. Koyuki had seen that expression on Haru's face countless times by now. That was how close they had gotten to each other.

"Anyway, this has been fun in a way. I'm glad I came here, after all."

"It's not like you to be so vulnerable with your feelings," Azuma teased.

"Well, these are our last moments together. There isn't much point in keeping up a show now."

"I guess not."

With that, Haru willingly thrust her hand out in front of herself. She was waiting for a handshake.

"Just don't think this means good-bye forever, not if I have anything to say about it," Azuma replied.

They all stared at him and then took a good look around. Haru smiled, bright and forceful.

"Good-bye, everyone. Until we meet again."

"That's right. Until next time."

Apparently satisfied with Azuma's response, she waved her hand and backed out of the room just as she was, never turning away from them.

"What are you looking so grim for?" Rindou asked, making a face Koyuki had never seen on him before. "She's right, you know. It's not like we'll never get to see each other again."

"Yeah... I know."

Koyuki was a little mortified that Rindou had picked up that she was feeling sad. Rindou looked away, unsure how to interpret her silence, and scratched his head.

"If this is about her...," he began in a comforting tone. Koyuki knew immediately who he was talking about. "Just let it go already. She was never really one of us to begin with. We just happened to spend a little time together due to a weird series of coincidences."

"True, but still..."

Kaguya had only been with Charon for a few short months. Koyuki was fully aware of how strange it was to obsess over such a short period of time. But it was the memories that were bothering Koyuki now. Her memories with Kaguya. All those precious memories that Kaguya had completely forgotten about.

"You know what? After I leave Charon, I plan to go back to normal life. I've had enough of this stupid-ass make-believe, I'm glad it's finally over."

According to Rindou, there was no need for them to remain so hung up on the fact that this farce, known as the Extermination Bureau, had taken away six years of their lives. A clean break—that was what was needed. It was just the kind of thinking you would expect from him.

"You too, Koyuki... You should try to look forward. You're not doing Kaguya any favors by letting this preoccupy you."

"Don't act like you're not sad, too."

Rindou didn't reply, either to agree or disagree. He just stayed silent.

"You got me there," he said eventually, agreeing after all. But from the sound of his voice, he was at peace. "I wish I could have spoken to her again, one last time. But hey, who knows? Maybe we'll meet again somehow."

"You think so…? That we might all meet again?"

For Koyuki, Rindou was someone special, different from the others. They were stuck with each other in the best sense of the word. Two peas in a pod.

"Of course we will. It's not like we're dying, is it?"

"You know…you're probably right. You probably are."

Rindou laughed, a little exasperated, before turning to face Azuma.

"Thanks for everything. I owe you one."

"I'm the one who owes you. You've given me lots to be grateful for."

Rindou smiled in response, a gentle smile that wasn't at all like him. He took a step back and then smiled at the both of them.

"See you! Stay chill!"

Before he left, he flashed them an upbeat grin. That was the Rindou they were used to seeing. And with that, he disappeared from Koyuki and Azuma's sight.

"Koyuki."

Koyuki grimaced when Azuma said her name. It seemed as if Rindou wasn't the only one who could see through how she was feeling.

"It's fine. I've already accepted she's not coming. When you think about it, Kaguya was only at Charon for a few months. There were others, like Sakura, who were here for much longer," Koyuki said, making a face to show that she was over it.

Azuma said nothing, staring at her with an inscrutable expression full of mixed feelings.

"In any case, I better go get ready," Koyuki added. "I still need to clean out my room."

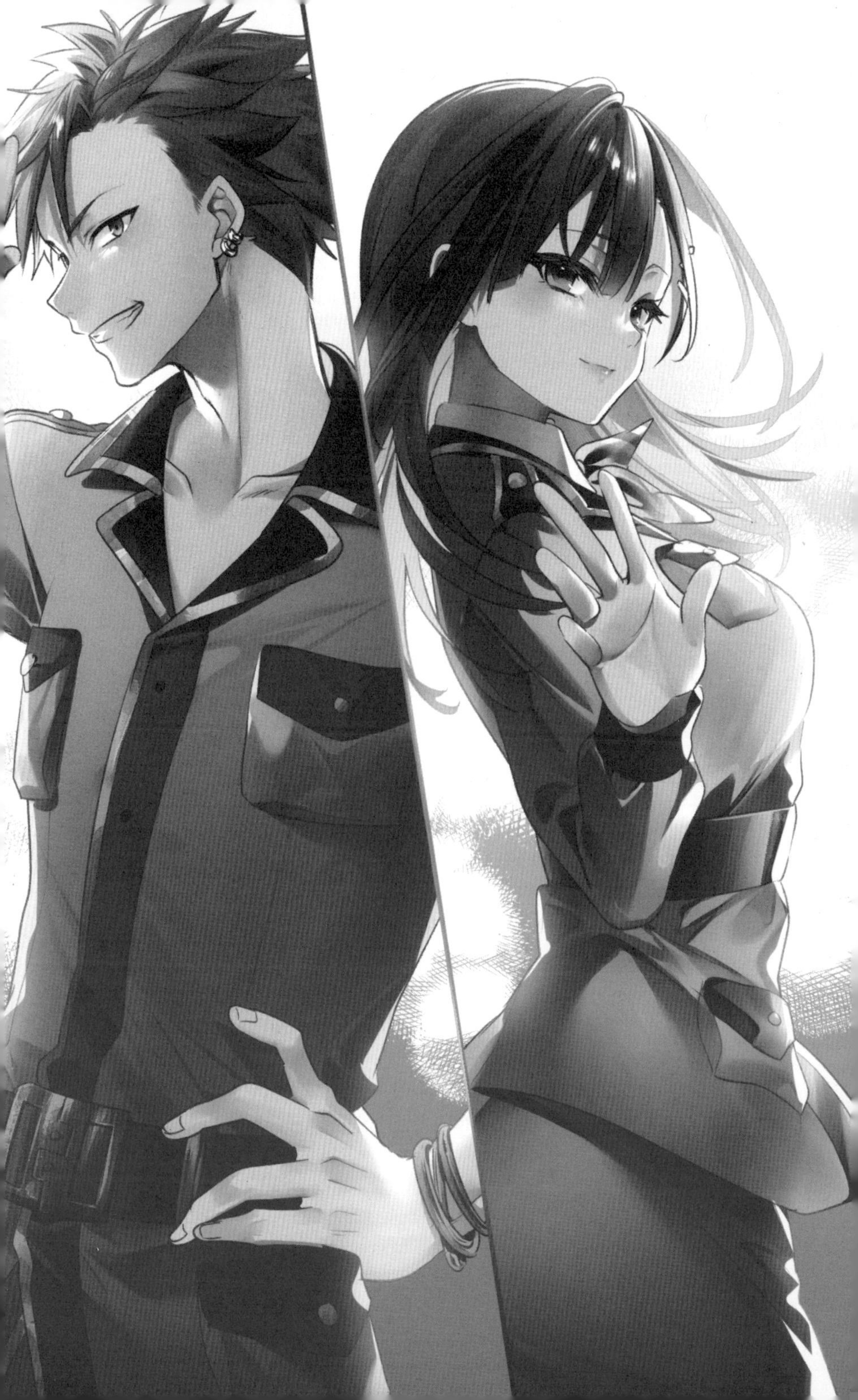

Azuma gave a noncommittal response as Koyuki headed back into the barracks. Once they were ready, it was time for Charon to disband.

She would be lying if she said she didn't feel sad, but—no, she was just sad. Very much so.

Even if this all had just been a sandbox for the development of Chronoses, even if it had all been make-believe. It didn't change the fact that it had been her youth.

"Ugh... This feels so strange."

She had spent six years of her life in these barracks. A lot of things had happened in that time. Now that it was over, they were all important memories for Koyuki.

At some point, however, even these memories would fade. As the experiences that were surely waiting came rushing in, the past would likely be pushed into a corner of her mind.

A time would come, eventually, when she would likely think of even Sakura only occasionally.

But that isn't necessarily a bad thing.

It was just what it meant to live.

"I'm sure we'll meet again."

Cradling her relatively light luggage, Koyuki exited from the barrack's rear entrance. The reason she didn't leave from the front, like normal, was because she didn't want Azuma to see her go.

She wanted to say good-bye with a smile at least.

"Ahhhh..."

She breathed in deeply and then exhaled. It was the only thing that was keeping her from crying.

Then she took a step forward. Just as she was about to set out, however, she turned around to get one last look at the barracks.

It had originally been a community center and would probably be torn down after they were gone. This was her last chance to see it. She tilted her head upward. Suddenly—

"Excuse me...," a voice said.

* * *

"Ah..."

Koyuki's eyes went wide. She spun around in the direction of the voice, coming face-to-face with a girl with scarlet hair and a worn-out expression.

"How...?"

Scarlet hair and pale violet eyes.

She must have been running. Her shoulders were heaving up and down. Her hair, which should have been neatly tied behind her head, was all over the place at the moment, making it obvious that she was flustered.

More importantly, however, was the question of what Kaguya was even doing here in the first place.

She had lost her memories; she shouldn't have remembered.

Major Mirai. Of course, she had brought Kaguya here. Koyuki shot the major an accusatory glance, but Mirai just smiled and shrugged. Some people never changed.

"You're...," Kaguya began hesitantly while Koyuki stood there at a loss for words. "You're Lieutenant Koyuki Asaharu, correct?"

"Huh...?!"

"I was, um, told your name...by someone named Major Mirai."

"I...see..." If Mirai had told Kaguya her name, then obviously... "Then I guess there's no need for me to keep up the act anymore."

Koyuki suddenly leaned forward and hugged Kaguya tight. Kaguya's body felt a little bit warmer than Koyuki's own. Kaguya was of course taken by surprise. For her this was their first time meeting, after all.

"That's right. My name is Koyuki Asaharu. I'm your friend."

"My friend...? But..."

"That's okay. We'll be friends starting from today, then."

It must have felt bewildering to hear that from somebody whose name you had only just learned. But Koyuki didn't care.

"It's okay if you don't remember. We can create new memories."

"Um, Lieutenant Asaharu..."

"Call me Koyuki." Koyuki stepped back. "I'll call you Kaguya, as well."

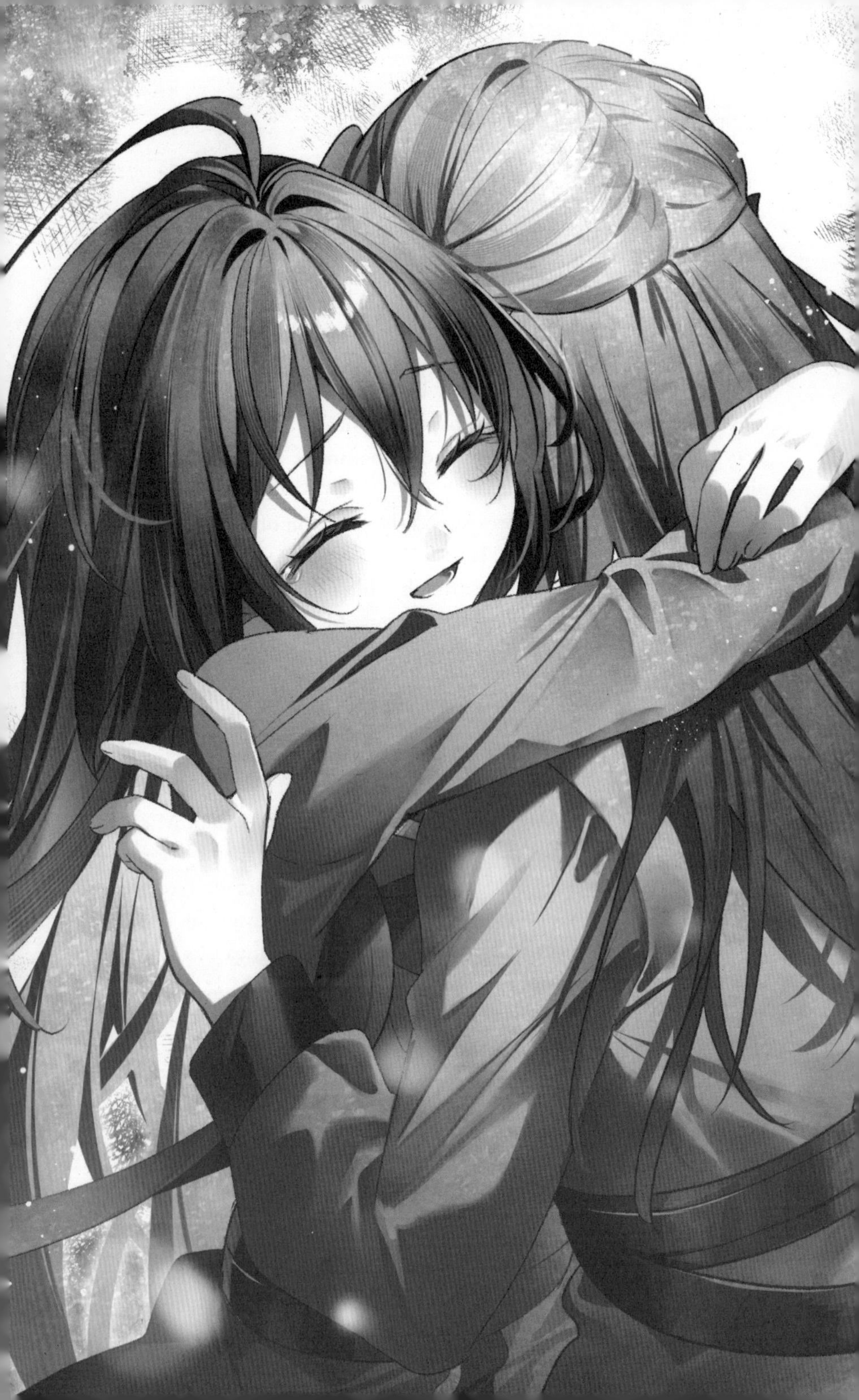

"...?"

Koyuki could tell that Kaguya felt hesitant. That was just her personality. But she could hardly refuse such a request.

"Have you seen him yet...?"

Kaguya shook her head vaguely. Just as Koyuki had expected, Kaguya apparently already understood who Koyuki meant by *him*.

"Then you should go now. I'll be waiting here."

"Umm...," Kaguya said, stopping Koyuki before she could leave. "Were you—? What were we to each other really...?"

"I'll tell you all of that later," Koyuki whispered, placing a finger to her lips. "For now, it's a secret. But there is one thing I'll let you know."

Koyuki knew this wasn't necessary, but she just couldn't help herself.

"He can be really lousy when it comes to being honest about the way he feels. So you're going to have to be honest enough for both of you. Trust me. I've been watching you two from the edge of my seat for a while now."

Something about the oblivious expression on Kaguya's face felt nostalgic to Koyuki.

"I will," said Kaguya, nodding emphatically. Koyuki watched her turn and walk away.

"They really do have some strange tastes over there...," Koyuki muttered to herself.

Those people from Technical.

• • •

The barracks were already cleared out and put into order. Apparently, the facility was going to be torn down once Charon was gone.

Azuma would be lying if he claimed that didn't make him sad. He had spent so many years here. But he believed it was better this way. There were too many reminders of his time with Kaguya. It had actually been a little painful in the end, staying here.

As he waited for Koyuki, Azuma let his mind wander to thoughts of what he was going to do next.

The system considered Azuma to be a minor, orphaned by disaster.

He assumed he would be shuttled off to a different facility once the Bureau was gone. After that, he wasn't sure yet.

"What's taking her so long...?"

He took a step forward, planning to go look for Koyuki. If she wanted to take her time, that was fine, but this seemed like a bit much, even for her. Just as Azuma turned—

He caught a flash of scarlet out of the corner of his eyes. Vivid, sparkling red.

He turned slowly. It couldn't be.

"H-how...?" he stammered.

There she was—the girl who had supposedly forgotten all about him. She looked away in embarrassment.

"I felt like I knew something after all...something about you," she said to him.

"You must be mistaken." That was the only answer Azuma knew to give. "News about Charon is shared with the Bureau on a regular basis. You probably just saw something on one of the screens and convinced yourself it meant something more. I've never met someone like you before in my entire life. This is all a mistake."

Even without proof, however, Kaguya was not so easily dissuaded.

"That's what I thought at first as well... But it seemed so vivid, especially that silver earring of yours."

Azuma touched the earring in his left ear.

"I feel like I recognize it. Like I've seen it once—no, many, many times before..."

"As I said, you must be mistaken." Azuma sighed and glared at her like he did the last time they had met. "If you've seen it many times before, then it must have just been on the Bureau's video feed. And then you just got things all mixed up in your head when we met... Honestly, I don't have time for this."

Azuma had already convinced himself that he needed to push her away. It was almost all over at this point—there was no real danger to her anymore—but even the briefest contact could get her wrapped up in things all over again. And what if that caused her to remember things?

To remember all the pain and hardship she had been forced to go through?

"If that's settled, would you please just leave me alone? For your sake, too, it would be better if you—"

"I'm sorry, but there's something I need to ask. And I need to ask it of you."

He was about to turn around when Kaguya's voice stopped him in his tracks.

"An elevated pulse. Whenever I'm in the same space as you, I feel something funny inside."

"What…?" Azuma was caught off guard by her words. "Are you saying—? Do you mean…?"

An elevated pulse—that was what she had said. Just like he, himself, experienced. Azuma wasn't stupid. He understood what that meant.

"I heard from Major Mirai that Charon is being disbanded today. Because the Extermination Bureau is being dismantled."

"Yes… What about it?"

"There was…something that I wanted to ask you before that happens."

Kaguya pulled out a single piece of paper.

Azuma's eyes went wide. It was from one of the physicals he had delivered to Kaguya. He thought he had gotten rid of that thing, but apparently, one page remained.

"Wh-what does this word here mean? Here, on the back?"

Kaguya thrust the back of the page toward him. A single word was written on the page's white surface. Azuma's interest was piqued as he realized that the word was in Koyuki's handwriting.

"*Love?*"

"Yes. You and I. I was thinking that maybe, once upon a time, I was—"

Kaguya suddenly froze mid-sentence. What was she saying?

"Oh, oh!! I'm sorry. Of course not. What was I thinking?! Really, I'm sorry. Forget it. Why would I say something like that…?"

"Are you…?"

The young man made an expression she had never seen from him before. But wait, wasn't this nearly their first time meeting? She was still trying to make it make sense in her head when Azuma spoke softly, muttering in a daze.

"Are you saying you're in love? You? With me?"

"…Oh!"

Kaguya suddenly clamped a hand over her mouth, shocked at what had just come out of it. But that was exactly what she was saying, wasn't it? And she didn't even have the decency to use a euphemism.

What was wrong with her? No one wanted to be told something like that by someone they were meeting for practically the very first time. It was creepy.

Kaguya was trying to think of something to say that would get her out of this situation, but before she could speak, the young man shook his head.

"No, you're not in love with me. How could you be? This is only our second time meeting."

"Ha-ha, y-yes, of course! I was just being silly." Kaguya sighed in relief. "I'm sorry. I'm just a little bit tired and confused. Something happened to me a little while ago, and I lost my memories, so…"

And so she was making excuses now—she didn't mean anything by it. Her memories and her thoughts had all just gotten jumbled together in her head. That was all.

"I must have just seen you somewhere before. That's all."

"Yes, that makes sense. Meaning you don't know me. This was clearly all a mistake. We can just forget about it."

"O-of course. Thank you so much. Um, by the way," she said, changing topics. She still wanted to speak to this person more. He might know her, after all. "I actually have a request—"

"It's different for me, though."

Kaguya blinked. What did he just say?

"Different...?"

"You may not remember, but we once fought together, side by side... It was only for a few months, but so many things happened during that time."

Kaguya responded with silence. She couldn't refute what he was saying.

"I know you won't want to hear this since this is practically our first meeting from your point of view, but since we're never going to see each other again after this, you can just forget about it later. I don't care. There's just something I need to say before we go."

A gentle smile, so gentle it didn't seem at all suited to the young man's face, formed on his lips.

"I need to tell you that I love you."

Kaguya gasped in bewilderment. That was not at all what she had expected him to say.

"Love? Do you mean—like as a person?"

"I mean as a man and a woman."

"But...this is almost our first time meeting."

"Not for me, it isn't."

"B-but for me, this is only the second time."

"I know that. I know this must make you uncomfortable to hear, so I hope you won't despise me for saying it."

But surprisingly, Kaguya felt nothing of the sort.

Rather, she felt a powerful feeling brewing inside herself. Similar to excitement but unlike anything she had ever felt before. She clutched tightly at her chest as if trying to control herself.

The young man, meanwhile, seemed much calmer. He began to change the topic, as if they hadn't been discussing anything out of the ordinary.

"So why did you come here?"

"Well...I—I guess I'm searching for my old memories." She pointed to a spot on the document. "I was told I had been in a coma for several months, but this document seems to contradict that. It shows my handwriting from a time when I was supposedly unconscious. And it had your name, so..."

"So you came here to ask me about it?"

"Well...something hasn't felt right for quite a while now."

Although he didn't ask, Kaguya began to explain herself. It was like all the words inside her had come bubbling to the surface and were spilling out.

"There were events I couldn't have possibly experienced. Emotions I shouldn't have had... I'm not the type to just let sleeping dogs lie. I thought that if I met you, I might start to understand things better."

However...

"That was a mistake...," the young man said firmly. "It won't benefit you to know those things. You'll just get wrapped up in Tactical's affairs again. Someone like you shouldn't waste her time on stuff like this."

"But the Bureau's being dismantled anyway, isn't it?" Kaguya insisted. "Once you leave here, you'll get to go back to being a normal teenager, won't you? Why can't I go with you, then?"

"But..."

The young man was tongue-tied, apparently unable to come up with a good reason why. Despite appearances, it seemed like he was actually a pushover.

"I want to be with you," she said.

Kaguya decided to put her real feelings on the line. This was all bound to work out so long as she just kept insisting.

"I want to be by your side and learn all sorts of things. About the memories I lost, all the things that must have happened, the times I shared with you. I want you to tell me what really happened over our months together."

She meant it. This wasn't just her scientific curiosity speaking. She felt as if she needed to know. It was too sad to choose not to remember it all.

"You remember, don't you?" The things she didn't. Those months she had lost. "Then tell me please. I'm not going to give up until you agree."

"No, you really won't, huh...? That is just like you, after all," the young man said, sighing in defeat. "You never were the type to give in. I always had to give in first."

The young man then extended his hand as if for a handshake. Although this was her first time seeing him extend his hand like this, it made her feel simultaneously nostalgic and melancholy in a way that was difficult to explain.

"The fight against the Goddesses is already wrapping up, so I doubt you'll be staying with us for long..." Kaguya felt like she had heard these words before. "But welcome to the unit, Technical Lieutenant Shinohara."

But something about his voice now seemed very different from whatever it was she was remembering.

"Actually, the Bureau is already gone now. If I'm going to call you anything, I guess it should be by your name, Kaguya."

Out of everything that had happened so far, Kaguya realized that hearing him call her by her name was what caused her heart to race the fastest.

It didn't seem to occur to her how rude it was for him to call her by her given name on a first meeting like this. Instead, she softly reached out to touch the hand held out for her.

For some reason, she suddenly felt like she wanted to cry. Besides her brother's, she had never touched a boy's hand before.

The sight of Azuma suddenly grew a little blurry. It took her a moment to realize it was the tears in her eyes. She wasn't sure why she was feeling the way she was feeling, but she knew immediately that these were not tears of sadness.

"Yes, thank you. Captain Az—" Before Kaguya could finish, a thought occurred to her. "Actually, would it be all right if I call you by your first name, too?"

"What?"

"It's just... If you're calling me by my name, it's only right that I do the same, right? It would be weird for just one of us to do it."

"Well, I mean, that is..."

"Your name is Yuuri Azuma, correct? Well, in that case...," Kaguya said, ignoring his distress as she extended her own hand.

Timidly, very timidly—yet firmly—the young man took her hand.

She smiled at him. "Nice to meet you again for the first time, Yuuri..."

Suddenly, Kaguya felt a little flustered.

"...Captain Azuma," she added.

She felt a rush of agitation upon saying his name. Strangely, her face felt flushed.

It was normal to call someone by their name, wasn't it? She had done the exact same thing with Koyuki Asaharu just moments ago. But now she felt confused in a way she did not understand.

Like she was someone else when he was there. She began to pull her hand away when suddenly—

"Ah—?!"

She was abruptly pulled in instead. No, not pulled—embraced. These arms now holding her were a little warmer than she had expected. As she looked up timidly, she saw that he was crying, too. She had her head down so she couldn't see, but tiny sobs were escaping his lips.

And then his lips parted. She realized he was trying to say, "It's nice to meet you," but for some reason, the corners of his lips lifted upward before he could speak—into a smile of joy.

"*Welcome home*, Kaguya."

The End

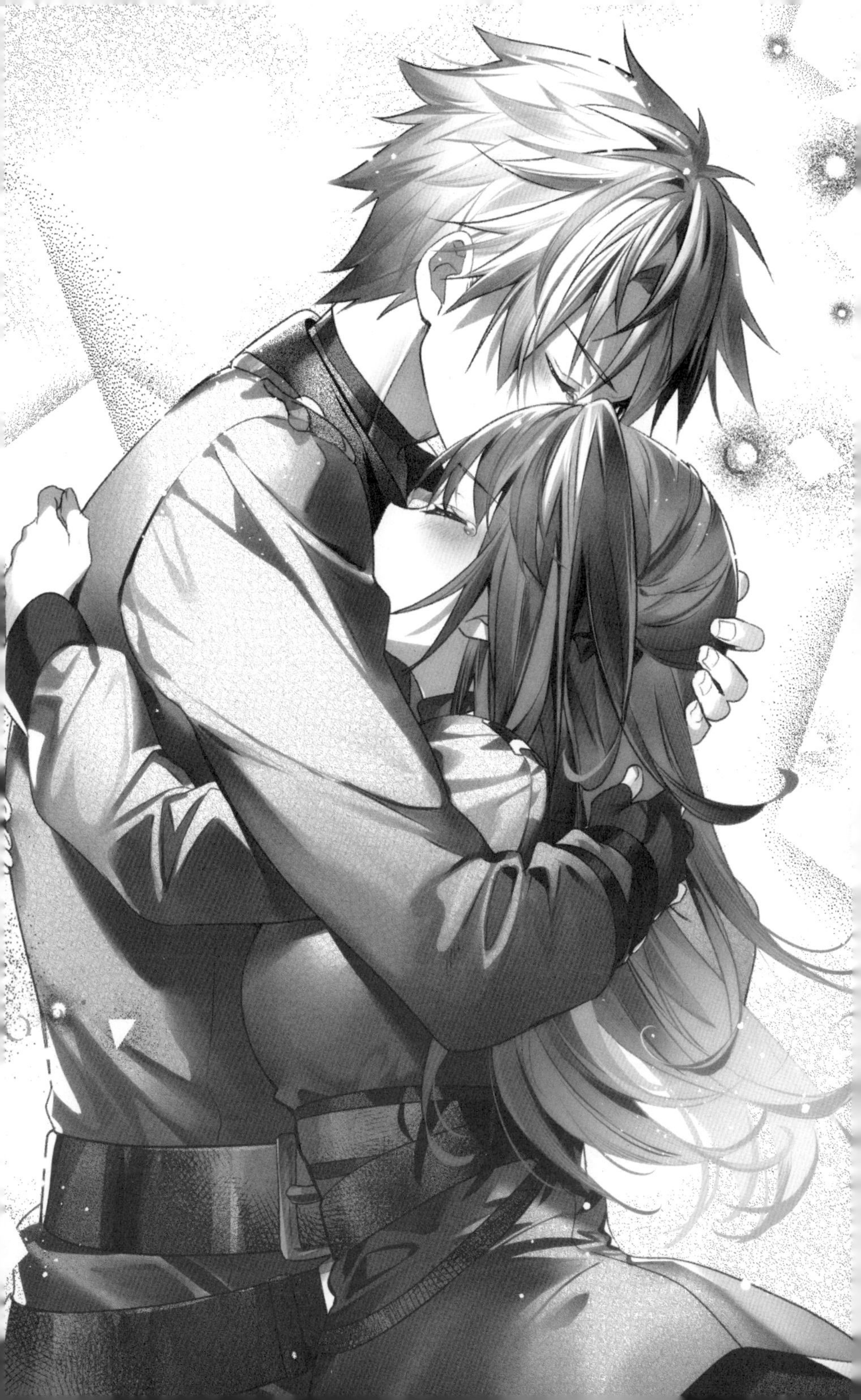

AFTERWORD

To those for whom this is our first time, it's nice to meet you. To old friends, it's nice to see you once again. It's me, Rei Ayatsuki.

Thank you very much for picking up Volume 3 of *Hero Syndrome*.

So the *Hero Syndrome* series has now reached three volumes. It's a strange feeling to think that a story I conceived of in autumn two years ago and which began in February of last year is still continuing, eleven months later.

By the way, dear readers, are you the type to read the story first, or do you prefer to start with the afterword? For my own part, I like to start with the story. So for the rest of this afterword, I'll just assume that everyone does the same.

As those of you who have already read the story should know, the tale known as *Hero Syndrome* has ended with this volume. While it is a little sad to see that it's over, I think this story was blessed to have been enjoyed by so many people. Honestly, thank you so much.

Now then, let's get straight to the acknowledgments.

To riichu, who was in charge of character design and illustrations. I was overjoyed by the many marvelous character designs you created, not least among them the adorable Kaguya. Thank you very much.

To GEKIDAN INU CURRY Doroinu. Thank you so much for

creating so many creepy yet extremely beautiful hero designs. It was truly an honor to get to work with you.

To my editors, M and N. Your willingness to always deal so pleasantly with the trouble I cause was a great help. *Hero Syndrome* only made it into this world thanks to its editors. Thank you very much.

To everyone involved in printing and proofing. I can never be grateful enough for your willingness to respond to important corrections. Thank you very much.

This will also be my last time writing an afterword for *Hero Syndrome*. But the work itself will continue to exist. A meeting between a book and a person is also a meeting between a person and a person. I think of it as a kind of connection.

Connections are often described as strings. But I have a slightly different way of looking at it.

A connection is like the flow of a river. People are like currents within that flow. The countless currents of a river come together in places and part again in others, over and over again, until they part into the sea. And once at sea, there are even more currents. More meetings and more partings.

It is the same when we meet a book. Books come into our hands for many different reasons, creating new connections each in their own time. And I am very happy if this book made one of those connections with you.

We are nearly out of pages, and it is almost time to draw the curtain. But I want to say, once more, that this story has brought a lot of energy and hope into my life. And it would please me more than anything if I was able to give some of that back to everyone in return.

We may have only been together for a short time, just a year. But thank you for supporting me every step along the way.

May our currents meet again.

3

REI AYATSUKI
ILLUSTRATION BY riichu
CREATURE DESIGN BY
GEKIDAN INU CURRY Doroinu

HERO SYNDROME

Eradicate the heroes who exact vengeance on the world.

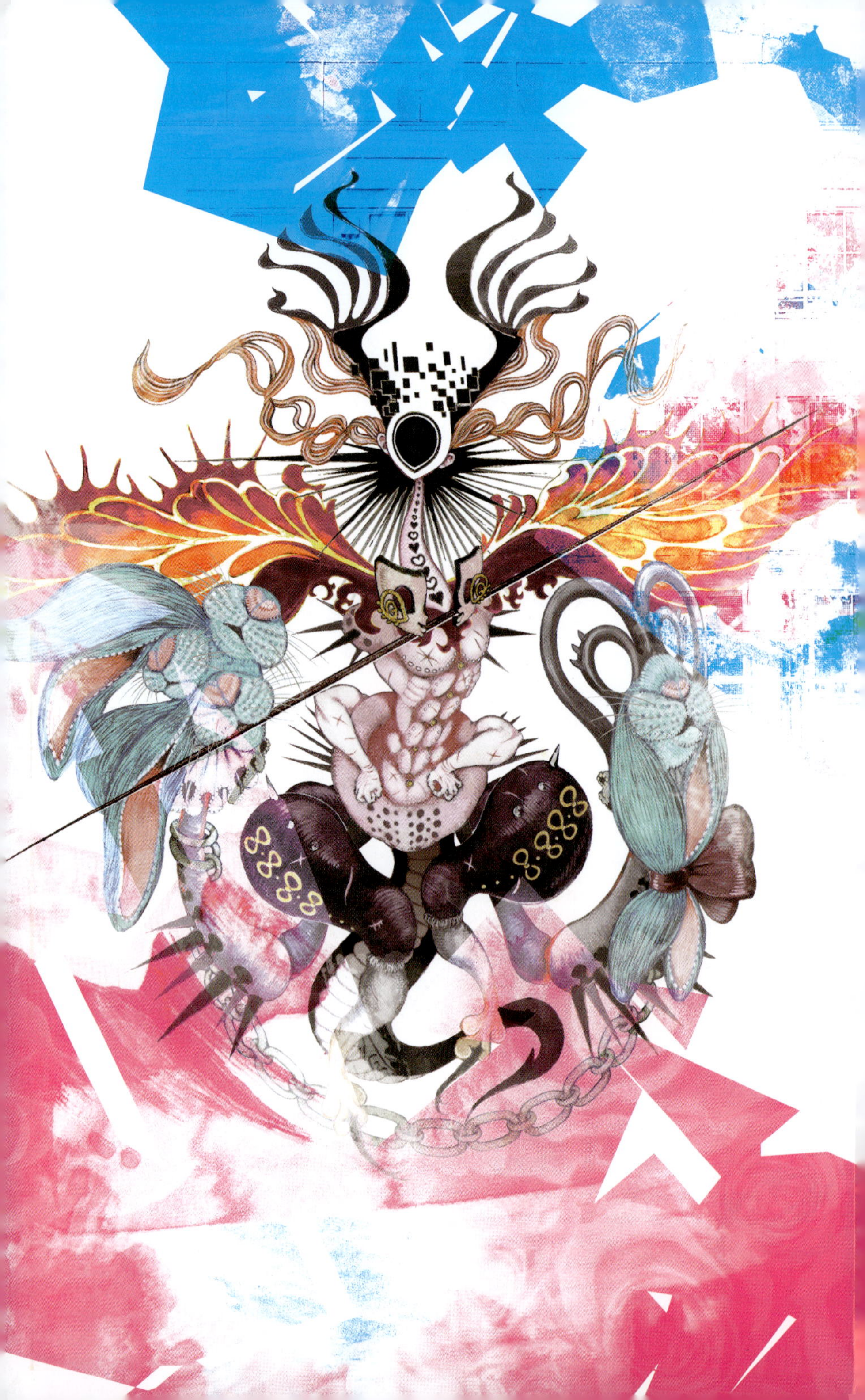